ALWAYS A BAD SIGN

A Case From the Files and Personal
Journals of Cheyenne Bruce,
Private Investigator, Book One

Lella Rae

MasterPieces Unlimited

*To my beloved friend, Barb Roberts, whose
unfailing support I treasure.
Thank you, dear friend.*

PROLOGUE

I n retrospect, aside from the fact that it was the last day of Jacob Levin's life, there was probably nothing unusual about that Monday in November, 1983.

This is the way I pieced it together later, after the final whispers had echoed into silence and the last of the blood had disappeared.

At 8:30 am, Jake had left his home in West Seattle. The sky had been overcast, with rain predicted by nightfall. *Good*, he may have thought, and let his mind wander over his favorite memories of Suzanne. He could have glanced into the backseat of his cream Lincoln Continental, noted the presence of his umbrella and moved it to the front seat. He was downtown by 9:00.

Jake spent most of the morning on the phone. He closed a deal with Greg Hood in Eugene. At lunch, he met with a client; fat, bald Cal Sloan, who sniffed incessantly which probably drove Jake to drink the two Manhattans when he normally would have ordered only one. He ate a spinach salad that he told Cal, was a "touch lemony" for his taste. He returned to the office, according to his secretary, Bea, at just after 2:00. She handed him a sheaf of messages when he walked past. One had been from Suzanne. Another from an attorney in Nevada. Jake shut the drapes against the clouds that hung outside his window and, for the rest of the afternoon, he may have battled sleepiness as well as the stubborn attorney from Las Vegas. Bea confirmed that he dozed off at his desk at approximately 4:30. At 6:30, he called Magda and told her he would be working late on the Vorza job and not to wait up for him. He might have felt a stab of guilt but dismissed it with the thought that he would make up for it at Christmas. At about 7:30, he took a cab to a new restaurant on Blanchard, ate stuffed sole and red potatoes, then headed back to work.

When Jake again left his office, it had been 10:25. He probably had no premonition he was about to live his final half hour. Instead, he undoubtedly looked forward to the night. He locked the outer office, rode the elevator down thirty-one floors, nodded to the security guard, who noted the time in his log, and walked out into the wet Seattle night.

The rain, which had started just as he had left for lunch, had been heavy all day. At 10:30, it rained as freshly as ever, making rivers of the streets as it danced frantically on the pavement. He *whumped* his umbrella open and jogged the half block to his parking garage.

The Lincoln skimmed over the shining streets, the radio blaring. A song by the Judds, perhaps? A late-night interview with Chuck Knox? He switched to KIRO and Talknet with Bruce Williams. Jake might have felt good during the drive. He liked his big car and felt one with it. Jake was an intelligent man who knew enough psychology to realize the significance of that and it probably amused him. He and his car moved effortlessly over the West Seattle Bridge, but instead of taking Admiral Way to his home, he exited to Harbor Avenue and turned toward Alki Beach. Suzanne would be waiting.

Jake eased the car into a parking space. Across the water, the lights of the city, dimmed by the rain, looked like dirty junk jewelry.

The beach was empty and over the roar of the wind, the radio and the drumming of the rain on the top of the car, Jake would have been unlikely to hear the choppy waves. In the summer, the avenue would be so crowded with jocks, bikinis and cruisers, he wouldn't be able to drive its length let alone find a place to stop. But, in dark November, the street had been empty and the beach loomed dangerous and forbidding. In summer, he knew, he and Suzanne would have to devise a different plan. Had he scanned the few parking spots for Suzanne's car? There *was* one car at the opposite end of the line of spaces, but it wasn't hers.

He turned off the engine, but allowed the radio to play on. The Lincoln's smoked-glass windows had steamed up almost immediately, but that would have been all right with Jake. He didn't want anyone stopping by to look inside, especially after Suzanne had arrived.

Had he looked at his watch and wondered where she was? Did he wonder if she couldn't ever be on time? Even as the thought hit his mind, he may have felt a stirring deep inside of him. When she arrived and he felt her fresh, youthful body and smelled her sweet breath, her chronic tardiness wouldn't matter. It never did.

He and Suzanne didn't have to meet at Alki like a couple of teenagers. He could have afforded a hotel. A good one. Suzanne had an apartment they could have used. Had used. Making love in the car was risky. More than once the police had shone their spotlights at the back window, but they never did more than that. Lincoln Continentals seemingly weren't suspect as hotbeds of teenage romance. Had that been what made it so thrilling, Jake? The risk? The smell of the rich leather beneath you? The young, beautiful Suzanne who played so willingly and was oh, so sexy?

Sometimes, perhaps, a twinge of fear would shoot through his stomach and he would wonder if she would ever tire of him. He wasn't a Don Johnson or even a Clint Eastwood. Hell, he knew he couldn't even touch most guys as far as looks went. But he and Suzanne had something together. They could laugh. They could laugh and they could screw. He might have deliberately thought of Suzanne's lush honey-colored hair and moist mouth and found himself with the beginnings of an erection.

Lately she had been pressuring him. Marriage. She knew he was married. She knew he would never consider a divorce. She knew. He hoped to God Magda never found out. What he and Suzanne had was separate. Thinking about it, his jaw might have tightened and his eyes narrowed. If Magda ever found out, there would be hell to pay. He had seen her jealousy flare a time or two.

He may have wished Suzanne would hurry up. He may have felt as though the inside of the car was pressing in on him. With her beside him, ripe and sweet, the whole world would disappear.

Had he thought he heard a rustle in the back seat? Silly. Had he glanced in the rear-view mirror? Maybe it was Suzanne outside the car. He heard something again, definitely behind him. But before he could turn around, an arm had slipped around his neck and forced his head against the headrest. Something rough rasped his chin. In panic he groped for the arm. Given another millisecond he might have been able to pull himself free, but the blade slashed into his carotid artery with a curious *crunch*. With an odd detachment he may have felt himself moving out of the man who struggled against the blade. He may have seen the fountain of his own life hit the windshield and run down in a grisly parody of the rain outside.

I think he felt no pain, just a growing numbness that started behind his eyes as his senses began to drift away. In blind response, he pushed against the horn, but the sound of it had faded even as he knew it wouldn't help. Dimly, his mind may have called to Suzanne, God and then, at the last, his lips may have formed the word "Magda."

ONE

Tuesday, November 15, 1983

Right from the beginning, my day went wrong. My ESP apparently hadn't been working that Tuesday morning. If it had been, when E.Z. Radford called me from West Seattle, I wouldn't have answered the phone.

Its ring sliced through a delightful dream about a girlhood summer in Oregon. My brother Larry had been in it, and my mother had still been alive.

"The Sign of the Cross," I answered. "Cheyenne speaking."

"Is this a religious establishment?"

"You never give up, do you, Easy?"

His laugh made me think of warm blankets and soft pillows. "I've got something for you," he said, as if he were holding up a delectable chocolate just out of my reach.

Easy Radford was the chaplain for the Seattle

Police Department. His name was actually Ezekial Zachary Radford. He hated it when I called him Easy, which was the main reason I did it. He and I had been friends for seven or eight years, since long before my agency was born.

We used to joke about opening a restaurant together and calling it Chey and Easy, but he always said that would be a better name for a brothel. He never stopped nudging me that "The Sign of the Cross" sounded more like a religious cult than a detective agency. The name, and the logo too, had come out of a time when people had laughed at my profession. One well-enough meaning guy had put his fingers into one of those anti-vampire crosses when I told him I was psychic.

"Okay, what is it?" I asked, sitting up. The red numbers on my alarm clock said it was 6:32 am.

"Murder."

"You know I don't handle that," I said trying to sound patient and not sleepy. "Missing persons, yes, injury claims, yes, but nothing heavy. No murder." I could hear the irritation creeping into my voice as I spoke. It was way too early.

"This is someone you know," he said.

"Easy, just spit it out."

"Remember when you looked for Angelle St. Martin?" he asked.

"I wish I could forget," I said. The irritation ramped up a notch. I didn't like to be reminded of that case. Angelle St. Martin had disappeared five and half years before. No amount of meditation, no amount of psychic ability, no amount of investigation could turn up any trace of her.

"Magda St. Martin's husband was found murdered this morning," Easy was telling me. "They found him, in his car, down by Alki Beach."

I winced. "Oh, poor Magda! But, Easy, why would I get involved in this? Surely the police are doing what needs to be done. They'll have it figured out long before I ever would."

"She asked for you."

"But, why? Tell her I don't investigate murders. From her point of view, I don't even do missing persons all that well. At least, I never found her daughter. What does she want me for?"

"She wants some protection and doesn't like what the police are offering."

"There a suspect?"

"In custody."

"Then what would I be protecting her from?" I swung my legs out of the bed and danced my feet on the freezing floor before I found my slippers.

"She's not sure the police have the right guy. And she's afraid the press will get onto it."

"She's got that right."

"She wants you," he said.

"Easy, I don't want to do this." I crawled into my

3

robe and gave the electric heater a nudge with my foot. "She wants protection? Does that mean she wants me to stay there? No way."

I pictured Magda St. Martin the way she had looked the last time I had seen her, petite and distraught over the disappearance of her daughter. Feminine, but tough enough to bend steel. I had never seen her cry.

"Chey, she asked for you. Besides, it's money." The bastard knew how to get to me. "You remember where the house is?" Easy asked.

"I wish I could forget that too," I muttered.

When I hung up, I padded into the bathroom for a quick shower. I pulled on a pair of jeans, a bulky wool sweater and some boots.

I grabbed a handful of trail mix and a glass of tomato juice.

My file cabinet held a shamefully slim file on the Angelle St. Martin case. I pulled it out and paged through the meager reports. Everyone has had an experience or two in her lifetime that she would like to forget. It beats on her in the morning and hits her in the face in the middle of the day. It creeps up and grabs her around the throat in the darkest hours of those nights when all old failures come back to haunt.

I blew the Angelle St. Martin case. Five and a half years before, that would have been the spring of 1978, Magda St. Martin, a now retired actress, had discovered that her teenaged daughter was missing. I couldn't find her. No matter that it was my first case. No matter that I hadn't learned some important things about investigating that only come with experience. I blew it. I couldn't find Angelle. I couldn't even get a mental fix on her. Eventually, I had to give up the hunt. As far as I knew, Magda had never stopped looking, though she had refused to bring in the police. I never did read about it in the paper, but I sure as hell thought about it.

I stuffed the file into my briefcase and switched on my answering machine. I was running a one-woman operation. And on a shoestring, too. My "staff" was an ancient mechanical device that answered my phone if I didn't get to it by the third ring and a tired old Adler typewriter that typed the "m"s too close to the next letter and made my reports look slightly foreign. But, for right then, that was the best I could do. I had a small income from doing insurance fraud investigations for Northwestern Life and what I made from my own agency. It was not much, though, and sometimes, what with paying off my mother's medical bills and my living expenses, there was nothing left over at all. Someday, I knew, I would have a posh office and a nice apartment and wouldn't have to worry every time my car got that strange little sound in the engine.

The streets still glistened from the previous

night's rain and the intermittent showers of the early morning. I pulled out onto Island Crest Way and drove the length of Mercer Island. I lived in a community of orthodontists, attorneys, airline pilots and a few oddball professionals like myself. Most people thought you had to have money to live there. You did. Unless you happened to accidently find a once-in-a-lifetime cheap basement apartment like mine. My home was also my office. There was a hide-a-bed and a corner which you could laughingly call a "kitchenette". It wasn't terribly attractive, but it was comfortable enough, private, cheap and perfect for me.

I've always had psychic ability. When I was a kid, I drove people crazy answering their questions before they had a chance to ask them and finishing their sentences for them. I gave that up. It seemed to annoy the hell out of most people. I got the idea for doing readings from watching television, and my "clients" wanted to believe what I told them so badly they were willing to pay me. I worked street fairs and just managed to balance on the edge of respectability, though I always felt like a fraud. I made it a point to only tell them the good news. Unless there was legitimately something the client could do about it, the bad news just wasn't good business. My mother had had the ability, and my brother too, though none of us had seen the cancer coming for her. Just before Angelle St. Martin had disappeared, I realized I was going to have to make some serious money to pay my mother's medical bills. I had trashed the stereotypical psychic accoutrements and gone to detective school. I had been in the business ever since. I tried to use my ability whenever I could and it often helped.

In November, Mercer Island was dressed up for fall and joggers had exchanged their shorts for Spandex tights. The car's heater still hadn't warmed up by the time I reached I-90. My car was one of those old Honda Civics that someone had painted a gawd-awful shade of penalty flag yellow before I owned her. It wasn't a very inconspicuous color for a PI to drive, but we seemed to have anonymity in our distinctiveness. She may not have had a lot of class, but I loved her. She and I went back even farther than my apartment and I did. I treasured her. Maybe because she had been my home for a little while after my mother's house had sold to help pay for her hospital bills.

To people who lived anywhere else, West Seattle was a different world. The best way to get there was via a relatively new bridge that sailed you up over the tide flats of Harbor Island. Below, you could see the old steel mill and, in the distance, downtown Seattle. Contrary to what everyone seemed to believe from watching TV and movies, the Space Needle was not visible from everywhere in the city.

I hit the Admiral Way exit hard and hoped the Civic would make it up the hill. No, I hadn't forgotten the way. Nor had I forgotten the house.

Who could?

I stopped my car at the curb and sat for a moment letting my gaze sweep the magnificent estate. It was an enormous monument to elegance, surrounded by lush green lawns, silver maples and evergreens. Several large rhododendrons guarded the bulkhead in front. I saw someone move behind the largest bush. Rolf Edmondson, the gardener, stepped out and watched me as he pruned. I wondered if he remembered who I was. His eyes narrowed while he pretended not to stare.

The house, creamy white with dark chocolate trim, was decorated with a glassed-in turret and gables like a giant cake. A wide drive circled from the street to a three-car garage on the side of the house. It was mostly hidden by stately trees and blended well into the background. A stained glass wall, a triptych of windows, graced the front of the St. Martin place by the front door. The three windows were immense, reaching from the ground almost all the way to the eaves. The artist had let his imagination soar and had swept the scene with ribbons of bright violets, electric greens, blues and vibrant reds. The figure of Medea, rich with color and flanked by the Furies, was cloaked in veils. She held aloft a gleaming glass dagger over the body of her slain child.

My last visit to this house had been a disappointment at best. Nearly every day since, I had wondered what had happened to Angelle. Shortly after her daughter had disappeared, Magda's second husband, Angelle's stepfather, had been killed in a parking lot downtown. It had been a random robbery and murder that never had been solved. Three years later, in 1981, I read that both Magda and her third husband had been involved in a fiery plane crash that had killed the man and scarred the woman forever. And now, Magda had lost another loved one. *Poor woman*, I thought, *I know what that's like*.

I left my car and nodded to Rolf on the way up the walk. The stained glass windows still had me in their grip when I stepped onto the porch. It was a fitting scene and the perfect house for an actress. One of the few mansions in West Seattle, it sat at the very top of Admiral Way and overlooked the whole of the city.

"Cheyenne Bruce," I said into the intercom. Almost immediately the front door opened and Laurel Gold smiled her welcome. She looked very much as she had five years before and exactly what she was. She was one of those women who moved from the thirties to the forties and beyond without changing. She was the only woman I have ever seen who had genuinely golden hair. Except for a few silver strands, it hadn't changed at all. She wore a plain sweater. The collar of a pink blouse lying neatly over the neckline. The thin gray line in it matched her simple gray skirt. Perfect attire for the nearing middle-aged maid-housekeeper-secretary of Magda St. Martin.

"Laurel." I took her hand. "I'm terribly sorry to hear about Mr. Levin." Laurel looked at the floor, swallowed, then moved so I could enter.

"I'm so glad you came," she said. Her voice was husky and tremulous. "It's been a long time, Cheyenne. How are you?"

"Keeping well," I said. Her fingers were cold and damp.

We stepped into the foyer. It was so familiar and though it had been five years, it seemed like yesterday that I had walked out of this same house, defeated. The room appeared unchanged. The floors and furniture surfaces shone like new patent leather.

"Magda and Mr. Radford are in the music room." Laurel's voice broke and she coughed to cover it up.

"Laurel, first tell me what happened," I said. I put my hand on her arm. Her nervousness leapt into me like an electric shock. Her eyes filled with tears but she didn't allow them to overflow onto her face.

"Jake was out late last night. We didn't think anything of it. He works late like that…often. Clients fly in from all over the world and he isn't home until three or four in the morning sometimes. Occasionally he even stays at the office overnight. Magda went to bed early. I watched a movie. Then, of course, the police…" She stopped and swallowed again as if fighting down her tears. "Please,

Cheyenne, go in to Magda. She wants to see you."

I crossed the living room and looked back at the windows. In the morning light, the intense hues spilled onto the floor like a colorful carpet. The music room door was closed and the house was quiet. Laurel opened the door and stepped back for me to enter, then she closed it softly, staying outside.

Easy sat next to Magda on a love seat, holding one hand and murmuring. Both looked up when I came in. I wondered why Magda had chosen the music room for this meeting when the living room would have been more cheerful. Was it because she saw herself presenting a more picturesque scene here than would have been possible in a more comfortable setting?

"Chey," Easy said. He released the hand he had been holding and rose to meet me. Magda's eyes looked stunned, but her mouth formed into a cool smile.

"Cheyenne," she said, lifting her hand. Her brilliant blue caftan covered all but the tips of her fingers. They felt hard and cool. "I'm so glad you could come. I asked Mr. Radford to send for you. I hope you don't mind."

If Laurel Gold had not changed, Magda St. Martin had changed enough for both. Five years before, Magda's hair had been a luxuriant brown. It had gone gray and though it was brushed into a short, becoming style, it had aged her. She was thinner and seemed somehow shorter than I remembered. I thought bitterness had burned into her eyes as well, and her hand trembled like a butterfly.

"I don't mind at all," I said and released her hand. "Although, I'm afraid I may not be of any help. Didn't the police come and take all of the information?"

"Oh, the police!" Magda brushed them aside as if swatting at a fly. "Yes, they were here. They told us what happened and asked us a million questions. They said they would be back for formal statements tomorrow. They think they have a suspect, but... oh, I don't know!" She got up from her seat and wandered about the room, touching her possessions as she went. On the piano, a bouquet of late roses caught the light and stained the dark wood with the color of blood. Magda paused before it and absently pulled one of the flowers from the vase. She resumed her pacing, methodically tearing the rose into shreds of ruby and emerald. I could see a small, rippled scar above the high neck of her caftan. It was a tiny peek of the extensive scarring below. I wondered just how far down her body it went.

"Jake brought me these flowers the day before yesterday," Magda said and glanced at the ruined rose in her hand as if just then realizing that she had torn it to bits. If she weren't Magda St. Martin, I would have said she looked helpless. She turned and appealed to us. "What am I going to do without my love?"

You're going to do exactly what I do, I thought.

You're going to wait until you can see couples enjoying each other without being so angry and jealous that it hurts. Only, for me, I knew, it had been almost twenty years and I was still waiting.

Easy went back to Magda's side. His job, to dispatch such news as death and dying to the innocent public, was sometimes an ugly one that I had never envied.

"I want to hire you, Cheyenne," Magda said, suddenly all business. "If you could stay here a few days…a week…for protection…"

"I understand they have a suspect," I said quietly, taking a seat in one of two winged chairs and drawing Magda into the other.

"Yes, a teenager who was seen in the neighborhood a couple of minutes after they found Jake. He was high and carrying speed and marijuana. I don't think he did it. He's a boy. What reason would he have for killing Jake?" Her eyes were clear and her voice strong. It was hard to believe that she was discussing her husband's death.

"Robbery?" I suggested.

"No, there was nothing taken," Easy said. He stood behind Magda and put his hands on her shoulders. I watched them kneading gently as if he were massaging his strength into her.

"Is he someone Jake knew?" I asked. She shook her head. "Is there anyone you can think of who might have wanted him…who would have wished him harm?"

She shook her head again. "Nobody dislikes Jake. Everyone loved him. I just can't believe that something like this could happen to such a sweet..." Her voice trailed away as if she was unable to go on. I stole a quick look at Easy.

"Do the police have a weapon?" I asked him. He shook his head but, before he could answer, Magda spoke again.

"No, they don't have a weapon," she said. "They said he...They said knife wounds..."

"It's all right," I said, not wanting her to continue. "I'll get the police report later."

"You know," Magda said. Her hands rested in her lap. "After the accident, I thought all of the bad things were over for me." She looked up at me. "You heard about the plane crash? Yes, I remember getting a card from you." I nodded and she continued. "I was burned so badly, I thought... The doctors thought I would die. And, of course, Mason *was* dead. I thought I couldn't go on. I've lost everyone I've ever loved. Everyone." She sat calmly, looking at the past. "It's as if someone is stalking my family. Peter was stabbed in a parking garage, you know."

"The police found the man who did that, I thought."

"They thought so, but had to release him. No evidence and he had an alibi," Easy said.

"Yes, it was an alibi," Magda said. "You know what I think? I think...no, I'm sure it was that Donald Tooley. That crazy man. They questioned him, when Peter died. And he threatened Mason!" She turned her head and looked up at Easy. "He could be the one who killed Jake, couldn't he?"

I looked from Magda to Easy. "Who is Donald Tooley?"

"He's a fan who wrote me letters and threatened both Peter and Mason." Magda's voice was ragged. She stopped and put her fingers to her lips.

"Miss St. Martin, the police will question him," Easy said.

"No. They have the wrong man. They won't bother looking for anyone else. Don't you see? They think they have the man, but they don't. Cheyenne, please say you'll stay and help me. The press will be surrounding the house as soon as word gets out. They'll hound me and follow me everywhere I go. I need you. The police..." Her voice trailed off.

"Magda," I hedged. "The police will do everything possible. If you need protection, a private security guard..."

"It's the money, isn't it?" she said, brisk and businesslike again. "How much do you want? What is your regular fee for something like this? A thousand? Two? Five? Tell Laurel and she'll have a check for you immediately."

"No, it isn't the money," I said. "My usual fee is $30

an hour and expenses. If you want me to stay here, that's going to run into quite a chunk. I honestly don't think you are going to need protection, Magda. If you don't have a security system, it would be cheaper to install one than to have me around full time." I looked at Easy. "Aren't the police willing to patrol the neighborhood?"

Easy nodded.

Magda swept all of my objections away with a wave. A huge diamond, surrounded by sapphires, glittered on her left hand. Her nails were blunted and short. "I want *you*," she said. Over her shoulder, Easy winked at me and nodded. Inappropriate as it was at the time, I felt a little thrill of pleasure. I had always been a sucker for a guy who winks.

"A security system—" I began again, but Magda interrupted.

"Security system be damned!" she said. Cold green fury flickered in her eyes. "I want a living, breathing, thinking human being here." She looked at her ruined hands lying in her lap. "Let me hire you for a week. For protection, yes, but primarily so you can look into the case independently," she said and raised her face to mine. "Please."

In the end, I agreed to it. Not because I wanted to but because I couldn't turn down the flat fee of five-thousand she offered, especially in view of the fact that it would just about pay the rest of my mother's bills. Besides, I owed Magda something. A long time ago, she had lost her child and I had failed to find her.

I gave her the forms and a standard contract to sign. "I'll have to go home for a while and arrange to be away. How about I come back later, say noon?" I put my hand on her shoulder, hoping to give her what shred of comfort I could. Underneath my hand, under the caftan, beneath her skin I felt fear and something else flowing along with her blood and I was glad I had given in.

I glanced at Easy and started to move toward the hall. When I opened the door, Laurel was so near I thought she might have been listening.

"Laurel, would you go in to Magda? I'd like to talk to Mr. Radford and I don't think she should be alone."

"Are you staying, then?" Laurel asked. Her eyes looked wide and frightened, yet she didn't look directly at me. I nodded, wondering if they had arranged for me to stay before I ever arrived.

Laurel went into the music room and Easy stepped out.

"Oh, God, Easy, I don't want to stay here!" I told him in a whisper. "What am I going to do that the police can't do?" I sighed. "Oh, that poor woman has been through so much." Even though I had agreed to help, I felt trapped.

The light from the stained glass window fell on Easy's shoulders. His hair was black and straight as if at some point an ancestor had mated with a Native. His strange denim blue eyes took the light from the window too. One eye was false, the result of a childhood accident. The pupil of that eye remained the same size while the other one dilated in moments of excitement. Easy was a good five inches taller than I and three years younger. At the time, that made him 34. I would have preferred to say I was not attracted to him, but that simply wasn't true.

"It's good money," he said. "Besides, you'll be in my city. I'll get to see more of you."

The thought of using the money to make a final payment on my mother's medical bills helped cheer me up. But only a little. Easy cheered me more. "Oh, shame on you. And a man of the cloth, too," I said, smiling. I got a terrible pleasure out of teasing him.

"Hey, I'm a chaplain, not a priest." I saw him frown slightly at what he had said.

"Hmm. You would think you were a priest, always turning me down like you do," I murmured. "Look, I told Magda I would be back about twelve. You going to stay here with her?"

"You know why I turn you down," he said, refusing to hear my question.

"Do I?" I bent my head and rummaged in my pocket for my keys. I knew. Easy hated his nickname because he wasn't at all easy. Not in the immodest meaning of the word, anyway. In disposition, he was as comfortable as a plush bathrobe, but his morals could have used a little unbending. I had almost succeeded in getting him to unbend a time or two but it almost wasn't worth it in view of the guilt he suffered. "It doesn't look good for the public to see such behavior from a police chaplain," he had said more than once. But that was only an excuse and a lame one at that. He firmly believed that sex should wait for marriage and he must have known by then that I was not going to be ready for anything like that for a long time. Maybe never. I was well aware that he wanted to settle down some day and have a family. Usually, when we were together, we had fun, teased, joked and talked about our work. Lately, though, I had seen signs of something in him that had caused me more than a little discomfort.

"I'll see you later if you're still here," I said. I knew he wouldn't be, though. In a city the size of Seattle, there was a lot of need for comfort and consolation.

I went back to my car and pulled away from the curb without looking back at the house. By the time I reached I-90, I felt guilty because I was still thinking about Easy and not Magda.

TWO

May, 1978

My first case had been a lot like the first day in my new school when I was in the third grade. I didn't know what the hell was going on, or why it should be important.

The disappearance of Angelle St. Martin had been my first case as a private investigator. Oh, sure, I had worked with a detective agency for a year and a half, long enough to pass the exams and meet state requirements. But Angelle had been *my* case. My first one flying solo. My license had been so new, the ink still smeared if I held onto it too hard. It had been so new that people were still hiring me as a psychic. Magda, in fact, had hired me as both a psychic and a private investigator and the St. Martin case had influenced every case that followed.

It had been May. Magda and her husband, Peterson Winthrop, were dividing the year between Los Angeles and Seattle. Magda had recently finished a film and was taking a vacation. Peter, a scriptwriter, presumably could work anywhere.

"I've never worked with a psychic before," Magda said to me that day after we had introduced ourselves. "Nor a private investigator." We stood at the front door of the gorgeous home. I was entranced by the house as well as Magda's ethereal beauty. At least, to me it was beauty. I had always been fascinated by the unique and that's exactly what Magda was.

The moment I walked into the house I could feel its life. I sensed there had been anger there, and suspicion. There had been deep love and some laughter, but very little joy. I felt a forlorn despair, too, but these feelings seemed to be more like echoes, as though they were from past occupants of long ago.

Magda ushered me into the living room. She wore a pair of peach satin lounging pajamas. I have never looked at that color since without thinking how perfectly it matched her skin. It was hard to tell where Magda St. Martin stopped and the garments began. If I had been a man, I would have been instantly in love. In fact, I'm not sure that I wasn't, a little. Her body, fluid and looking incredibly vulnerable under the fabric, moved smoothly each time she crossed her legs or swept her dark hair out of her eyes. It was hard to believe that she was heading toward fifty. It was difficult to say exactly where her beauty lay. Taking her features one at a time; her mouth was too wide and her nose a bit large, but absolutely perfectly shaped for her face. Perhaps the beauty lay in her green eyes that were very nearly the color of emeralds, or possibly the serene self-assurance with which she made every move.

I had smiled at her, hoping to reassure her, but at the same time feeling dull and inadequate. I also hoped I looked more confident than I felt. There seemed to be nothing of Angelle in the house. Nothing of real youth. At least that I could sense.

"When was the last time you saw Angelle?" I asked, wondering if she hadn't already told me. I had soon learned to carry a notebook. And, later, learned to listen carefully and remember as well. Some PIs liked to tape their interviews and, when I was in training, I had done it for a while too, but had given it up. People didn't say the same things when they were being recorded as they said when they were not.

"We had lunch together the day before yesterday," Magda said. Her eyes glinted like hard, cold gems. "But I know she was home that evening because I heard her in her room. It's across the hall from mine."

"May I see her room?"

"Of course." Magda had stood in one flowing ripple of peach silk. I have never understood how some people do not seem to generate wrinkles in their clothing.

The woman I had supposed was Magda's housekeeper stood in the doorway. "Mr. Winthrop is home," she said, her voice timorous. She pulled at her blouse and smoothed her skirt.

"Laurel, this is Cheyenne. She's going to help us find Angelle. Cheyenne, Laurel Gold. She's my right hand." Magda had breathed a soft laugh. "And my left."

Laurel gave me a prim smile. In contrast to Magda's sensuous fluidity, she looked almost too tidy. Where Magda was made from silk, Laurel was made of finely woven wool. In fact, she resembled Magda enough that the two women could have been sisters. Half-sisters, I decided. They both had beauty. Laurel, however, looked more functional than beautiful. She shook my hand. In her handshake I felt a momentary sense of something hard. Not strength, exactly, but a quality that didn't match her aura of timidity.

"I'll take you up to Angelle's room," she said, and looked questioningly at Magda.

She led me upstairs to the second floor. I ran my hand along the banister. The rich wood was as smooth as mink. At the top of the stairs, I glanced back in time to see Magda slide her arm around the waist of a tall, solidly built man.

Angelle's room was orderly and I caught the sweet smell of flowers in the air. I spotted a bottle of Jungle

Gardenia on the dressing table, picked it up and held it in the palm of my hand. I let my mind empty and focused on the bottle in my palm. Nothing.

"Did you see Angelle at any time after Mrs... Miss St. Martin saw her?" I put the cologne back on the table.

Laurel moved the bottle to the exact spot where it had rested before I had picked it up. She shook her head. "I saw her the day before yesterday too. At lunch," she said. She glanced around the room as if to assure herself that everything was in perfect order.

It was a very feminine room. Too ruffly for my taste. The double bed was covered with white lace and, underneath, a blue coverlet showed through. A dust ruffle swept the shining hardwood floor, though I was reasonably certain no dust was ever allowed to touch it. Dark blue drapes had been drawn back and white organdy curtains hung over the windows. The wastebasket was empty and the desktop had been cleared. Except for the bottles and boxes on the dressing table, it could have been a guest room awaiting an occupant.

I opened the closet door and peered inside. Expensive looking jackets, pants, dresses and blouses hung in a neat row. Shoes rested in pouches, and sweaters, folded and stacked, occupied most of the compartments. I ran my hands along some of the clothing. For a second, I felt a breath of youth and heard a note of faraway laughter, but then it was gone. I felt much more of Laurel there than Angelle.

"If she ran away, she hadn't planned to change her clothes," I said.

"A few things *are* missing," Laurel told me. "Her casual clothes mostly. A few pairs of shoes." You couldn't have proved it by me. The closet looked like a well-stocked women's clothing store.

"What about her bank accounts? Do you know the name of her bank and her account numbers?" I asked, feeling like I was prying. When I had first started working as an investigator, I suffered agonies of embarrassment feeling that I was intruding. It had taken me a while to get over that.

"I can get them for you." She stood nearby with folded hands, as though she was afraid to reach out and touch anything.

"And her social security number?"

Laurel nodded.

"The police have been notified, of course," I said. It was funny how some people overlooked the obvious and would rather spend money than go the simple, traditional route. I opened a drawer and noted stacks of panties and stockings.

Laurel moved to the window and peered anxiously down. Her alertness was like a taut wire. A mere touch and she would have begun to hum with tension.

"The police wouldn't take this seriously," she said.

"They have so many runaways, they don't bother with the ones who are as old as Angelle." She turned her back to me, but I had seen that her eyes were blank.

"Do you mean it hasn't been reported?" I shut the drawer. I was beginning to feel a bit cranky. I felt as though Laurel was jerking me around, and Magda too, withholding information and being agreeably uncooperative. She nodded, but offered nothing further. "Yes, it has been reported, or yes it hasn't been reported?" I asked, hoping I didn't sound as impatient as I felt.

"It has not been reported," she said. She seemed sure that I would get any necessary explanation from Magda, but I wasn't so sure I would.

"I'll need a list of her friends," I said, wondering how much information, psychic or otherwise, I could get from Angelle's family if I could get so little from her own bedroom.

Laurel stood by the door until I had finished another walk around the room. I felt as if I had done nothing at all. I almost always got some feeling of a person when I have been in his or her bedroom. The only feeling I got about Angelle was so fleeting as to not be there at all. Her room was ordinary; full of clothing and furniture but little else. It was almost empty of Angelle herself.

We left the room and Laurel shut the door silently behind her. Downstairs, she left me in the living room. Magda and Peter sat side by side on the sofa. Sunlight was beginning to break through a spring storm's clouds and it washed through the windows above their heads. It would turn out to be a nice day.

When I entered, Peter stood.

"Cheyenne Bruce," Magda said. "This is my husband, Peter Winthrop."

"I have always thought of psychics as being old hags," Peter said. "Frankly, I'm surprised to find a good-looking woman like you doing this." Magda glanced at him quickly and her forehead creased into an instantly erased frown. I ignored his comment, as it deserved.

"Mr. Winthrop," I said.

"I hope you're going to find our little girl for us," he said when we both had sat down. He sat closer, if possible, to Magda than before. They seemed the perfect couple. His big masculinity complemented her like a rich gold setting does a diamond.

He insisted that I call him Peter. He smiled but the concern never left his face. I searched his brown eyes and found only worry. I wished too late that I had held out a hand for him to shake.

"When did you last see Angelle?" I asked him. The concern flickered for a moment and was replaced by something foreign. I only had a second to wonder about it.

"I saw her on Sunday afternoon," he said and turned as if to have Magda confirm it. She nodded.

"On Monday, I was at work all morning in my study and I had lunch with an agent. That evening Angelle didn't appear for dinner."

"Are you very close to Angelle?" Again, just the briefest flicker in his eyes.

"I married Magda when Angelle was eleven. Seven years ago. Yes." Again, he looked at Magda. "I would say that I know her quite well."

"Peter helped me raise Angelle," Magda said, laying a smooth, youthful looking hand with long tapered apricot nails onto Peter's knee.

Laurel returned and silently handed me a piece of paper. On it she had written a list of Angelle's friends and their phone numbers. Her handwriting appeared as tense as she. Her letters were oddly squared. She started to retreat but Magda called her back.

"Stay, Laurel," she said. "You might be able to help." Laurel hesitated and looked uncertain, then chose a chair opposite the couple and next to me.

"Thank you," I said and pushed the paper into my pocket. "Do you know of any problems Angelle might have been having?"

"I think she is having some difficulty with a boy," Magda said. Curiously, both Peter and Laurel objected.

"No," Peter said, emphatically shaking his head.

"I don't think so," Laurel said.

"Why do you say that, Miss St. Martin?" I asked, ignoring them for the moment.

She gently tapped one of her nails against her chin. "When we had lunch together that last day, I thought she was looking tired. I teased her about it at first." She stopped and thought for a moment, then resumed. "She kept drinking water. That's what she always did as a child when she had something bothering her or something to hide. She would drink water. Glasses and glasses of it. The colder the better. We used to keep a glass bottle in the refrigerator and I'd always know when Angelle had something on her mind because that bottle had to be refilled constantly." Peter folded Magda's hand into his. I saw a diamond the size of my thumbnail on his wedding ring finger, so big it looked fake, but I knew it wasn't.

"Just because she drank up her water, darling, doesn't mean she is having boyfriend trouble," Peter said. He smiled, showing teeth too perfect to be natural.

"Well, I think she is," Magda insisted. "When I asked her, she didn't deny it."

"Do you have any idea who the man might be?"

She frowned and thought a moment, then shook her head. Her hair brushed Peter's shoulder and I saw him smelling it. "She has lots of friends. Boys and girls." Magda laughed softly and a little sadly. "I guess I should say 'men and women.' She isn't exactly a girl any longer. You'll be getting in touch with her friends, won't you?"

"Yes. Laurel has given me a list. Do you recall what Angelle was wearing the last time you saw her?"

Both Magda and Peter looked flummoxed.

"She was wearing her white cable knit sweater," Laurel said. "And those red plaid bell-bottoms." She said "red plaid bell-bottoms" as if she was describing pants made out of live lizards.

Peter and Magda nodded together. "Yes, that's right," Magda said.

"Does she have any piercings or tattoos?"

"Oh, heavens!" Magda said. Peter stayed mute and Laurel looked as though she wanted to say something. "She would never do anything to mar her body," Magda continued with a short laugh.

"Laurel, do you have anything to add to that?" I asked. Laurel shook her head, her mouth taut.

"I don't want you to spare anything in finding her for us," Peter said. "No matter what the expense, we want her found."

"Maybe you should tell me a little more about Angelle. What does she like to do?"

"She likes to do all of the normal things that girls like to do. She rides horses, swims, sails. I can't think of anything she doesn't like." Magda again creased her face into a frown for only a second. It was as if she wouldn't allow herself to hold any one expression for long. My grandmother used to tell me to quit making faces for fear my face would "freeze" that way. Magda apparently subscribed to the same theory. She seemed afraid to leave her face in a frown or a smile for more than a few seconds.

"She doesn't like living in Seattle," Laurel said, her voice barely audible. She looked up. "At least...But, I could be wrong."

"What Laurel means is that Angelle thinks Los Angeles is more fun than Seattle. She doesn't particularly like spending her vacations here," Peter said.

"Why does she, then? Surely she's old enough to be on her own." Magda and Peter looked at Laurel, who in turn looked guilty. I had a feeling I was about to learn why the police had not been notified. No one voiced any opinion so I pressed on. "Does she have her own car?"

They all looked at each other again. "Yes," Peter said finally. "She has a Mustang. It's still here. In the garage."

"If she were leaving," I asked, "why wouldn't she take her car?"

Again, they exchanged looks. I was getting more cross by the minute. "She doesn't have her driver's license," Magda finally said. "Angelle was in a little trouble last year." Magda moved her other hand to Peter's arm as if he infused her with energy. "She was into drugs and alcohol for a little while. We had quite a time," she said, laughing lightly, as if she were talking about a disobedient toddler. "When she had a tiny run-in with the police—it was all just a complete misunderstanding—they gave her probation."

"Not probation, darling," Peter said. "They called it 'parental control'".

"Anyway, part of the conditions of it were that she was to have supervision for a year and loss of her driver's license. Until she's eighteen. There are actually still a few weeks...less than a month to go."

So, there was another thing they hadn't been strictly honest with me about. Angelle was only seventeen, not eighteen.

"She hates the supervision, Cheyenne," Peter told me. He grinned winsomely. "She despises it. We think she's probably gotten a little rebellious idea in her head and has run off."

"Well, she's always been rebellious," Magda said. "That's part of her charm."

"Did you call any of her friends in Los Angeles?" I asked.

"Immediately," Magda said. "None of them know anything. They all promised to call if they hear from her. Of course, whether they will or not..."

"We want you to find her before we have to report it," Peter said. "Do you understand? If it becomes official that she isn't with us, she might have to go to jail."

"Oh, Pete, they wouldn't do that!" Magda said with a shocked laugh. Nevertheless, she looked worried. "Well, that's why we find it so strange that she would run away," she said. "I don't think she would do anything to violate her probation." She glanced at her husband. "Her 'parental control.'"

"Does she have any money with her?" I asked.

Again, they all looked at each other. "She has a generous allowance," Peter said.

Magda nodded. "She could easily have some cash."

"She would need quite a bit," I said. "For her to disappear for very long, unless she's staying with friends, she would need a substantial amount."

"We don't monitor her spending habits," Peter began. "She may have..." he shrugged, "several thousands." He looked at Magda and she nodded.

I let the question drop then, intending to check her bank account activity later myself.

"Mr. Winthrop," I said, "you told me you are close to Angelle. You're her stepfather. Sometimes having a stepparent is a strain on a teenager. Are you sure she feels as close to you as you feel toward her?"

"Yes, indeed!" he answered, his voice hearty. I thought I heard a sniff from Laurel, but when I glanced at her, she was sitting quietly looking toward the stained glass windows in the foyer.

"Angelle's father was Roger St. Martin," Magda said. "He died from a stroke when Angelle was only five. I married Peter when she was eleven. He's practically raised her."

Peter nodded. "She isn't happy about her supervision, of course," he said. "But we didn't have any arguments about it."

"You see, Cheyenne," Magda said, as if she were about to admit to something shameful. "I've always wanted to give my daughter everything I could. Every advantage. I was raised..." She broke off and smiled sadly. "I was an unhappy child. We were quite poor. I lived with an alcoholic mother and father who...well, he abused me. And so did she. I was locked into the attic or the basement for hours at a time. Once, it was two days." Her voice choked off and Peter pressed her cheek with the palm of his hand.

"Don't, darling," he said. He looked at me. "My wife has overcome her childhood."

"Not quite, Peter," she said with a faint smile. "You see, I can't go into attics or basements, even now," she said to me. She seemed to give herself a gentle shake. "However, my daughter has had a wonderful life. I've seen to that. I can't imagine why she would want to run away." She spread her hands into a gesture indicating helplessness. For a moment, I saw worry and strain line her face before it vanished.

"What are her goals? Does she want to be an actress, like you, Magda? Or is she a writer, like you, Peter?"

Magda's laugh was the sound of crystal bells. "I once wanted her to be an actress. She's very pretty, though not beautiful. She looks too much like me for beauty." Peter murmured something and Magda briefly leaned her head on his shoulder. "You're sweet," she said. "I wanted her to try modeling too, but she didn't want to. Said it was for empty headed mannequins." She laughed again. "She has a mind of her own."

"You haven't had any arguments with her lately?" I asked,

"None," Magda said firmly. Peter shook his head.

"Laurel," I said, "do you have any ideas?" Again, she looked like she wanted to say something, but ended by shutting her mouth and folding her hands firmly in her lap. Then she shook her head. Her soft blonde hair swung into her face.

"Miss St. Martin, Mr. Winthrop," I began, "I strongly suggest that you report this to the police."

Magda had begun to shake her head before I had finished speaking. "No," she said. "I will not risk my daughter ruining her life by being arrested for parole violation." She glanced at Peter when he started to say something. "Yes, Peter, I know it's 'parental control'!" she said, her voice sharp with impatience. "She has lived on her own before, she knows how to take care of herself. She isn't a child. I insist that the police do not become involved." This time her frown was not so quickly erased.

"One more thing, then," I said. "I'll need a picture of her. Later tonight, I'll try to get a clear mental image of her. It would help if I could have a recent photo."

Laurel rose and went to the mantel behind me. She handed me a framed photograph. In it, a young woman with an impish grin stared at me defiantly. She seemed to be thinking, "Find me if you can." She had Magda's wide mouth, but her cheekbones were higher, giving her a more traditional beauty than her mother's.

"May I take this one?" I asked. "I'll bring it back unharmed."

"Certainly," Magda said. "And we've to write you a check as well." Peter went to a small antique desk in the corner and switched on the stained glass lamp. While he was busy there, Laurel removed the photograph from the silver frame. We hadn't discussed fees and I wondered what Peter's idea of a retainer would be. That was in the days when I was shy about charging for something as intransigent as psychic feeling and I was not yet used to charging for investigation. I eventually learned to quote my price before I asked too many questions; just enough to determine whether or not I wanted to accept the case.

I needn't have worried. With a hefty check and a photo in my possession, I headed out into my first real case.

Later, I would again stress to Magda and Peter that police investigation was warranted. Bank records showed that Angelle had not withdrawn any funds after her disappearance and I had not been able to reach her mentally or otherwise. But Magda remained adamant, convinced that Angelle's reputation and future would be destroyed if the police became involved. For a while, I persisted in trying to find the elusive girl, but eventually I had to admit that nothing further could be done. It had become the case that never stopped haunting me.

THREE

Tuesday, November 15, 1983

When I got back to my apartment, I had a message from Mrs. Lockett at Northwestern Life who wanted to know when I would finish up with Mr. Houston. Northwestern Life hired me from time to time to investigate insurance claims. Mostly, the jobs were straightforward; someone claimed a disability that proved to be uncomfortably real. But occasionally a Mr. Houston came along.

Clovis Houston had probably been one of those kids in baggy pants and suspenders who nagged his mother to buy the cereal just for the prize inside the box. I could imagine him dumping his Cracker Jack onto the ground so he could get to the trinket. He spent his time looking for the bonuses in life without wanting to deal with having to pay for them. He claimed that his ex-wife, a little thing of maybe ninety-five pounds if she was retaining

38

water, had deliberately rear ended his car with him in it. The resulting whiplash, he claimed, had left his temporomandibular joints permanently damaged. He claimed he couldn't open his mouth more than ten millimeters. He was grandly willing to forgo pressing charges against her if his former wife's insurance company, my Northwestern Life, would pay him a more than generous sum of money for current and future damages. Thus far, none of the dentists or specialists he had seen had persuaded him to open wide. My feeling was, and it concurred with the insurance company's opinion, that Mr. Houston wouldn't weigh the three hundred and fifty pounds he did if he couldn't open his mouth any farther than ten millimeters. My job was to catch him in the act. I had spent hours watching him lug home bags of groceries containing Sara Lee cheesecakes, loaves of Wonder Bread and dozens of doughnuts and maple bars, but I hadn't snapped a single picture of him eating them. Of course, those things could be broken into small pieces, but I didn't see Mr. Houston's patience stretching that far. I wrote in my organizer to call Mrs. Lockett and tell her I wouldn't be able to watch Mr. Houston eat for the foreseeable future. They would either assign someone else to him, or he would be waiting for me when I finished up with Magda.

I briefly thought about taking my pistol with me. I lifted it out of its case and held its cold danger in my palm, then placed it back into the cabinet and locked it. "No reason to take guns along," I said to no one. "There's been enough killing already." I rarely, if ever, carried my weapon. I had learned long ago that, though I had had enough training that I was proficient in its use and more than qualified to carry it, I was not prepared to take another person's life. Nor did I believe that my judgement was such that I could make life or death decisions in the space of one or two seconds. For me, protection must come from whatever knowledge I had gained in self-defense classes.

My tool kit was my briefcase, an old doctor's bag that Easy had found for me. In it, I had a flashlight and batteries, an assortment of plastic bags, latex gloves, my compact camera, extra film, a ruler, binoculars and, for disguise purposes, a couple of scarves, a baseball hat and sunglasses. I put my portable typewriter into its case and found an empty loose-leaf binder and added plenty of filler paper. I added my organizer, a few clothes, toilet articles and shoes to my suitcase, realizing the last person who had used it was my mother when she had gone to the hospital for the last time.

I opened the door of my apartment and very nearly ran headlong into my landlady, Mrs. Sacks. It wasn't yet noon. This was not a good sign.

"Oh, Cheyenne," she said. "I'm glad I ran into you." She looked guilty and I got the feeling she had been waiting for me to come out.

"Good morning!" I tried to sound cheerful, but the

day hadn't started out well and it looked like it was going further downhill.

"I need to talk to you." She cleared her throat. She obviously had something unpleasant to say and wanted to get it out of the way as quickly as possible. She was a small woman of sixty or sixty-five. I knew she and her husband were antique dealers and their home, upstairs, was crammed with priceless treasures. I've always thought they had let me have the basement apartment so cheaply because they liked the idea of a private detective living downstairs as a sort of security measure.

"Would you like to come in?" I stepped aside and she entered into my minuscule living room. I put my suitcase down and she looked at it absently, then got right to the point.

"Mr. Sacks and I are...uh...we're going to be moving to Spain. We'll be leasing the house and the new tenants will want the apartment too. I'm afraid you're going to have to move." She said it all in a rush, and then looked relieved that her ordeal was over.

"Oh," I said, completely at a loss. My little apartment had been something of a security blanket for me. A little ball of anxiety began to form in my stomach.

"I'm sorry," she said and looked like she was about to cry. Well, hell, so was I! "We both have enjoyed having you as a tenant, you know. Mr. Sacks and I both, well…"

"Spain!?" I said, hoping to head off any demonstrations of feeling that might embarrass both of us. "That sounds so lovely. I guess I should start looking for a new place, then. How soon do you think…?"

"The first of the year, I'm afraid," she said. "We're moving to our home on the coast of Spain and the new tenants want to move in as soon as possible." Once she had imparted the bad news, she seemed in a hurry to leave. She made her excuses and I was left to deal with the fallout. The anxiety in my stomach threatened to turn to panic.

◆ ◆ ◆

By the time I had pulled out onto I-90 for the third time that day, the sun was gone and there was a definite November chill in the air. Except for the drenching rain of the night before, the weather had been far too nice to indicate a coming winter. The darkening sky began to match my mood.

As I crossed the floating bridge, the wind was blowing from the south. To my left, Lake Washington was restless and choppy. Occasionally spray reached over the railing and batted at the traffic. I shoved an old John Denver tape into the tape deck but took it back out when he began to sing *Back*

Home Again.

Before the I-5 entrance, I moved over and merged onto the Dearborn exit. I had decided to stop by the Public Safety Building and get a copy of the police report.

At ten in the morning, the downtown traffic wasn't heavy. I parked in a lot where I knew the attendant. He waved and I headed on foot to James Street. In the records department, the clerk told me the report hadn't been filed yet and I knew I'd have to make the trip up to the detectives' office.

If Harlan Quiller is there, I'll just turn around and leave, I told myself. *No, that's cowardly, Bruce. Get in there and be a woman.* I tried in vain to subdue the irritation the thought of him always generated in me.

Harlan Quiller was indeed there. He looked up when I entered and his eyes lit up like a snake's when it spies a mouse. There was something oily about Harlan Quiller that made me want to wash my hands after I talked to him. I never sat down in his office. Partly because he never asked me to and partly because I didn't want to get grease stains on my clothes. I was pretty sure he had somehow heard that I might be involved in this case and had withheld the report on purpose. Or maybe I was being paranoid.

"Well, well, little lady," he said loudly enough so the other two detectives in the office looked up from their desks. I recognized Perce O'Dell and threw him a twitch of the eyebrow. "What can I do for you? Someone steal your lipstick?"

"Cut the crap, Quiller," I said. "You assigned to the Levin case?" I wished too late that I'd gotten Easy to find out ahead of time who had been assigned. If I had known it was Quiller I might have given Magda's case even more serious second thought.

Harlan Quiller was a handsome man. He looked like a tall cherub with his boyish blond curls and dimples. Once upon a time, when I had first met him, I had been attracted to him for about ten or fifteen seconds but had quickly realized that he was nothing but a scary clown in a cheap suit.

"Oh, are you going to 'help' us?" He curled his fingers into quotes around the word "help". "Wonderful!" I saw the other detectives go elaborately deaf and return to their work. "But you're too late, dear. We have a suspect and he's coming down off his high over at the jail right now."

I let out a sigh. "Who is it?" Out of the corner of my eye I saw Perce leave his desk and go out the back door.

"Well, you know I can't tell you that. Don't you worry, though. We've got everything under control." He moved to put his arm around my shoulder but I stepped away.

"I'll need a copy of the police report," I said, knowing it was a futile hope. The man laughed, sounding nasty.

"Gee, I don't think I have it right here." He patted his pockets and made a great show of looking around. "Nope. I think it's misplaced. Sorry. I'll let you know if we need any knitting done or anything like that." His dimples deepened; tiny sinkholes in the asphalt of his face. Even though I knew he was merely showing off for the benefit of the other detective, I stared at him long enough to make him blink, then left.

Outside, in the hall, I nearly ran into Perce.

He laughed and held up his hands. "Hey! It's me and I'm not Quiller!"

"Oh, sorry, Perce," I said. "You know, someday guys like Quiller are going to get into serious trouble for the things they say and do." The idea made me smile.

Perce O'Dell towered over me by at least a foot and a half. He towered over everyone. His almost seven-foot body was full to the top with kindness. He had a perpetually sad face, as if by looking down on most people he was able to see more than he cared to know. Some, seeing his unkempt awkwardness, took him for stupid, but he was a crack detective. One of SPD's best. A long time ago, I had found his lost son. He would be my friend forever. We'd had dinner together and cried on each other's shoulders once or twice for various failures of marriage and career. We hadn't been lovers, though I wouldn't have minded. Maybe we knew each other too well for that.

"I saw you in there," I said. "How come you didn't say 'hi'?"

"Didn't want to remind Quiller that I know you," he said, waving a Manila envelope under my nose. "If he had remembered, then maybe he would find out that I got a copy of the report for you."

"Oh, Perce!" I grabbed it and peered inside. "You are a good man."

"Yeah? If I'm so good, how come I'm not rich?"

"Are you on the case too?" If he was, my job would be a cinch.

"It's Quiller's case," he said. "I'm on that Greek restaurant thing. But I just happened to be going by when Levin's body was found. Brower and I hit the scene just about the time the blue and whites showed up and I did write part of that report."

"What else can you tell me?" I stuffed the envelope into my briefcase. There was a sudden loud voice from the detective room. "He's going to come out here and see us," I said. "I've had enough of him to last for the next five years."

Perce leaned over and pressed the elevator down button for me and the up button for himself. "I'll call you," he said.

I scribbled Magda's phone number on the back of a business card and handed it to him. "This is the number of the victim's widow. I'll be staying with her for a week. A few days, anyway." The down elevator arrived and I stepped in. "You call me tonight."

He nodded and the elevator doors shut.

I n a few minutes I was back on I-5. I passed the Rainier Brewery and merged onto the West Seattle Bridge heading back to Magda's.

The St. Martin mansion was in one of the most beautiful parts of West Seattle, but the world didn't look so good to me that afternoon. When Angelle had vanished, it had been late May and the yard a showplace of color. Now the rhododendron bushes were devoid of blossoms but the late roses and chrysanthemums glowed with ruby and topaz. Whatever else he was, Rolf Edmondson was one hell of a gardener. I made a mental note to talk to him.

No one answered my ring and after a moment I stepped off the porch, walked around the house to the back and tried the door knob. The door opened and I stuck my head inside.

"Laurel," I called softly.

"In here," she said. She put her head around the corner and motioned me into the house where I found myself in the laundry room. Laurel was removing articles of clothing and towels from the dryer, inspecting them and placing some of them back into the washer. A line stretched across one end of the room and from it hung a dripping slicker and a sweater that looked like it would take days to dry.

"Aren't you doing that backward?" I asked. Laurel

didn't smile. Instead, she turned a solemn face to me.

"Magda is very meticulous about her home," she said. "You know that."

I noticed a line of strain under her eyes. Jacob Levin's death had affected her deeply. More, perhaps than the death of an employer normally would. I wondered if he had been more to her than that. But, then, she'd been part of Magda's family since before Magda had even married Jake. Undoubtedly, she had felt close to him.

"She won't tolerate even one stain on the linens," Laurel was saying. "If there are any at all, they go back into the washer. If a second washing doesn't remove the stain, the item is thrown out." Laurel spoke as if reciting a lesson from rote.

"Where is she?" I asked. "Is she all right?"

"Oh, yes." Laurel sighed, sounding tired. "She's lying down upstairs. As soon as I'm through here, I'll show you where to put your things."

"Did Easy...Mr. Radford take her down to identify the...uh...Mr. Levin?" I put my bags on the floor and picked up a pair of clean gardening gloves. Laurel took them from me.

"Please, let me do it," she said. "Yes, they went just after you left this morning. It took a lot out of her. I wanted to go but she said she wanted to do it."

"She's a very strong woman," I said. Laurel looked at me quickly but said nothing.

Laurel's slender hands disposed of the towels and linens, either by folding them or placing them back into the washing machine. She still wore the neat sweater and skirt, an odd uniform for a laundress.

"You do a lot around here," I said. "Maid, secretary, laundry woman…what else?"

"Anything and everything," she said, smiling. "It really isn't that much. There's just Magda and Ja… Just Magda now. It doesn't take much to whip together a quick meal or do a little laundry or correspondence. If I didn't do it all, we would have to hire someone else who would have to be trained and would probably get in the way."

"You're very devoted," I said, meaning it as a compliment.

"Oh, I know everyone thinks I'm a fool for doing all this, but Magda needs me. Especially now." Her face reddened and her eyes filled. She fidgeted with the corner of a hand towel.

"Of course, she does." I was surprised at her outburst. I, for one, had never thought of her as a fool. Far from it. "Laurel, what happened? About Jake, I mean. Were there any indications that he was in any trouble? Any threats, perhaps that Magda knew nothing about?"

She shook her head. "No. I can't think of anything." She inspected a filmy garment, either a nightgown or a slip, placed it aside and picked up another that looked so fragile, it seemed to be made of cobwebs.

"I never met him. What kind of a man would you say Jake was?"

"Jake Levin was one of the nicest men I have ever known," she said. She continued to fold clothes and didn't look up when she spoke.

"What kind of business was he in?"

"He was a products manager," she said. "Whatever that is." She smiled sadly. "It has something to do with advertising and promoting products."

"How had Jake been lately? Did he seem worried about anything?"

She stopped sorting as she squinted at the window. "Yes, now that you mention it, I'd say he was worried. Maybe not worried, exactly, but he wasn't his usual self."

"In what way?"

"Well, he's always so friendly and outgoing. He *was*," she amended. "He didn't have an enemy that I know of. But it seems lately he had been quieter than usual. I really didn't think anything of it."

"What do you think of it now?"

She pulled her gaze back to mine, then resumed folding. "I don't know. Nothing, I guess. He probably had something important going on at his office."

I wondered why she had mentioned it at all. "Do you think he and Magda were having trouble?"

She shrugged. I waited. Finally Laurel sighed.

"They weren't having 'trouble' exactly. They had... words a few times."

"All couples have 'words.' Do you mean they were fighting more than usual?"

"Oh, no. They didn't fight. I could sometimes hear them talking and when I came into the room, they would go quiet. Or sometimes, at breakfast they would just sit there and eat. Not talking, you know?"

"So, nothing more than any other couple? You didn't actually hear any conversations?" She shook her head and looked miserable, as though revealing even that much seemed disloyal to her. "And you have no idea what any of the disagreements were about?"

"No, I didn't hear...Once, I heard them having a... well, not a fight. I heard them having words."

"You mean, they were having loud words?" *Lord*, I thought. *How hard does she want me to pull?*

She nodded.

"Where were they when they had the loud words?" I felt like a kindergarten teacher interrogating one of her students.

"We had all gone to bed."

"So, it was loud enough for you to hear them through closed doors. How far away from their room is yours?"

"Across the hall." She kept her head down, folding and sorting, folding and sorting. I decided to let the matter drop for now. I wasn't getting anywhere anyway.

"What do you know about Rolf Edmondson?"

She glanced at me quickly. "Rolf? Why? He doesn't have anything to do with this."

"Probably not," I said. "But I have to check out everyone if I'm going to earn my fee. Besides, the police will undoubtedly be interested in him."

"Look, if you think Rolf was involved in this at all, you're wrong. He has nothing to do with it. I suppose you and the police will be asking him all kinds of questions. He's off this afternoon," she added, as if hoping he would escape my questioning altogether.

I backed off. There was no sense in distancing her. I could find out later why Laurel Gold was so defensive about Rolf Edmondson. The last time I'd talked to Rolf, his hands had been filthy and he'd looked sweaty and unshaven and smelled like dirt. And the glimpse I'd gotten of him in the front that morning had told me he had not changed much in five and a half years. I saw him as a small, quiet man who looked something like a grimy camp counselor.

"I thought the police had a suspect," Laurel said, after a moment.

"Yes, they do. A teenager who was walking by last night approximately when the police showed up on the scene. They held him for a little while, but if he isn't free by now, he will be soon. I don't think he's the man."

She nodded and whipped a pillow case into the air where it cracked like a gunshot. Then she folded it and turned on the washer. She collected the small stack of clean items. "Come on, I'll show you where your room is."

She led me through the kitchen, down the hall and up the curved staircase to the second floor.

"My room is right here at the top of the stairs. Magda's is the master suite here on the right. You know Angelle's room right next to mine and next to Magda's is one of the guest rooms. This is the servants' quarters here on the left. Obviously, we don't use them for anything." She stopped in front of a door across from the servants' rooms. "Yours is this one. You have an *ensuite*."

So, Magda has never given up on Angelle after all, I thought. *Angelle still has a bedroom.*

My room was big and airy. Lace curtains covered the windows that looked out onto the side yard. The walls, a pale blue, were trimmed in rich cream. The room was furnished with a desk, a large dresser and a carved antique armoire in addition to the bed. A comfortable looking armchair upholstered in royal blue sat near the window.

"This is lovely," I said. The room, not including the bathroom, was maybe slightly larger than my entire apartment on Mercer Island.

"Yes, the house really is beautiful," Laurel said. "Magda's second husband, Peter, bought it for her and Angelle, you know. They had to have it cleaned out. It was a terrible mess. The artist who lived here was something of a recluse. He let the place go almost to ruin before he died." She fiddled for a moment with tucking in her perfectly straight blouse, then smoothed her already neat sweater over it. "They said he killed himself." She looked around as if to make sure everything in the perfectly appointed room was in order. "If you don't mind," she said, "I still have some chores to do. You can rest here until Magda wakes, if you wish. Do you need anything to read? The library is on the third floor. Feel free to use it. Just go up the stairs that are right outside here, and it's just above you."

When Laurel had gone, I hung my black dress for the funeral in the roomy closet and peeked into the armoire to discover a television hidden inside. I unpacked the rest of my clothes and set up a work station at the desk. There was a check and a house key waiting for me on top of it. I got my typewriter out of its case and put my notebook nearby. There was a telephone on the desk, too, but I wished that I had my own. I had heard of a few people having mobile phones that didn't have wires and could be carried around, but I had never seen one. When I was finished, I had to decide which I wanted to do, go over the police report or make a quick tour of the house on my own. I settled on the police report. It would be better to explore the house by myself. I planned to wait for an opportune moment when both Magda and Laurel were out.

I settled into the chair by the window, opened my loose-leaf notebook and began to add notes under five divided sections.

Once upon a time, I took a novel writing class. I never wrote the novel, but I learned a valuable lesson in organizing my notes. I made divider headings for suspects, motives, alibis, scene and clues. Everything was cross-referenced. I always sorted out my notes that way with variations for the type of case I was working on. I was not very organized by nature, so it helped to have everything written in one place. At the back of the notebook, I kept a running ledger and time sheet showing time spent, expenses and money received. When I finished with it, I began on the report.

The police report stated that at 11:07 pm, a nearby resident, Jason Philbrick, had reported screaming coming from across the street. When the police arrived at 11:16, they found Miss Suzanne French, 23 years old. She had discovered the body of Jacob Levin in his car parked on Harbor Avenue, just before it becomes Alki Avenue. Mr. Levin, according to Miss French, had been waiting for her. She had opened the passenger door and stepped into the car before realizing that she was sitting in a pool of blood next to a dead man. She had then leapt out of the car and screamed until the police arrived. They found her at the scene, covered with blood and still screaming.

Did killers panic after their attack and draw authorities with their screams? I thought not. Although the woman could have been acting. I doubted that, too, but wrote her name under the "suspects" heading. I added Rolf Edmondson's name as well as Magda's and Laurel's and the Donald Tooley Magda had mentioned. Right then, everyone was a suspect and would remain so until I had eliminated their names from the list one by one. Of course, there was always the possibility that it had been a random killing, like Peter Winthrop's had presumably been, but I didn't think so. The fact that Mr. Levin had been sitting in his car made that seem unlikely. Had a stranger jumped into the car with him, I believed there would have been more signs of a struggle. He apparently had been taken completely by surprise. And nothing had been taken. His wallet, credit cards and cash had been left intact.

I saw no reason, other than the drug possession, for the police to hold the teenaged boy they had questioned. I finished up entering the information, drew up a time sheet and noted my hours. Though I was being paid a flat fee, I felt compelled to stick to my good habits.

I put in a quick, reassuring call to Mrs. Lockett at Northwestern Life. I told her I was still watching Mr. Houston and I would have his case settled soon. Since I had impending homelessness to worry about, I couldn't afford to pass up the small bonus I would receive from finishing it. I would have to find some time to get it done. I had just hung up when I heard a door open and close down the hall. I went to my door and found Magda about to go down the stairs.

She heard me and turned. "Oh, Cheyenne, you're here," she said. Her gray hair was perfectly in place and there were no wrinkles in her clothing. She put a cool hand on my arm as we descended the stairs together. "I want you to feel completely at home here," she was saying. "Anything in the refrigerator is fair game, whatever you need. If you can't find something, tell Laurel."

"I hope I can be of some help to you," I told her.

"It helps just having you here," she said.

When we reached the bottom of the stairs, Magda moved toward the music room. At the door, she stopped and stiffened. "Where are they?" she asked, her voice rising. "What's happened to my flowers?"

Laurel appeared in the doorway from the living room.

"Laurel," Magda said with an edge of hysteria creeping into her voice. "What have you done with my flowers?"

"I threw them out, Magda," she said quietly. "They were wilting."

Magda stabbed Laurel with a look then pushed past her through the living room and into the kitchen.

Laurel watched her leave. She twisted her hands as if she carried an invisible dishrag. "She'll go fish them out of the garbage now," she said, "and she'll see that they're too wilted to keep. I get rid of them when they start to die and she gets upset because they can't stay perfect forever." She dropped the invisible cloth and clutched her own elbows. "Sometimes I'm afraid...I"

I waited only a moment. "What are you afraid of, Laurel?"

"I think she might be going insane." She looked chilled.

"She's upset, Laurel. You both are," I said.

"No. It isn't just that. She's..." Laurel glanced at the door. "She acts crazy. Everything has to be absolutely perfect or she has a screaming fit. Well, you saw it. She'll expect those flowers to last forever." Tears trembled on the woman's lashes.

"She said they were from Jake."

"If I hadn't thrown them out, she would have blown up anyway."

"Laurel, while she's busy, I'd like to ask you a question. Do you mind?"

"No, of course not. Why should I?" She threw her head back. I could see her willing the tears away.

"This Suzanne French who found Mr. Levin in his car. Do you know her?" I watched Laurel carefully.

"No, I don't," she said. She pressed her lips

together and went back to holding her elbows.

"You didn't know she was Mr. Levin's...That she was seeing Mr. Levin?" Laurel didn't look shocked. At least not shocked enough.

"Okay. Yes, I knew. But I didn't know her name." She looked at me defiantly.

"Does Magda know?"

Laurel moved her gaze to the window, then to the floor, then back to me. She bit her lip, looked at her hands and said, "She does now."

FOUR

Tuesday, November 15, 1983

Laurel had said Rolf had the afternoon off so I turned down the split pea soup and chicken sandwiches she offered and headed for his house. I wondered whether he was still home and what he did with his free afternoons.

Laurel had told me he lived in what was called the Caretaker's Cottage. It shared the lot with Magda's house as the only other building on the block. The cottage itself was charming. The multipaned windows sparkled and the outside of the house looked well cared for.

He opened the door immediately, as if he had been standing on the other side waiting for me. He wore jeans, a belt sporting a buckle made from a huge agate and a denim jacket. He was leaving. If I had waited another two minutes, I would have missed him. If he was surprised to see me, he hid it well.

"Mr. Edmondson, I don't know if you remember me. I'm Cheyenne Bruce. I investigated the disappearance of Angelle St. Martin five years ago."

Fine lines netted his sun-browned face and his eyes looked like he had seen too much of the underside of life. "I remember you," he said, not too graciously. He edged me out of the doorway and shut the door behind him. "I didn't know anything about it then and I still don't."

"I want to ask you a few questions about Mr. Levin's death. Would you mind?"

"Look, this is my time off. My free time. I'm not staying around here. If you want to ask me questions, you can wait until tomorrow." He loped down the walk and I had to trot to keep up.

"Where are you going?" I asked. He continued toward his car; a battered station wagon parked at the curb. I followed along behind him, probably looking like an anxious puppy.

"Junction," he said.

The "Junction" was the main intersection of the community. Thirty or forty years ago it had been the downtown of West Seattle. But, in the first part of the 80s with the addition of the Jefferson Square shopping center, just one block east, the Junction had been on its way to becoming just another intersection. There were still diners, drug stores, video arcades, record stores and taverns there that hung on and probably always would. I imagined that a lot of West Seattle residents might have resented the hell out of Jefferson Square for taking business away from their beloved Junction. I could foresee a time, however, when the Junction, with the addition of some hip restaurants and maybe a theater or an art gallery, could flourish once again.

He got into his car and started it up. Just as he was pulling away from the curb, I opened the passenger door and jumped in. He stepped on the brake, forcing me to brace myself on his dusty dashboard. "Look," I said. "I was hired to investigate the murder of Mr. Levin. Would you rather answer my questions while you're at work tomorrow or do it right now, on your day off?"

He gave a disgusted grunt but continued ahead, not looking at me. His car smelled like cigarettes and mildew and gave off an aura of past violence and sex. I thought he was probably more dangerous than I had been led to believe but I hadn't gotten any concrete feeling from him at all. Yet. I kicked aside a Seven-Eleven cup with a trapped straw that was rolling around on the floor.

He parked in a lot behind the main business area and I trailed after him into a dismal looking walk-through whose tiled walls were decorated with graffiti and what looked like a large mustard stain.

I imagined he was heading toward one of the taverns and I reconciled myself to drinking a beer. I was wrong. The Silver Dollar was a video arcade, somewhat cleaner and possibly newer than any of the other establishments sharing California Avenue with it. At 2:45 it was nearly empty. There were a couple of preteens, skipping school, and a three-piece suiter who might have been taking a late corporate lunch, though from what corporation I couldn't imagine. At least, his video proclivities were possibly less harmful to his liver than a martini lunch would have been.

The unique aroma of the Silver Dollar was a mixture of sweat, the grime of money, and stale cigarette smoke. Though smoking was prohibited by an authoritative sign, I imagined the combined exhalations of hundreds of smokers over the years had taken a toll on its permanent air quality. The place probably hadn't been aired since it had opened. Rolf shoved a five-dollar bill into a money changer and scooped up a handful of gold, quarter-sized tokens.

With an unlit cigarette hanging from his mouth, Rolf poked two of the tokens into a nearby machine that had the words "Double Dragon" and something in Chinese painted on the front. While he concentrated on the screen, I stood next to him watching the action before me.

"You got questions, ask," he said finally, the cigarette bobbing with each word.

"It's a little hard to talk in here," I said.

He took his eyes away from the screen and squinted at me. Then he turned back and smashed a whip-bearing female figure with a computer-generated baseball bat. The machine made a squeak very much like a trapped rat. "You didn't have to come in here," he said.

Across the room, brilliant lights flashed in succession. I glanced over and saw "Retina Scan" scanning my retinas. I turned back to Rolf's game.

"How about I buy you a beer," I said.

"I thought you wanted to talk about Mr. Levin's murder," he said loudly. The two boys abandoned their game and glanced our way.

"Rolf, keep your voice down, please!" I said. I wasn't about to put on a show for the regulars. "If you don't want to talk here, we can go somewhere else, but I'm not going to question you in front of an audience no matter how macho it makes you feel."

"What do you want to know?" He actually flushed a little.

"For starters, you can tell me what you were doing at eleven last night." On the screen, an apparently indestructible female figure offered kicks and jabs with her spike-heeled boots.

"I was right here."

"I suppose you have several dozen friends who will be glad to corroborate that," I said, wondering for the hundredth time why I had ever gotten involved in this thing. I knew the police had not yet questioned Magda and her staff but they would soon be asking him the same questions I was. "Did Mr.

Levin have any enemies that you are aware of?"

He said nothing. His game was over and we moved to a machine with the words "Altered Beast" painted on the side in fluorescent yellow. He fed a token into it and the brilliant eye adorning the screen changed to a mostly naked man at odds with several horrific looking monsters.

"As far as I know he didn't have any enemies. I didn't kill him. I was right here. Yes, people saw me here, I guess. There are a few people who come here all the time but we don't go staring at each other. We're here to play the games and when we do that, we're looking at the screens, not each other." He turned and looked at me. His man got disintegrated by a devil-thing throwing its own regenerating head. "Anything else?"

"Yes. How did you hurt yourself?" I gestured toward the network of scars that covered the backs of his hands.

He looked in the direction of my gaze and shoved his hands into his pockets. For a moment, I thought he was not going to answer.

"What happened?" I pressed.

Finally, he pulled another token out of his pocket and dropped it into the machine.

"Fire."

"Fire? When?"

"That doesn't have anything to do with Mr. Levin,"

he said. "You don't have any right to ask questions just out of curiosity, even if Mrs. St. Martin did hire you."

He was right, of course. Magda had hired me to protect her and to look into Jake's murder. That didn't include asking her gardener about his scars. But there was something about Rolf that didn't fit with Magda, Jake and Laurel. I couldn't imagine him as part of the household. He was too...crude. And too dangerous.

"Look, could we go somewhere else and talk? How about I buy you a cup of coffee?"

He didn't answer. I watched him for a minute more, then turned to go. He surprised me by abandoning the machine and following me out. Next door was a little café that sold soggy looking tacos and that kind of chili you would expect to burst into flames when you dip in the spoon. Normally I didn't drink coffee but I ordered it partly because the pot of hot water sitting on the burner looked cloudy and I didn't want to look like a wimp in front of Rolf by ordering tea. He let me buy the coffee and we found a seat near the window.

"How did you feel about Mr. Levin, Rolf?" I asked. The coffee tasted like it was in danger of spontaneous combustion too.

"He was my boss. I guess he was okay," he said. He watched the sidewalk for signs of life.

"A good boss, would you say?"

"Sure. I didn't hate him or anything, if that's what you think."

"I don't think that. I don't think anything. I just want to know how you feel about the family. What about Magda? Do you know her well?"

"Look, mostly I stay outside and do my job. I do the gardening and some repairs around the house. Something big, they call a plumber or an electrician. I don't hardly know them." He kept his eyes focused everywhere but on my face. I didn't think he was telling the truth.

"What about Laurel?" At last, his expression changed. I could have sworn his eyes went soft for a moment before he covered it up with a frown and a sip of the murderous coffee.

"What about her?"

I sighed. "How well do you know her?" Maybe he'd had an affair with her or something. No crime in that, although he didn't seem at all Laurel's type.

"Like I said, I stay outside, do my job and *hope* to get a relaxing afternoon off once in a while." I stared at him over the rim of my cup. Finally, he said, "Okay. I know Laurel pretty well. We've both worked for Magda for a long time. We're both part of the staff, so we tend to, you know, stick together."

Suddenly he shoved his chair back and dug into his pocket for a tip. He was out the door almost before I had a chance to react. Probably he was sorry he had given me any information at all.

I saw him re-enter the Silver Dollar. I thought about following but decided to let him have the day off he wanted. I left him there and walked south on California Avenue, peering into some of the shops and stopping to browse in Northwest Art and Frame. In the Pegasus used book store I spent more time and money than I had intended. I crossed the street then headed back up the other side. I stopped at the bank to deposit Magda's check and continued north on California Avenue in the late afternoon, glad I had worn comfortable shoes. I caught a late lunch/ early dinner at a little *sushi* place near Admiral then walked the rest of the way to Magda's. It was a long, brisk walk but I needed it. I wanted to sort out all that I had heard so far, such as it was, so I could enter it into my notebook in some kind of order.

By the time I got back, Laurel and Magda had settled down for the evening. Their bedroom doors were shut and I could see lights under both. The only other light burning in the house was the one on the stairs, presumably for my benefit. I turned it off and closed my own door to work on my notes. I had to admit, there wasn't much.

My notebook was still painfully bare of notes when the phone on my desk rang. In a moment, Laurel tapped on my door to say the phone call was for me. It was Perce.

"Chey," he said. He always sounded glad to talk to me. A guy like that was nice to have around sometimes. "Got a few minutes to talk about the

Levin case?"

"There's nothing I would like better," I said. "Where are you? Home?"

"Yeah. Even the police get to knock off sometimes."

"While we PIs are always on the job."

"Okay, you got the police report. They let that kid go. Hassled him a little about the pot but didn't hold him. I, frankly, don't know why they picked him up in the first place."

"Tell me about Suzanne French," I said.

"The girlfriend? Apparently, they met right there in that parking space once or twice a week for a little...what you could politely call a tryst. The windows are tinted so no one can see in. They've been doing it for a couple of months now."

"Right down there on Alki? That's really risking it, don't you think?"

"Sure, it is. I wouldn't do it," he said. "There are a lot of things we civilized folks would do and a lot we wouldn't do. I guess he was pretty hot for her."

"How come they didn't go to her place or a motel or something? Jeez, that's kid's stuff."

"I guess it was the thrill of the risk," he said. "Anyhow, I think Quiller really raked her over the coals when he questioned her."

"Do you think she had anything to do with it?"

"No, not me. Quiller does, though. But you know

him."

"Magda was saying something about a fan of hers. What do you think about him?"

"Could be. They'll be checking him out. Let's see, the techs were out at the St. Martin's this afternoon looking at Miss St. Martin's car. Laurel Gold, it seems, doesn't have one. They didn't get a look at Rolf Edmondson's. It wasn't there and he wasn't at home. You probably saw them there."

"No, I was out. Talking to Rolf Edmondson, as it happens."

"Get anything from him?"

"Nope. He told me absolutely nothing. Why?"

"He's an ex-con, you know."

"No, I didn't." I had that old feeling again that Magda and Laurel had been jerking me around. They might not have been lying, exactly, but neither one had been telling the whole truth. I had been planning to do background checks on all of them, but it was good to have the information early. "So, what was he in for?"

"Aggravated assault. He tried to kick a guy to death in the MacDonald's parking lot five years ago. Did two years and now he's on parole until the end of December. Oh, and the guy, the one who ended up in the hospital with four broken ribs and a depressed skull fracture? He was going with Miss Suzanne French at the time."

"Shit," I said. "Does Rolf know her?"

"Apparently he used to be engaged to her. We got a file this thick on Mr. Rolf Edmondson." I couldn't see his fingers but I could imagine.

"She must have been pretty young," I said. "She's only twenty-three now."

"Sixteen," he said. "Needless to say, it didn't last very long."

"What in the hell was Magda thinking when she hired an ex-con? She's asking for it."

"He, Mr. Rolf Edmondson, saved Miss St Martin's life. You happen to notice some bodacious scars on my man's arms? The plane crash three years ago? Rolf was on the plane too. That's what did it. He'd just gotten out of prison and she hired him back. Lucky for her that she did. He pulled her from the wreckage. At great personal suffering to himself, I might add. She has a lot to be grateful for."

"But he worked for her before that," I said.

"Yes, he did." I heard paper rustling on the other end.

"He's been working for her for more than five years," I said. "Since before Angelle disappeared, anyway."

"Disappeared?" he asked. "Who?"

"Magda's daughter. Over five years ago. According to Magda, she ran away, but I've always had a few questions about that."

"I wasn't aware of that," Perce said.

"No, Magda and her husband—that was Angelle's step-father—didn't want the police involved. *Insisted* that the police not investigate."

Perce "*tsked*" a couple of times.

"Magda must know Rolf is an ex-con."

"Sure, she does. Her job offer enabled him to make parole without having to go to a half-way house or take some crap job slinging burgers," Perce said.

"Maybe Magda doesn't care that Rolf has done time but, knowing her, it doesn't seem likely."

"That give you enough to chew on for a little while?"

"It does indeed," I said. "Listen, Perce, thanks for calling. I'll be in touch."

I hung up and debated about whether to go up to the library to look around, read one of the treasures I had picked up from the bookstore or just go to bed and get the whole miserable day over with.

The house was quiet except for the normal creaks and moans an old house makes during the night. It was cold in my room, but I was reluctant to leave the relative warmth of the bed to search for another blanket. Annoyed with myself for being unable to fall asleep, I tried deep breathing for relaxation. Generally, it took me fewer than twenty breaths before I lost count and dozed. That night I reached fifty-six before I yanked back the blanket and pulled on my robe.

The living room was lit with the streetlights outside. I thought of my tiny apartment and the pride of ownership I usually felt for my meager store of furnishings. What magnitude of owner's pride did Magda feel? I really didn't think the house could be worth less than a couple of million. The furnishings another million. I wondered if Magda had put Jake's name on the deed. Either way, with Jake's death, it all belonged to Magda.

I saw the flowers Laurel had thrown away, now gracing the table in the foyer. They looked tired but not too bad. Magda's tirade of the morning had apparently evaporated entirely.

In the kitchen I found a plastic bag holding a handful or two of walnut meats. I poured a glass of orange juice and, carrying it and the walnuts, I wandered into the living room. The huge windows loomed over me.

I ran my hand over the lower portion, feeling the texture of the glass and the smooth lines of metal running between each piece. Some of the glass which looked one color in the daylight, with the sun shining through, took on an entirely different appearance at night. The artist had cleverly used glass which had its own character in the dark. The window took on new meaning depending upon the amount of light that hit it and from what direction it came. Even to my untrained eye, the windows before me were obviously superior pieces.

As I stood gazing at the windows, the house whispered around me. Faint voices, far away, echoed into the darkness. Somewhere deep in the house, I heard the garage door rumble into life. In a moment, the kitchen light came on and Magda appeared in the doorway.

"Oh!" she said, her frown relaxing instantly. "I thought it was Laurel standing there. Cheyenne, is something wrong? Couldn't you sleep?"

"Magda," I said. I let out my breath, amused at how much she had startled me. "I thought you were in bed. I'm sure you generated at least a few premature gray hairs. I'm supposed to be protecting you."

She laughed, a little guiltily I thought, and murmured an apology.

"I was hungry," I said. "I hope you don't mind that I drank some of your juice and ate a few nuts."

"Not at all. You know you have free rein in my house. I told you that." She pulled off a pair of gloves and shoved them into the pocket of her coat, then unbuttoned it. "That's a wonderful window, isn't it?" she said, nodding toward the triptych.

I had the feeling she was deliberately steering the conversation away from herself, though where she had been or what she had been doing was hardly any of my business.

"I wish I had the talent to create something as beautiful," I said, falling into her neutral conversation. I would be getting personal soon enough.

"Talent is a gift," she said. "I had it, you know. I guess I still do, but the desire is gone. Talent without desire is the biggest waste there is. And now, with Jake gone…"

"Do you feel like talking about him?" I asked her.

She looked at me, seeming to consider the question. "I think I do," she said. "Let's sit down." She knelt to pick up a tiny speck from the floor. I wondered if it had been a crumb of walnut. Magda put it into the pot of the huge palm by the front door.

The house seemed to settle around us while we went into the living room. She switched on a lamp and we sat at either end of the sofa. She still wore her jacket, an expensive looking brocade, so smooth and unwrinkled it could have been new.

"I know it may be difficult to talk about him this soon," I said, "but I've found that talking about the… the loved one who is gone, sometimes helps. Why don't you tell me about Jake, Magda?"

"Jake is…was everyone's friend. He was the only man I ever met who was completely without selfishness. He loved everyone. And everyone loved him."

Not everyone, I thought.

"We met after the accident. The plane crash?" She

looked at me. I nodded. "I didn't care about anything then," she continued. "Mason was gone, Angelle was gone and Roger, her father. Peter was gone. Even my looks were gone. It seemed to me that everything that had been important to me was gone. I had lost them all and for some cruel reason, I was forced to live on." She waved her hand. "Oh, I don't mean I was suicidal. I don't think I could do that. But I just didn't care to live anymore. And, by all rights, I probably shouldn't have. I should have died in the crash with Mason."

She stared at the past for a moment, then laughed softly. "Typical story of the actress. Married four times. This one, though, was never divorced. That's odd, isn't it? Married four times and never divorced? I suppose it makes me look guilty in a way." She turned to me. "Do you understand what I mean? Have you ever lost someone you cared deeply about, Cheyenne?"

I said nothing for a moment. I had lost my mother, but I knew that wasn't what she had meant.

"Yes," I said, wondering if I should continue. But, if I wanted her to be honest with me, I knew I had to be honest with her. "Once, I was deeply in love with a wonderful man. We planned to be married." I swallowed. I so seldom spoke of David that I almost couldn't do it at all. Magda murmured a sympathetic word or two. "He went to Vietnam and never came back."

"Killed," she breathed.

"Missing and presumed dead. There had been an explosion... They never found him."

"Oh, my dear!" I saw a twinkle of tears in her eyes. She put her hand on mine and I felt her warm, honest sympathy. "Have you ever tried to use your... power...your psychic ability to...?"

"Find him? Oh, yes. We actually had a psychic connection, David and I," I told her. "I think if he was alive, I would have been able to reach him. It was like a light went out one day. At one moment David was alive and in the world. The next, he wasn't." I cleared my throat. "Then, a few years later, I found another man I thought I loved. Did love. Very much. We got married." I didn't want to talk about Cam either.

"But it didn't work out," she said.

"No. It didn't work out."

Neither of us spoke for a moment, each thinking about our own problems. "But you were going to talk about Jake," I said finally.

She smiled and nodded. "You know, when I first met Jake, we were at a night club. I was with a group—not with anyone special. He asked me to dance. Well, that day, I had had a crown come off one of my lower front teeth." Magda laughed at the memory. "I was so self-conscious about it! And I was already terribly self-conscious about my scars. I suppose the tooth wasn't all that noticeable, but I thought everyone in the room could see it. He asked me to dance and then he asked me my name. I was surprised that he didn't know it, but that was Jake. Anyway, I leaned way over and whispered into his ear, 'My name is Magda'." She closed her eyes, still smiling at the memory. "I didn't want him to see my missing tooth. He thought I was coming on to him. After that, well, it was love! Pure and simple." Magda looked down at her hands. The scarlet coat covered most of them but her deformed nails plucked at the wide cuffs.

"You are helping me so much. I want you to find out who is destroying my family." The high neckline of Magda's dress showed only a hint of her scars. Above it, her face was a mask of carefully applied make-up and years of acting experience. I felt conflict emanating from her. She wanted me to find out what had been happening to her loved ones, yes, but there was more to it than that. I sensed that she had secrets as well.

"I don't know how much I can help, Magda," I said. "Especially if you go out at night without telling anyone." She had the grace to blush, but it, too, could have been part of her act. "I promised to help mainly because I never found Angelle for you."

"Why, I've never blamed you!" she said. Her eyes opened wide. "If anyone, I blame myself."

"But you shouldn't. She was almost old enough to do as she pleased. If she chose to run away, that was her decision." Even as I said it, I hoped that she *had* run away. I had never felt that she had gone deliberately.

"I suppose you're right," she said, but didn't look convinced.

"And, I can't help you if you refuse to tell me the truth."

She looked startled but said nothing.

"Why didn't you tell me that Rolf Edmondson had been in prison?"

She frowned, one of those instantly erased expressions she had, and looked guiltily down at her lap. "I didn't think it had any bearing on the case."

"But it certainly could have. I'm going to have to know everything if I'm going to help you with this."

"I guess I thought the police would question him and discover that he didn't have anything to do with it, because, of course, he didn't."

"Maybe yes, maybe no. Even so, I need to have all the information you and Laurel have."

"I'm sorry," she said with a charming little pout. "Am I forgiven?"

I nodded, but found it difficult to smile. I wanted to believe her. I wanted to like her. I felt that if circumstances were a little different, we could have been friends. But, if she wasn't out-and-out lying, she *was* avoiding the truth.

"Did you ever suspect him in Angelle's disappearance?"

She looked startled again. "Of course not! Why, that's absurd. You mean you think he helped her run away?"

"No. Not run away. That he might have done something to her."

"No. Absolutely not. I refuse to consider anything so ludicrous." She suddenly pulled a tearing yawn and I got to my feet deciding to put off the rest of my questions until another time.

"Let's get to bed," I said. "It's almost two now. In the morning I'm going to talk to a few people so we can find out what's going on here."

"Do you have any ideas yet?" she asked.

I shook my head. "It's too early. I want to check out that fan of yours." I stopped and appraised her. "And I want to talk to Suzanne French." Instantly her gaze iced into a hard, frozen stare.

"It's a shame, isn't it?" she said. She turned away from me to head for the stairs. When she faced me again, the ice had vanished. "It's a shame she isn't the one who is dead."

She climbed the stairs ahead of me and we said goodnight outside her door.

"I enjoyed our talk, Cheyenne," she said. "I have very few women friends." She smiled at me and it was so warm and seemed so genuine, I smiled in return but I left my guard firmly in place.

I got into bed and stared at the ceiling. Alone in the dark, I tried to get a mental fix on David as I had done thousands of times over the years. My mind probed, retreated and probed again, but it met nothing but deep, deep black. Usually, I got some sense of the person I was concentrating on. There would be a flash of feeling or a brief glimpse of surroundings. Something. Getting nothing never boded well. I tried again. Nothing. That was always a bad sign.

FIVE

Wednesday, November 16, 1983

The next morning. I woke with hundreds of little blacksmiths making horseshoes inside my head. I knew immediately, without using any psychic ability whatsoever, that it was going to rain. I got headaches from eating peppermint too. I don't sleep well away from home, either. I preferred my own bed, even though it felt like the entire Seahawks football team kept its shoes under the mattress. Needless to say, I was cranky.

It was early, not quite light. The clouds hung over the house like dirty cotton batting. People who don't live in Seattle said, if you don't like the weather, then wait fifteen minutes. They also said that people in Seattle don't tan, they rust. Neither statement was true, nor were either of them funny, but that's what they said.

I stretched, which was the closest I ever got to true exercise, which I disliked intensely. I thought the people who said they got high from it were liars. A good warm-up without ever getting into the perspire-y stuff did just as well for me. Fortunately, I had inherited a body type that doesn't gain weight easily.

I dressed in sweats and went quietly down the stairs planning to take a short walk before the rain started. The morning was dead calm, as if the clouds were pressing all life flat and nothing could move. I went out anyway. It wasn't for exercise. It was just a short, thinking walk.

So far, we had one dead person—two if you wanted to count Peter Winthrop, and I had to count him because he was dead too and his murderer had never been found. Okay, three, if you counted Angelle, but I hadn't completely given up on her yet. Well, maybe I had, but I wasn't ready to admit it. Say, two deaths and a possible third and at least five suspects if I included Donald Tooley. I had to get to Donald and talk to him. I imagined Quiller would be questioning him very soon.

On California Avenue, cars whipped by. I dodged them and made my way across the street then headed west to the other side of the bluff that constitutes the Admiral district of West Seattle. The wind picked up and pulled what leaves remained off the trees and danced them to the ground. Underfoot, a few inches of soggy ones had accumulated. They weren't the kind of crunchy fall leaves that one kicked. That told me it had rained in the night too.

Again, no psychic ability needed.

Of course, Rolf, Laurel and Magda all had to be considered as suspects as well as Suzanne French and an untold number of people who had known Jacob Levin. I didn't have any idea how many people that was or how many of those had perhaps carried a grudge for some unknown or forgotten slight. Had Suzanne's father resented his daughter meeting a fifty-ish man for a teenaged romp in public? Maybe she had another boyfriend who was the jealous type. And, thinking about jealous boyfriends, Rolf Edmondson had been jealous enough to kick the living shit out of a guy once merely because Suzanne was going out with him.

I needed to talk to Suzanne and I needed to dig up a copy of the Peterson Winthrop file. I could go downtown and get it myself or I could give Perce a call and let him do it for me. That thought was more appealing, though not quite fair to Perce. He had his own work to do.

A picture of Peter standing in Magda's living room greeting me with his winsome smile came to mind. He had been full to the brim with life and vitality. When he had died, I had seen it in the papers, but, of course, I was off Angelle's case by then. He had died right after my mother had, and I hadn't even attended his funeral.

Jake's funeral was that evening. I *would* be there.

It was nearing ten when I got back to the house.

The rain was just then starting what looked like a long day's deluge. Several strange cars and assorted vans had pulled up in front of the house and onto the drive when I turned to go up the walk. It looked like I was just in time. I recognized one of the cars as Quiller's. The rest belonged to reporters. I pushed aside a microphone and brushed past men and women hurling questions at me. They didn't know who the heck I was, but it appeared they didn't care. I ran up the walk and into the house.

"Quiller," I said, finding the man in the living room. "What the hell did you do? Alert them? Take your press conference out of here."

"Well, Miss Bruce, I didn't expect to find you here," he said. "Did your seventh sense tell you that we'd be over or did someone call you on that horribly mundane thing, the telephone?" I didn't bother to answer him. He peered outside as if just noticing the throng of eager reporters and camera operators congregated in the yard. "When and where the press gets its information is no concern of mine," he said.

"What made you change your whole *modus operandi* by coming out here to get a statement?" I couldn't resist pointing out to him that his deferential treatment was showing. "Don't you usually have people come down to your office for that? It makes you look just a teensy bit star-struck and that's not a good look for anyone."

Laurel appeared behind Quiller. "Oh, do you know, Mr. Quiller, Cheyenne?" she asked. She sounded

worried. "I didn't know you worked with the police."
I heard Quiller snort.

"I *try* to work with them," I said. "The man's
funeral is tonight, Quiller. Couldn't you hold this off
for a day?"

"She does pretty well," Quiller said to Laurel,
ignoring me. "Actually, Miss Bruce, we came out to
talk to Rolf Edmondson and process his car, but I
wanted to talk to Miss St. Martin and Miss Gold first."
He arched his fakey, penciled-on looking eyebrows
at me. "Now, can we get down to business?"

Magda stepped forward, cool, confident and
serene. She wore a blazing orange morning gown
with full, long sleeves and a neckline that went to
her chin. As usual, she looked regal and composed.

"Miss St. Martin." Quiller came so close to bowing,
I almost laughed.

"I hope you don't mind having Cheyenne in the
room with us while we talk. She's been a tremendous
help to me," Magda said, extending her hand. For a
moment, it looked like he was going to kiss it.

Quiller barely glanced at me. "Fine, fine," he said,
though I doubted that he had heard her. He normally
wouldn't have allowed me to be anywhere close to
the person he was interviewing, but Magda had all of
his attention. I thought he was going to ask for her
autograph. I wondered if I should go get him a pen.

"I thought you had a suspect, Detective Quiller. I
want to tell you right now," she continued. "I don't

think that young man did it. The one with the drugs. And I can guarantee that Rolf Edmondson had no more to do with it than I did."

Quiller's eyebrows shot up. "You can guarantee?" It looked like he had swallowed down the wrong tube and didn't know whether to breathe in or out.

"Yes. I'm certain he didn't. I do have a lead for you. That's what you officers call it, isn't it? A lead?"

Quiller nodded. He looked so flustered, I wished that I had my little camera in my hands right then. He succumbed to every bat of her eyelashes and flash of dimple she threw his way. I had worked as a consultant with the Seattle Police several times over the years and I had nothing but deep, sincere respect for them. Quiller makes them all look like a cadre of super-heroes by comparison. He took a tape recorder from his case and set it up on the coffee table.

He spoke his name, the date and time into the recorder then instructed Magda to do the same. Then he had her repeat what she had told him.

"Several years ago, I was being harassed by a man named Donald Tooley. I believe he may be the one who killed my husband."

"Have you heard from him recently?"

"Oh, no. I'm only telling you that since he once threatened my husband—not Mr. Levin, but Peter —, Donald Tooley should be questioned. Your people talked to him once after Peter was killed but he was never charged. They didn't even hold him after he threatened to kill my third husband. He most certainly could be the one! I'm only suggesting that you check him out."

"Could you tell me what you were doing the night Mr. Levin was killed?"

"Yes, indeed I could. I was in bed, asleep. I had gone to bed early that night as I was having one of my headaches."

"Headaches?" Quiller repeated.

"Yes. I get them every now and then. Jake called about six or six-thirty to say he wouldn't be home until late and I had a headache so I went to bed." She closed her mouth into a tight line, as if she knew what was coming next.

"Are you aware of the circumstances of the discovery of your husband's body?"

"Yes. I understand that he was found by a Suzanne French who was to meet him on Harbor Avenue that evening."

"Then you know Miss French?"

"Indeed, I do not. I do happen to know the circumstances. That was the question you asked, wasn't it, Mr. Quiller?"

He swallowed, but said nothing.

"I'm sorry," she said, bowing her head as if she had been acting but the whole effort had suddenly become too much for her. "I do know that the woman was his...that he was involved...seeing her.

Yes. I wish I didn't know that, but I do." I could almost see the steel in her. "Jake loved people," she said. "He loved everyone. Women, men, everyone. I don't mean that he was attracted to men," she said quickly, seeing the expression on Quiller's face. "I mean he was friendly with everyone. He was a little too friendly with women sometimes, perhaps, but he loved me, Mr. Quiller. Don't ever think Jake didn't love me. He never would have left me. Never."

"You don't sound like you're jealous, even though you say he was 'too friendly with women,'" Quiller said.

"On the contrary, Detective," she said. "I'm extremely jealous. But I'm not a killer. Even though he was unfaithful to me, I certainly couldn't have killed him. I loved him very much. You see… Jake married me and loved me when many men couldn't stand to look at me." She made a pathetic gesture toward her chest and the scarring hidden under her clothing. "I had to love him for that. I will always love him for that." She sat quietly, lost in the past and in her own grief. I thought that if Quiller had any sense of decency at all, he would go away and leave her alone. He didn't.

"It would be hard to take, having your husband go wandering after a twenty-three-year-old woman," he said.

Magda looked up at him, expressionless. "Is she that young?" she asked, but didn't watch him long enough to see him nod.

"It could make a woman crazy, couldn't it?" he asked, conversationally, "having your husband throw you down for a cheap tramp?" Magda looked stricken, but only for a second. A mask fell over her face and the serene woman was back.

"Of course, people will think that," she said. "Unfortunately, we'll never hear my husband's side of the story."

Quiller looked ashamed and must have felt he had drawn enough blood. "Thank you, Miss St. Martin," he said finally. Magda glanced at me then swept from the room. I had the impression that it was nothing more than a stage exit.

Laurel fluttered in, looking like a trapped butterfly. I felt sorry for her. She sat down, looked at Quiller, then me, then Quiller again. When he told her that she was not under arrest but that this would be a taped interview, she looked positively terror stricken. I wanted to reach out and touch her but settled for a wink. Quiller again stated the date and time and his name, then had Laurel state hers. It seemed to calm her some when he jumped in with the questions.

"Miss Gold, do you remember what you were doing the night that Mr. Levin was killed?"

"Of course. I was in my room watching TV." She looked quickly at me as if she wanted me to corroborate her story. I hadn't been there.

"Do you remember what you watched?"

Her answer was immediate. "Yes. Night Gallery is on Channel 22 at eleven." She looked confused momentarily. "Um, that's when they said the...Mr. Levin was found."

"Do you know who discovered the body?" he asked. She winced at the word "body".

"Miss Bruce told me it was Suzanne French." She looked down at her lap and began to play with a fold in her jersey dress.

Quiller threw me a look that, if he'd had his way, would have put my eyes out.

"Do you know who Suzanne French is?" he asked.

Laurel nodded, still looking at her lap. Suddenly, she looked up and right into Quiller's sneaky little eyes.

He requested a verbal answer and she managed a soft "Yes."

Quiller studied his notes for a moment and the lapse seemed to unnerve Laurel completely.

"Do you think I did it?" she asked. Her eyes were full of terror but I saw something else there as well. Defiance?

Good for you, Laurel, I thought. I moved to her side and slid my arm around her. I have to admit that my gesture wasn't completely humanitarian. I wanted to know what she was feeling. All I felt from her was discomfort.

"We have to suspect everyone, honey," Quiller

said. "I just want to get your statement. For the record, that's all. All right?"

She nodded again, then whispered another "Yes." I wanted to punch Harlan Quiller's lights out.

"Did you see Miss St. Martin that night, Miss Gold?" he asked. She thought for a moment. A tiny jolt went through me when I realized she was about to lie.

"Yes, I checked on her about ten." Quiller missed it, but I saw Laurel throw a frightened glance at the door Magda had exited from. "She was asleep," Laurel continued. "I...we...everyone loved Jake," she said in a rush. "I can't think of anyone who would do anything to hurt him. Anyone." She broke into sobs and Quiller looked as uncomfortable as any man does when he is confronted with a crying woman.

"I think that will be all for now," he said. "We do want to talk to Mr. Edmondson."

"Of course," Laurel whispered, composing herself, though she looked defeated. "I'll take you to him." She hurried away like a rabbit let loose from a trap. I walked to the door with Quiller and barely refrained from telling him what I thought. I tried to give him the benefit of the doubt. After all, the man had been doing his job. I had almost forgiven him when he turned around.

"You're a mind reader," he said. "Who do you think did it?" I saw his sneer just in time.

"Kiss off, Quiller," I said and shut the door. I hoped

it hit him in the ass.

Quiller and company had been gone about a half hour and Magda had pacified the press with a short statement when the mail arrived. Normally, I didn't pay that much attention to it, since all I ever got were bills and junk. Besides, I wouldn't be receiving anything at Magda's house anyway. But that batch stirred things up more than Quiller had.

I was just heading up the stairs to make some notes when I heard Magda gasp.

"I...I don't understand," she said. "I don't...." She handed me the paper. It was a letter. The handwriting sprawled all over the sheet.

Dear Mothermine

I know you have been terribly worried about me but things will be all right! The trouble between you & me has hurt us all. I can't take it anymore & must do something about it. You are the strong one. I love you. I don't want to take away one you love but can't help it. At first it will hurt but if you know I'll be happy that should make you happy too. Forgive

Love Angelle

I read the note twice, then over again. "I don't understand either," I said.

"My darling girl!" she said in a sad sounding

whisper. She looked at me, but didn't seem to see me. It was more like she was looking through me to another place and time. "In a way, this is just like Angelle," she said.

I watched her carefully. Surely, she could see that the letter was bogus. It was obviously an old letter with the margins cut off to make it take on a meaning quite different from the original.

"Magda," I said. "I don't think this is…" I hesitated, wondering for a moment how to tell her that someone was playing a cruel trick on her. "It doesn't say anything about where she's been or what she's been doing. It's pretty vague after five years. And what does she mean, 'take away one you love'?" *Surely, someone as intelligent as Magda St Martin wouldn't be taken in by this*, I thought. But, then, sometimes we believe only what we want to believe.

"Why, I imagine she's referring to herself. She's a very selfish girl, Cheyenne. Anything she has done or has wanted, she has simply taken. She believes anything is all right as long as it's something she wants. But you must understand that she loves me. She's come back," she said woodenly, then turned and headed for the stairs.

"Well, she hasn't come back," I said, but Magda was already halfway up, seeming to walk in a daze. "She had to have mailed the letter from somewhere," I said to myself. At least someone had. It bothered me. It was wrinkled as though it had been discarded at some point. It was sloppily written and there was no date. Yet, Magda had said that it was Angelle's style. I wondered where the envelope was.

At lunch, I asked Laurel if she had seen the letter. Magda had not come down to eat.

"I opened it," she said. "I open all of Magda's mail."

"And you read it?"

"Oh, yes. I read her mail and if it's something she needs to concern herself with, I leave it for her or hand it to her." She took a bite of her salad. She seemed entirely unconcerned about Magda ostensibly receiving word from Angelle after more than five years.

"Magda seems to think it's genuine. What did *you* think of the letter?"

She looked up in surprise. "I think that Angelle is a very selfish girl and that she hasn't changed at all."

"You don't think it looks a bit suspicious?"

"Suspicious? How? This is exactly the kind of thing Angelle would do. She loves being enigmatic. Mysterious. She's having fun." She broke a bit of crust off her French bread and sopped up a smear of salad dressing with it, looked at it and put it back down.

"I wouldn't call it fun," I said. "I would call it cruel."

She shrugged. "Angelle can be that way."

"Where is the envelope?"

"I threw it away," she said. Her eyes were round and surprised. "Did you need it?"

"Where is it? I'd like to see it."

Laurel looked around her as if the envelope was waiting on a countertop to be picked up. "I...I took it out to the garbage can, I think," she said. "Do you want it?" She asked again. "I could get it for you. Do you need it right now?" She stopped and looked at her watch. "The trash has been collected," she said. "I'm sorry, I didn't realize you would want it."

I almost made a comment about the convenient timing of the garbage collection, but held my tongue.

"You know," she began, as if she was about to make some deeply personal comment, "Magda's mother was insane. She committed suicide when Magda was fourteen. She almost killed her husband once too." She stood and began picking up the plates. Silverware clattered and almost fell to the floor.

"Laurel, what are you saying?" I asked. She sounded a bit out of round herself.

"What I'm saying is, Magda may have passed along some of that to her daughter. I think Angelle might have done it. I think Angelle may have killed Jake."

"Why would she do that, Laurel?" I asked. "Why would she disappear for five years, return, kill Jake, then write to her mother? She didn't even know Jake, did she?"

"Not that I know of." Laurel actually looked disappointed. "Angelle was pretty jealous, though." She bit her lip and looked up. "Maybe she killed both

Peter and Jake."

"Was she jealous enough to kill two of her mother's husbands, one that she had never even met? Whatever for? What could she hope to gain? Her mother's permission to return? I'm sure not. She could have come back at any time in those five years."

"Maybe she wanted to come back and thought Jake wouldn't let her."

"But she didn't know him," I said. "Why would she think that?"

"I just think she did it," she said, and pressed her lips together as if to indicate she was finished speaking. "Of course," she said finally, as an afterthought, "I hope she didn't."

SIX

Wednesday, November 16, 1983

I had gone up to my room when Laurel summoned me to the phone. It was Easy. I barely said hello to him but told him that I would call him back in a few minutes and asked him where he was.

"At my desk," he said. "What's up?"

"Nothing. I'll call you in a few minutes." I hung up, got my jacket and went out to my car.

There was a pay phone on the corner of Admiral and California and I called Easy from there.

"What's going on?" he asked. "Are you outside?"

"I don't want to use the house telephone anymore," I told him. "It's too easy for someone to listen. Strange things are going on there. In the future, call my pager and I'll call you back."

"What's happening?"

I told him about the letter and that I could instantly see that it was faked. "The thing is," I said, "she was never found. The police never looked for her. Remember? Magda and Peter didn't want the police to know she was missing. Laurel, it seems, is convinced that Angelle, for some reason, killed both Peter and Jake, then sent a letter to her mother."

"You would think Angelle would be the last person in the world they would want to pin a murder on."

"Magda, maybe. I'm not so sure about Laurel. Magda is acting strangely too, though. It's as if she's trying to convince herself that the letter is genuine. She must think it's as fake as I think it is. If she doesn't, she's not nearly as smart as I thought she was. It's crazy. Angelle's been gone for five years. Why would she turn up now, a raving homicidal maniac, then write her mother a letter that's cryptic to say the least? The whole thing doesn't make any sense."

"Homicide never does," he said.

"Of course, it does. People who commit cold-blooded murder think they have a perfectly legitimate reason to do it, even if it's just because the victim made them as mad as hell."

"Who do you think sent it?"

"I honestly don't know. Magda herself? Laurel or Magda? Laurel is acting pretty uninterested in it. I want to tell Magda that it's obviously not a recent letter actually sent by Angelle, but I'm all but certain that she already knows. I want to wait for a while and see what she does. For all I know, she sent it to herself, hoping to throw suspicion away from Angelle, not that anyone has seriously thought about Angelle being the killer, except Laurel. Magda swears in one breath that Angelle's disappearance has nothing whatever to do with the murder and then in the next she says someone is stalking her family. She doesn't know that Laurel suspects Angelle. It's a mess, Easy. I told you I didn't want to take this case."

"And yet, you did," he said. "How was your date with Quiller this morning?"

"Some date. He spread his obnoxiousness around for a while then went out to terrorize poor Rolf. From what Magda says, it sounds like they're doing some heavy questioning of Donald Tooley as well."

"The fan, yes," he said. "What do you think?"

"I haven't talked to him yet. I would lean toward Rolf Edmondson, myself, if I could think of some motive. Frankly, I don't think any of us are on the right track at all. No one seems to have a real motive. And everyone was sitting around at home or at least in familiar territory the night of the murder," I said, thinking of Rolf's idea of home away from home. "Or at least, that's what they've said."

"He give you any trouble? Quiller, I mean?"

"Just the usual. Nothing I couldn't handle. I thought I would go over my notes and organize events and people as I know them so far. I'll see you at the funeral later," I said, hoping I didn't sound too enthusiastic.

When I was back at Magda's, I found Laurel still in the kitchen. I grabbed a dish towel but, as usual, she wanted to do everything herself.

"Laurel," I said, "I'd like to ask you a few more questions, if you don't mind."

She didn't answer, but looked pained. The way a cat does when you want it to eat its food from a dish instead of the floor. She had washed the glasses, rinsed them and dried them, and now was beginning on the plates.

"Well, I know you have to, and I'd much rather answer your questions than talk to that awful man who was here this morning," she said. She folded the dish towel between each drying session.

"Why do you think Mr. Quiller is awful? He was pleasant enough." I wondered if she had a little psychic ability herself.

"Oh, I don't know," she said. She bent her head to scrub a particularly stubborn bit of food from the edge of a plate. "I hate to have to talk to any of them. I...I know what they think."

"What do they think?"

"I know they think I killed Mr. Levin."

"But, Laurel, he doesn't think that. Besides, you were here at home that night." The idea of her killing anyone was almost laughable, though killers rarely look like what they are. Consider Ted Bundy. I had once helped in the search for a lovely, tow-headed young man who had run away after killing three of his classmates for their lunch money. My motto: You never know.

"Mr. Quiller doesn't think I did it?" she asked, looking hopeful for the first time since I had arrived.

"No, I don't think so. The only questions I want to ask are so that I can know you better." I put my hand on her arm and she offered me a shaky smile. I felt a bit of openness, a bit of something hidden, a bit of distrust and a bit of fear. Typical things to feel from almost anyone.

"Okay, then," she said. "After that, maybe I can ask you a few to get to know *you* better."

"Fair enough. You know, it seems as if we *should* know each other. After all, I worked on Angelle's disappearance. That was how long after you started working for Magda?"

"I've known Magda a long time. I'd been living with them a few years by then. Magda was helping me in modeling school."

"Oh?" I hadn't known that.

"Oh, yes. I was an aspiring actress then, too." She laughed. It was such a soft sound, it barely reached me. "Magda and Peter... He was killed too. Oh, my! They've all been killed." She sighed. Had she just now realized that?

"It was a long time ago," I said. She attacked the silverware and I stood there like a dud, not allowed to help.

"Yes. Well, Magda and Peter were helping me through modeling school and acting classes. You see, our mothers were friends when I was a baby. Magda is ten years older than I and she always thought of me as a younger sister. She and Peter wanted me to have the best and, of course, I couldn't afford to attend modeling school, so I came here and worked for them in exchange for the tuition to school. They did so much for me. I owe everything to Magda."

What, 'everything'? I wondered. There she was, a virtual servant in the big house and she was talking about owing Magda.

"What was your childhood like, Laurel? You said your mother and Magda's were friends."

"I had a perfect childhood," she said, "My mother and I were very close. She taught me how to cook, how to sew..." She shook her head and laughed softly. "My childhood was wonderful."

"Why didn't you continue with the schooling?"

She laughed again. When she did, I could see traces of beauty in her face. Otherwise, she wore habitual worry lines and frowns. "I didn't have any talent. You can take all the lessons you want, but if you don't have a little natural talent, you aren't going to make it. Oh, sure, I did some modeling.

I still do, sometimes, but I'm a little old for it now. Although," she hesitated then continued. "Nordstrom is having a modeling competition for 'the mature woman.'" She made finger quotes for the last three words. "I was thinking about entering it when Mr. Levin was killed."

"How old are you, Laurel?" She was one of those women who will grow into her late eighties and never seem to age after sixty.

"I'm forty-one," she said. It must have been her petiteness that made me think she was younger than I was.

"I think you should go for it," I said. "You certainly have the looks and figure."

She blushed. It made her more attractive than ever. "Thank you," she said and turned away to wipe down the stove.

"Tell me about the crash that killed Magda's third husband. Mason. I never knew him."

"Oh, Mason was a wonderful man. He was a writer. At least he wanted to be a writer and I think he would have made a great one if he hadn't been killed. It was just a miracle that Magda wasn't also. She was sitting right next to him. They said he was thrown from the plane, seat and all. Magda's seat stayed in and that's why she was burned so badly. Rolf saved her."

"Rolf Edmondson?" I pretended ignorance only to keep her talking. Some people clam up if they think you already know what they're going to tell you.

"Yes, he went along with them because Mason had broken his ankle the week before and they needed Rolf to help him get around. You know, in and out of the shower and things like that. He was on the plane when it went down and everything was burning. He's the one who pulled Magda from the wreckage. He got his arms burned very badly, too. She was on fire, you know."

No. I hadn't known any of the details and wished I hadn't had to hear them.

"Maybe Magda will go back to acting now," I said, thinking out loud. "She's alone. It might be good for her."

"She's hardly alone!" I had been unprepared for her indignation. It was like a bucket of it had been dumped over her head.

"Well, of course not," I said, rushing to correct my error. "She's fortunate to have you! You will be the one to get her through this. But I thought she might think about going back now that her husband is gone."

"I doubt it very much." Laurel banged open a cabinet and began pulling down jars of olives, pickles and bowls for chips.

"Why not?

"Obviously, she is in no physical condition to appear in movies," she said as if my mental acuity were suddenly reduced to a two-year-old's. "She's covered with scars."

"I know that, of course, but physical beauty isn't everything."

"You are talking about a woman to whom perfection *is* everything. It's very cruel of you to even suggest she go in front of the public again."

"You're very loyal," I said. "You know her much better than I. I hope you will forgive my unthinking suggestion." Frankly, I thought Magda was much more confident than Laurel apparently did.

She looked startled. I supposed she hadn't expected an apology from me. Maybe she was used to rebuttal.

"I like it here, anyway," she said. She sounded doubtful, but she visibly relaxed. She must have seen something in my face because she laughed softly again and I was once more impressed with her attractiveness. "Magda's difficult to work for," she said by way of explanation. "She's a perfectionist, like I said. But I like working for her all the same."

She removed carrots, celery, and snow peas from the refrigerator and opened a jar of pickles. I would have offered to help her prepare for the expected post-funeral guests, but she would have refused. I smiled in agreement.

"You should see how upset she gets when there's dust on anything," Laurel went on. "I try to keep things like that out of her way. I know how she can get. I used to be afraid she was going to have a heart attack because she got so upset about little things. Magda thought we should have this catered." She swept her arm over the crudités she had been working on. "But that would have been a disaster. The caterers wouldn't have done everything exactly like Magda wanted. It's much less complicated if I do it myself."

"How did she feel about Mr. Levin having a girlfriend, then?"

This time Laurel did not smile. She looked frightened, then glanced about her as if Magda could appear at any moment.

"I think she pretended that Suzanne didn't exist. It would be like her. Almost anything Jake did was all right with Magda."

"Almost?"

"Of course, she hated it, but Jake was everything to her. I think he truly loved her."

"He loved her but had a woman on the side?"

"Well, that's true." She moved toward the stove and lifted the steaming kettle, sank a teabag into the pot and filled it with boiling water. "I think...," she continued. "I think it was some kind of mid-life crisis or something, and I'm almost certain that Magda did too. She was just waiting until he got over it."

"Tell me about this Donald Tooley. He used to be in love with Magda?"

"Oh, yes, He sent her love letters."

"Really!"

After she had poured us both a mug of tea, she sipped hers, scalding hot, without a wince. "Donald Tooley is a disturbed man," she said. "He wanted her to divorce her husband—that was Peter—and marry him. He was married himself. Still is as far as I know."

"Do you think he really has mental problems? Does he drink? Take drugs?"

"Oh, I suppose he could be crazy," she said. "But he's also not too heavy in this department." She tapped the side of her head. "The letters he sent to Magda are still here if you want to see them."

"You have them?" I couldn't believe she or Magda would have wanted to keep them.

She nodded and we abandoned the kitchen. I followed her upstairs, past the bedrooms and the servants' apartment, to the third floor. At the end of the hallway, beyond the library and the ballroom, was a narrow stairway that led to the attic.

"Magda didn't want to throw them away," Laurel explained. "Her fans are very precious to her. She couldn't keep all of the letters she had ever gotten, of course. There were thousands! But she did keep some."

The attic was unlike any I had ever seen. There was no clutter, no dust, no cobwebs. It was as clean as the kitchen. Everything was neatly stored in labeled boxes and trunks. One bore the word "Costumes". I longed to rummage through it and a large cardboard box labeled "Toys". I knew there were bona fide treasures there and not the Goodwill variety. There were other boxes and trunks bearing Laurel's, Angelle's, Magda's and Jake's names as well as Mason's, Peter's and even Roger's. It appeared that Magda never threw anything away. The attic was large—the entire footprint of the house, I imagined, with walls that slanted to the roof peak. There was plenty of room for decades worth of accumulation.

Laurel's voice dragged me to a small chest near one corner. It was, like the others, labeled with tidy, tight penmanship. Magda's? Laurel's? We pushed aside layers of cards, pictures and mementos until we found a modest, bundle of letters. She glanced at one then handed it to me. The handwriting was cramped and thin, as if written by a person in deep pain. I read the letter then handed it back. She passed me another and then another. Each one made me feel as though I had somehow stumbled into the private chambers of someone's heart.

"These are so sad!" I said.

She nodded. "He was in love with her."

"I guess I thought these letters would be threatening in some way. I didn't realize they would be so heartbreaking." They had been written by a man pouring out his soul. "And this is the man Magda thinks killed Jake?" I asked. I handed the letter back and waited for another. To my surprise,

Laurel snapped the rubber band around the bundle and dropped it back into the chest.

"There are more," I said.

"They're all the same." She brushed off her knees as if the attic had been shrouded in dust.

"Do you think Donald Tooley would be capable of killing Magda's husband?" I asked her. "Those letters are heartbreaking, but I'm not sure they were written by a murderer."

Laurel's gaze swept the attic, landing on a trunk labeled "Angelle." She shook her head. "I know you don't think Angelle did it," she said, "but I still do."

SEVEN

L ater that afternoon, I found Magda in the kitchen surrounded by empty jars and mounds of apples. Laurel's preparations for the coming gathering were crowded into a corner of the counter and covered with a snow-white dish towel. Magda, chopping apples with a large chipped knife, smiled. The knife made a *ka-thunk, ka-thunk, ka-thunk* sound on the wooden board. "I suppose it must look a bit foolish for me to be making applesauce on the day of my husband's funeral," she said.

I shook my head. "Of course not. I think it's wonderful that you have found something you wanted to do. I didn't realize you knew how to do this. I'm impressed!"

"I love to can," she said. "I love to preserve things. When I was a child, we were always hungry. Always trying to scrape together enough to eat. Sounds cliché, I know. Like a bad headline: 'Actress Acquires Wealth After Poor Beginnings'. But, you know, I love the sight of things in great quantities. I do my own grocery shopping when I can, just because I love to see bins full of fruits and vegetables and the shelves lined with cans and cans and cans." She flushed and ran an arm over her dewy forehead. "Does that sound silly?"

"Not at all," I told her. "I was going to ask you if you wanted to go for a walk with me."

"Thank you," she said, looking pleased. "I'm afraid I'll have to pass, though." She gestured at the apples.

"Do you mind my leaving for a little while? I don't think I'll be gone long," I told her

"No, by all means, go ahead. I have plenty to do to keep me busy."

I picked up an apple and lifted my eyebrows. She nodded and I took a bite. The windows ran with moisture and there was a warm, cinnamon-y smell in the kitchen that reminded me of my mother.

She wiped her hands on a striped towel and followed me to the foyer.

"Take a slicker," she said. "It's going to rain."

I found one in the closet and shrugged it on. The clouds were indeed heavy with rain. The air rushed at me and grabbed at my hair, not playfully, but to bully me around. Before I had reached the curb, Easy pulled up in his car and rolled down the window.

"Hey, lady," he said. "Know where I can find a good private detective?"

"Young man, I hardly think the officiating minister of a funeral should be flirting openly. Especially with the young, and, shall we say, attractive, private investigator on the case." I laughed. He actually looked guilty for a second. Easy carried his guilt around with him like an overcoat. Sometimes it was slung over his arm but at a moment's notice, he could open it up and climb into it.

"I came to tell you I got a copy of the autopsy report."

"Oh, great!" I went around the car and jumped in with him.

Easy talked while I read. "It seems Mr. Jacob Eban Levin was murdered by an instrument of some kind, and not a very sharp one at that. Not the quickest, cleanest way to die. The wound had ragged edges as though the weapon was dull and there was some kind of debris present."

"Someone killed him with a dirty, dull knife? Good Lord! It's almost as though the killer wanted him to suffer." The idea made me shudder. "I hate to say this, but Magda is in the kitchen right this minute chopping apples with a very large chipped knife."

"You should let Quiller know," he said, looking worried. "The report doesn't specify a knife, though."

I thought for a moment. "I'll get the knife and take it in. I would prefer that Magda and Laurel not know that they might be under suspicion any more than they already believe. Laurel is paranoid enough as it is." I patted the pockets of the slicker for a pad of paper and a pen. "Easy, do you have something I can write with? Unless you're going to let me keep that copy."

"Your friend, Perce, said to give it to you with his compliments. I think the guy likes going behind Harlan Quiller's back any chance he gets, especially if it's to help you out. Sometimes I think I'm a little jealous of O'Dell." He smiled and I knew he was kidding. Still...

"I think I'm going to forget about my walk. I've got some notes to make. Are you going to stick around or are you on your way to the church?"

"I'm going up there to make sure everything is getting done. Shall I come back and pick you up?"

I shook my head. When I got out of the car, the wind whipped the hood of the slicker around and my bangs whisked across my face.

"Magda will be riding in the limousine. I'll follow it in my car and see you later, back here. You are coming to the...what *do* they call that, anyway? A wake?"

"Sure. I'll be here."

I didn't stick around to watch him leave. I tossed the remains of my apple under a bush for the local wildlife to finish up, then headed back into the house and up to my room.

My notes were still on the desk. I spent the better part of an hour putting them in order and adding new ones. I wondered if it was a good idea to continue to leave them lying around. I had a lock on my briefcase and carried the key on my key ring but rarely used it. Nevertheless, I put the notebook and reports inside and put the briefcase into the closet.

L ater that afternoon, after I had had my walk after all, and Magda and Laurel had gone out to the limousine to be driven to the church, I ducked into the kitchen and found the knife in the knife block. I photographed it carefully and slid it into a plastic bag. Even though it had probably been washed more than once since the murder, it needed to be logged in as evidence. I carried it upstairs and locked it into my briefcase. I would take it downtown to Quiller the next day.

◆ ◆ ◆

T he funeral was no more surreal than funerals generally are, considering there were so many famous people in attendance. It wasn't so much a funeral as a memorial service, as Jake's remains were not there and there would be no graveside ceremony.

There were hundreds of people both inside and outside the large church. So many, that some were forced to remain outdoors in the rain during the service. Jake, it seemed, had been known by many, well-respected and truly liked.

Thankfully, Magda was adept at dealing with the press. Even in her grief, she was capable enough to give the reporters and camera crews just the right amount of information and emotion to keep them from being too troublesome and disruptive.

I sat next to Laurel. Magda was surrounded by old friends who had come from New York and Los Angeles for her husband's funeral.

"That's Littler Coe," Laurel said in an undertone, nodding at a tall, rather stooped man guiding a girl of about fourteen down the aisle. "And I think that's his wife." I tried not to stare. The last six books he had written had topped the best seller lists for months. He looked like someone's uncle. It was hard to believe that such a brilliant mind lurked under that ordinary sandy hair. I personally didn't care for his breezy "I'm-so-much-smarter-than-you-that-I-can-get-away-with-anything" style, so I had only read his first two novels.

"See the bald man with the red tie? That's Larry DeCamp, the actor," Laurel said.

I nodded. "I think I've seen him. He has hair on television."

"He usually wears a toupee. I don't know where it

is today, or why he even wears it. Everyone knows he's bald."

"Maybe he's afraid of the wind..." I whispered to Laurel and was gratified to share a quiet laugh with her.

There were many people I didn't recognize, but I knew they must be wealthy and influential. The men wore summer-tans, in spite of it being November, and that pressed suit look. The women had professional nails and expensively careless hair. The value of the clothing alone of that congregation could have fed the entire enrollment of the Children's Home Society for all eternity.

I listened to Easy speak, forgetting for a moment that this was a funeral and he was a minister. His dark hair fell into his eyes and it probably looked like fervor to the mourners. To me, he looked adorable and boyish and made me want to hug him. He spoke glowingly about a man he hadn't known, glossing over his faults.

After Easy had finished and hymns had been sung, and several people had shared fond memories of Jake, Laurel and I stood up with the rest to leave. She turned toward Magda as if to help her. She was being held at the elbows by two men I didn't recognize but felt as though I should. They did look vaguely familiar. I knew if I had watched more television or gone to films more often, I would have recognized more people.

Magda climbed into the limousine with the two men and Laurel rode with me. She was silent all the way back to the house. I put my hand over hers and she smiled at me. With a heavy sigh she turned and looked out over the wet landscape. I felt her hurt like a burn. I knew she felt she should have been in the limo with Magda.

Limos and Mercedes-Benzes were already gathering in the street outside Magda's like a herd of expensive mechanical sheep. There were members of the press there too, though they did seem a little more subdued than they had earlier in the day.

As quickly as I could stop the car, Laurel escaped and ran up the walk. She was in the house before I could lock up. When I got to the front door, she had taken her place beside Magda and was receiving guests. I wandered through the room, watching as each group entered, greeted Magda and Laurel, then self-consciously moved toward the ranks of food lined up on the sideboard. It looked as if everyone had brought at least one cake and a hot dish. There would be food to last a month. I had always thought the obligatory crowd at the home of the deceased a barbaric custom. Didn't, after all, the bereaved have enough to worry about without having to deal with guests as well?

Gradually, the room became crowded. The smell of expensive perfumes slowly began to overtake the aroma of cinnamon from Magda's applesauce frenzy.

"Magda St. Martin is a pillar of courage." The man

next to me dipped his hand into a bowl of tortilla chips and breathed his boozy sentence right into my face. My eyes watered. He obviously had gotten a head start. "M' name's Al," he said and bowed, still munching on chips. He dug into a breast pocket and extracted a card. "Wonderful party, isn't it?" His card bore his name, "Alphonso de Las Alas", a phone number and address.

"Did you know Mr. Levin well, Mr. de Las Alas?" I asked. This man didn't seem to be too broken up that Jake was dead.

"Nope. Actually, I didn't know him at all." His Latin good looks were slightly roughened around the edges by the amount of alcohol he had consumed. His shock of silver hair hung limply on his forehead. He had loosened his tie.

"Are you an actor?" There had to be some reason for the man being there. He wasn't a neighbor. His card said his office was in north Seattle.

"Yes, I'm in real estate." He seemed to think that was terribly funny but all I could manage was a weak smile. "de Las Alas Real Estate, that's me." He nodded toward the card then leaned over to me conspiratorially. "I've cared for Magda St. Martin all of my adult life," he said, eyeing the bowl of chips again. "I've loved her through four marriages now. Knew her when she was first married to Roger. When he died, I was married. He died of a stroke when he was only 42. Imagine!" He looked astonishingly pleased. He had a peculiar habit of shaking his tortilla chip as if trying to dislodge clinging germs. He plunged a chip so far into the onion dip that he had to lick his fingers. "When my wife left me, Magda was married again. To Peter," he continued and peered at me over the top of a smeared looking gin and tonic. "Did you know Peter?" I nodded. "Terrible things have happened to my little lady. Terrible things."

I knew about the terrible things but I wanted to hear more about his "little lady".

He lurched a moment, then almost put his hand squarely into a pan of *chile rellenos.* "Why do you think she chose Seattle?" he asked. "An actress like her with the world on a stick should be living in LA. In Hollywood. Why do you think she chose Seattle?"

"She retired here," I said. "I imagine she likes it."

"No. She doesn't like it. No, ma'am." He took another chip, shook it and tapped it twice against the side of the bowl for good measure. "She moved here because of the climate. Want to know what she likes about the climate?" He leaned over to me and blew his ginny breath into my face again.

"What?" I confess, I couldn't help myself. After all, I was supposed to be finding out who killed Jake. For all I knew, Al did. Or, if he didn't, maybe he knew who did.

"She has to live in a mild climate where she can wear long sleeved clothes all the time." The word "clothes" came out somewhat slurred but he didn't seem to notice. I saw Laurel on the other side of the table watching him with the dead eyes of a shark.

"You know," he said. "I love her even if she does have the skin of an alligator. To me, she's beautiful. So what if she can't wear short sleeves? I don't care!" He waved his arm expansively and knocked a fragile looking glass bowl onto its side. It rolled to the other side of the table, laying down a path of potato chips. It hit a heavy silver plate, cracked and smashed onto the floor. Laurel leapt back before it landed. I would have tried to catch it, but it hadn't come in my direction.

The bowl hit the polished surface of the floor like a water balloon, spraying bits of glass and potato in all directions. When it had hit the silver plate, a chip had flown to the top of the mound of shrimp salad next to it, staring up toward the ceiling like the forgotten contact lens of a giant. I picked it off with my nail just as Magda appeared at my side. She looked angry and Laurel looked terrified.

"There's my little dove now," Alphonso said. He draped his long arm over Magda's shoulders and breathed into her ear. Her mouth curved into a tight smile and she bore him away to another part of the room.

"Magda is going to have a fit," Laurel said just before she fled for a broom and dust pan. I tried to find larger pieces of glass to pick up but they were all the size of small diamonds.

When Laurel returned, she quickly dispatched the shattered glass. After she had borne away the crystal dust, and returned, she still looked guilty as if she had personally flung the bowl to the floor.

"Who is he?" I asked her. She was searching the crowd for Magda and Mr. de Las Alas.

"I have no idea," she said. I could see in her eyes that she intended to find out.

"Laurel," I said, hoping to divert her. "Who is that?" I nodded toward a woman wearing a black suit embroidered with large orange poppies.

"That's Morgan," she said. Her face was glowing like a hot coal. She snagged the passing woman. "Morgan, I'd like you to meet Cheyenne Bruce. Cheyenne, Morgan Chatfield is Magda's sister."

I shook hands with the tall woman. She looked me over as if I were in a display case at Bloomingdale's. Her hair was cut short and was so shiny it appeared to be made of metal. I'm not sure how she got it that way but I had never seen hair that actually looked like brass.

"So, you're the private investigator," she said. Her loud voice carried. A few people turned to look. "I *hope* you will clear this case up soon. It's making me extremely upset that *anyone* could think that Magda has *anything* to do with this. It's simply *preposterous*."

"I wasn't aware that anyone thinks Magda is responsible," I said.

"Of course, *everyone* knows that our mother was, well, I'm sure Magda has told you the story." Morgan's tight mouth tightened even further. She twisted her linen napkin. Her nails looked like shining chips of plastic. "But just because our mother had man troubles and a little depression, I don't think *anyone* should go around accusing my sister of *anything* like this. It's simply *intolerable*." She caught sight of a photographer outside the window and was instantly diverted. "I thought more of the press would be here," she said, heading closer to the window and the photographer. Though she had moved away, her strident voice easily carried to me. It was as if she were making the rounds and announcing the impossibility of anything but Magda's complete innocence.

"I didn't want to come here." I turned to look at my neighbor, a lady who was wearing a dress and a matching hat made from a large black and white checkerboard fabric. I knew her son and his family, the Grafts, were Magda's neighbors across the street. I had seen her the day before. Her son had been putting her into the car for what appeared to be a reluctant outing. There had been words between the two, though I hadn't heard what had been said.

"My name is Cheyenne," I said, holding out my hand to her.

"I'm Iola," she said shyly, and let me shake her hand for a second or two. Her family; her son, his wife and child had all been baked in the same pan, as colorless and pale as bread. Only Iola appeared to have any character.

"Didn't you like Mr. Levin?" I asked her. Her glasses were those white cat's eye kind with rhinestones in the corners. Exactly like the ones I had worn in high school.

"Sure, I liked him. The only reason I came over here is because I liked him. I would have expected him to come to my funeral. I did expect him, in fact. I sure didn't think I would outlive him. Why, he was nothing but a pup."

"But you don't like coming here?" I offered her a cup of punch. She grasped it in both hands and swallowed it greedily, then looked around. She looked almost guilty, but held the cup out for a refill.

"There are ghosts in this house," she confided to me.

"Ghosts?! Really?"

She nodded. "I've seen them."

"Mrs. Graft, I've been staying here and I've never seen any ghosts."

"I guess if I can call you Diane, you can call me Iola," she said. "But I have seen them. Three times."

I let the error of the name alone. If she wanted to call me Diane, that was fine with me. I wanted to hear more about the ghosts. It was the most interesting conversation I'd had that whole day. "Tell me about the ghosts, Iola," I said.

"Once, I saw someone dressed in white come out the front door and disappear into thin air," she said in an overly dramatic tone. "She had on a long dress and her hair was all wild and every which way." She leaned toward me. "I could see *through* her," she whispered, then turned toward the stained glass window behind us. "Another time, I saw that woman up there?" She gestured at the frightening Medea. "I saw her move and climb down from there. And another time, I saw a huge black dog, with red, fiery eyes, as big as a horse. It was in the—."

"Mom, you know better than to talk like that," Ben Graft interrupted his mother. He had a perpetually harried look, as did his wife and son. "I'm sorry," he said to me. "My mother's been dreaming up a lot of things lately. She swore she saw elves in the yard this past summer and now this. We've been looking at...uh...alternative living arrangements." He put a volume of meaning into the arch of his eyebrows.

"It's so sad when the mind begins to go," Morgan Chatfield said over the fading voice of Ben Graft. She had drifted back and stood near again as if she had never been gone. Ben had steered his mother toward the front door. I managed to throw her a wink before she turned away. "Our mother was like that, you know," Morgan said. "She was crazy too."

She isn't the only one, I thought, and I wasn't thinking about Iola.

EIGHT

Thursday, November 17, 1983

First thing the next morning, after Magda had assured me that she felt secure enough for me to leave, I headed out toward Burien to have another talk with Morgan Chatfield. I suspected the lady could give me a lot more information about Magda and Angelle than I had been getting from Laurel or anyone else.

As I turned the car off Roxbury and headed toward Ambaum Boulevard, memories started creeping into my mind. They poked their fingers into my heart and waggled them around until it had begun to hurt.

Morgan Chatfield lived out beyond Seattle in the suburb of Burien. The last time I had been there was when my mother had still been alive. I pulled my thoughts away from the day of her funeral and let them wander over the time she had spent at the Burien Terrace Nursing Home. I would be going right past it. I wondered if any of the residents who had known my mother would still be there. I doubted it. Except for James, everyone else had seemed old enough not to have survived.

I tried to drive right past Burien Terrace and focus on Morgan's address. Instead, I found myself urging my car up the driveway and around to the back of the building. I parked and sat behind the wheel trying to get my bearings. In the past, I had always done that. I never went in cold to Burien Terrace. It was a place you had to work up to.

In the rear-view mirror, I saw Mrs. Wheeler sitting by the back door. After five years, she, at least was still there. She appeared to be sitting in the same place she had been sitting the last time I had seen her. It was as if she had been waiting the whole five years for me to return so I could steer her wheelchair out the door and down the hill to freedom. I took a deep breath and got out of the car.

Mrs. Wheeler brightened the minute she saw me. Her mouth turned up on one side in the deadly grimace I knew was her smile. I doubted that she recognized me. She was happy to see anyone. She wore a dressing gown with a thin line of oatmeal dribbled from chest to waist. I pressed her good shoulder with my hand and asked her how she was today. She said something that I couldn't decipher so I complimented her new shiny black pumps with the strap across the instep. She grinned. I waved and stepped into the past.

Farther in, by the day room door, as if he couldn't decide whether to go in or out, sat James. I had seen him sit that way a hundred times. At first glance, James looked like an orderly who had taken a moment to sit in an abandoned wheelchair and watch the movie playing in the day room. He turned his head when he heard me, but his expression didn't alter. I knew he could see me—he wasn't blind—but nothing behind his eyes changed. There was no recognition at all. James' case was one of those tragedies you saw from time to time. His body and mind have been ravaged by a disease I didn't know the name of beyond its initials. Poor as I was, whenever they held telethons for that illness, I got out my wallet and thought of James. He had wonderful red hair and a hefty peppering of orange freckles that looked like they belonged on a surfer or a skier but not a blank young man who was suffering who knew what kind of horrors. I smiled at him and said hello, not knowing if he had heard me.

My mother's old room was still the color of dirty Thousand Island dressing. She had had the bed by the window. I never asked, but always wondered about the logic of giving a blind woman the bed with the view. Maybe they had known that Mama saw with more than just her eyes. There was someone else now in the bed Mama had occupied.

I stood just outside the door for a moment letting the past rise about my ankles, splash to my waist then cover my head like a flood. I could remember the day perfectly. I had gone to talk to Mama the day I first met Magda and Peter. The day I had gotten my very first case—Angelle's.

◆ ◆ ◆

"Mama," I had said. She had opened her eyes instantly and unerringly found my face, making it difficult to believe she was blind.

"Cheyenne, darling," she had said and raised her arms for a hug. She had always sounded happy to know I was near. Even after her surgery, when pain had been wracking her poor little body, she had been glad to hear my voice.

"Mama, I've got a case," I had told her.

"A case! Oh, honey, that sounds so important. I'm so proud of you! Are you going to make some money?"

I had laughed and wondered if she could hear how hollow it had sounded to me. I didn't think so. She had never let her smile falter for a second. All of the money I got would go toward keeping Mama in Burien Terrace where there would always be someone who could take care of her needs. The staff had been caring and Mama had liked them. I would always be grateful for them but her medical bills had reached beyond anything I had imagined in my worst nightmares. Even though my brother Larry had shared the burden with me, it had weighed me down beyond measure.

I mentally shook myself free of the memories. I turned and walked, without looking back at James, past Mrs. Wheeler and out the door.

Eventually, I had had some real news about cases I had solved and people I had found, but my mother never knew. By the time I was off the St. Martin case, having failed to help in any way, my mother had contracted pneumonia. When Peter had been killed downtown a short time later, my mother had just died.

◆ ◆ ◆

Morgan Chatfield lived in one of those small post-war houses in South Seattle. A short brick wall surrounded her property as if to keep out very small trespassers. I noticed she had chunks of ceramic embedded at random in the concrete of her walk giving it a whimsical look. The doorbell played part of a tune from *Carmen*. When Morgan herself answered the door, she looked as if she had been awake and ready to receive visitors for hours, though it was only ten o'clock.

She extended her hand to me.

"Cheyenne," she said. "Please come in." I was surprised she recognized me. At our first meeting, at the post service gathering, she had seemed to be one of those women who don't ever see anyone else, just their own reflection as it bounces off of other faces.

"Mrs. Chatfield," I said.

"I suppose you've come to find out what you can about Magda," she said before I had a chance to say anything else. She turned abruptly and led me into her living room.

Her house was the opposite of Magda's. Where Magda's had character and age, Morgan's was done in JC Penney *Haute de Uncertainty*. She had a glass and chrome coffee table and a blue-green carpet that looked like a well-kept lawn from another planet.

I've always been suspicious of people who own commodes as end tables. After all, they once were used to hide chamber pots. Morgan had perched one at either end of the sofa. One whole wall was glass, making the room look bigger and more open than it was. It also brought the chill from outside right indoors. I preferred a little more coziness than that.

I settled on a strawberry yogurt colored sofa that had no arms. I imagined her sitting there in the evenings with her feet up on the glass coffee table and munching on a bowl of buttered popcorn.

"I'm actually glad you came," she said. She wore a shocking pink jumpsuit and earrings the size of saucers dangling from coasters. Her penciled eyebrows arched delicately when she spoke, like horizontal parentheses. Her black lashes stabbed at the upper part of her eye after every blink. "I don't want there to be *any* question about Magda's having done this thing. No matter *what* kind of man Jacob Levin was, Magda would *never* have done anything to harm him."

"Mrs. Chatfield, first of all, I'd like it known that Magda is not under suspicion by the police." *Yet*, I thought, remembering that I had to stop by Quiller's office to hand off the knife. "They are questioning a man in connection to the murder. I'm merely trying to sort out whatever information you have that could add to what we already know."

"They have a man in custody?" she asked. She let go a sigh that deflated her entire body. "Well, *that's* a relief!" She fanned her face with her hand. She wore a ring with a stone the size of my eyeball. I figured it for a CZ.

"Why are you so afraid that someone will suspect Magda?" I didn't correct her mistaken impression that there had been an arrest.

"Well, because it's *completely* preposterous. No matter *what* kind of man..." She let the sentence trail, apparently becoming aware that she had already said it.

"What kind of a man was Jake?" I tried to cross my legs, but the depth of the seat on Morgan's ultra-modern furniture threatened me with varicose veins so I had to uncross them. Instead, I was forced to sit with my rib cage pressing into my hipbones and my knees apart. I knew I looked like a hunched old crone out of a fairy tale. She didn't. She had planted herself on a slim blue and chrome affair that looked like it had been tailor made with her flattery in mind. I could see from where I sat that it was gen-u-wine virgin Naugahyde.

"Jacob Levin was *not* what everyone thinks he was," she was saying. She looked self-satisfied, as if she had been waiting years to make that statement.

"What does everyone think? From what I've heard, he didn't have any enemies whatsoever."

"That's it *exactly*! You heard them talking at the funeral yesterday. Everyone paints him as this *saint* whom everyone loved. He wasn't like that. Why he was *cheating* on my sister. Have you met that little tramp he was involved with? I have *underwear* older than she is."

I doubted it. I couldn't see her as a woman who would let her underwear get old enough to turn color in the wash.

"Have you met her?" I asked.

"No," she said. "But I—"

"Was there some other way that Jake treated Magda badly? Did he abuse her in some way?"

"I call cheating abusive, don't you?" Her eyes flashed with indignity. "Magda is…well, she's a *jewel*. A ruby. A *diamond*."

"What did you think of Angelle?"

"There's another ruby. They were a pair. Beautiful, talented." She shook her head. "What a *waste*! What a *crying* shame. Don't you think?"

"Magda seems to handle her retirement very well," I said, assuming that was what she was talking about.

"Oh, no. She's not at *all* happy. Would you like a drink?"

I shook my head. "No, thanks. But, please, go ahead," I said, thinking it might be easier for me if she did.

She swept to one wall where a bar was cleverly hidden behind some imitation wood paneling and one of those starving artist paintings that is really done by assembly line workers with paintbrushes. After a moment of clinking ice and glass she settled again in her chair.

She wore the top of her jumpsuit open, revealing a freckled chest. Her hair, cut very short, was as sleek as a short-haired dog's. Her feet were bare and she had painted her toenails a splendid shade of cranberry. She dabbed at the edge of one eyebrow with a well-manicured hand and took a sip of her drink.

"Magda is very unhappy," she said. "My mother, you know, was plagued by depression *all* of her life. I have pictures of her taken as a child where she looks positively *miserable*." She took a healthy swig from her glass.

"Magda said her mother...your mother was an alcoholic."

Morgan laughed a little too loudly and a little too long. "God, no! Magda *would* say that. Anyone who takes a sip of wine is automatically pegged by Magda as an alcoholic. No. Absolutely not!"

"Do you know if your mother was abused as a child?" I asked.

"Oh, no. She was an *adored* only child. Her childhood was perfect," she said. "She simply had these spells of manic depression where she would go almost crazy talking a mile a minute and then a few days later, she would be talking about suicide." She peered at me over the rim of her glass. "You know that's how she died, don't you?"

"How old were you and Magda when it happened?" I asked, ignoring her question.

"Magda was fourteen and I was twelve. We were living with our father's sister by then. That was in Tacoma. Mother had tried to kill Father, and his sister *insisted* that we go stay with her. It was during one of Mother's bad times, obviously. She had tried suicide before but bungled it. That last time, it worked." She ruminated over her drink a moment, crunching one of the ice cubes. "I always wanted them to make a movie of it."

"Did your father abuse you or Magda?"

"Of *course* not! He *adored* us!"

"That's not what Magda told me," I said. "She says she's never quite gotten over the abuse she suffered as a child."

Morgan actually laughed. "That's Magda for you," she said, dismissing the subject. "She's always making things up to make herself more dramatic. No, Magda and I were *adored*. By both our parents." She half closed her eyes as if she were remembering a golden youth.

"So, you think that manic depression runs in your family," I said. "Do you see any tendencies in yourself?"

"Oh, God, no!" She laughed and it sounded manic to me. But then, what did I know?

"What about Magda? Do you think she inherited any of that?"

"Well, now, I don't know. Her husband *is* dead, isn't he? I'm sure Magda would never...that is, I *know* her. She's...or at least...she *was* madly in love with that bastard. *Why*, I'll never know."

"What did Jake ever do to you?"

"Nothing," she said immediately. I imagined Jake had turned her down at some point. "It's just the way he treated Magda so shabbily with that slut."

"You knew about Suzanne French?"

"Of course! Didn't everyone? Really! But I still don't think Magda had *anything* to do with it. Of course, it would be a terrific publicity stunt. She hasn't had much of that lately. Have many reporters been hanging around her house?" She looked eager.

"That lumberyard fire has pretty much distracted

the reporters," I said. "But Magda's retired. She, I'm sure, doesn't want any publicity."

"Ridiculous, isn't it? I mean with the *make-up* and photography tricks they have these days, why, she could be right *in* there." She batted her false eyelashes twice.

"Right in where?"

"Right in the middle of the Hollywood scene. I don't know why she isn't. She was *known*. She was *some*body. I would certainly be willing to move back down to LA with her. This is a terrible place to live." She swept her hand indicating the house and the city at large.

"Why do you live here, then?" I asked.

"Why, to be with my sister," she said. She raised both eyebrows.

I had the impression Morgan Chatfield wouldn't be at all disappointed if her sister did turn out to be the murderer of Jake Levin. She apparently had followed Magda wherever she had lived, absorbing Magda's fame like a fruitcake soaks up brandy.

"What is your theory about where Angelle disappeared to?" I asked.

She brightened immediately. "I have no doubt she went to Los Angeles and is right now trying to make it in films."

"But wouldn't she have contacted her mother? Her best friend? Someone?"

She shook her head and sipped at the drink at the same time. "No. She was like that. She'd decide to do something and would just *jump* in, feet first. She probably doesn't want to tell anyone until she has some kind of success she can parade." She wiped at her eyebrow again. "Frankly, I don't blame her."

"Oh?"

"I'd *grab* at the chance to act. I would give everything I have to be able to have the opportunities that my sister is simply *throwing* away." She looked momentarily guilty at what she had just said. "Of course, I wouldn't *dream* of leaving my husband, though I have had offers, you know."

I stood up. I had had enough. "Morgan, here is my card. If you can think of anything that might be of use, will you give me a call? You can either leave a message on my machine here," I said, indicating my home number, "or call me at Magda's. My pager number is here. Would you do that?"

She studied my card. "Of course." She looked disappointed. "I hope I was of some help," she said on the way to the door.

When I got into the car, I looked back and imagined her peeking from behind the curtain. She obviously was viewing her childhood out of a different window than Magda was. One of them wasn't telling the truth.

I wanted to talk to Jake Levin's secretary. I glanced at my watch and saw that she would probably be on her way to lunch by the time I arrived. I swung down to Alki to talk to the young man who had reported Jakes's car horn blaring and Suzanne's screams on the night Jake had been killed.

I parked in the same spot where Jake's car had been found, but the day was too light, too ordinary for me to get any sense of what he had seen or felt that night. I would have to come back in the evening.

There was nothing to be learned from Jason Philbrick. He was a beach bum waiting out the winter in one of those cheap houses across the street from the water that got buried under mud slides from time to time. He had told the police that he had been watching a special on TV when first, Jake's horn, then Suzanne's screaming had interrupted it. I talked to him a few minutes, then left, hoping to catch Jake's secretary downtown. I was curiously exhausted after talking to a woman who thought of murder as a possible publicity stunt and a man who called me "dude".

NINE

Thursday, November 17, 1983

O n rainy days, the sky hid the top of Seattle's tallest building, but in the sunshine, it gleamed like a chunk of obsidian. I wondered if anyone would be in Jacob Levin's office on the thirty-first floor of the Columbia Tower. What, after all, happens to a business when the boss is dead?

I stopped in the lobby to see if the security guard who had been working the night Jake had been killed just happened to be on duty. He wasn't.

A young man who couldn't have been over seventeen in spite of the official looking uniform and gun, assured me that he knew Frank Poplawski well, and Frank had given a thorough statement to the police. He, Chris Montrose, according to his uniform shirt, in fact, knew the whole story which he was delighted to relate to me. It added nothing to what had been on the police report. Apparently,

Jake had left his office and the building at about 10:30. Suzanne had found him at 11:07. Assuming it takes approximately fifteen minutes to travel from downtown to West Seattle in nighttime traffic, death occurred between 10:45 and 11:07. I thanked Chris, gave him my card to hand to Mr. Poplawski and took the elevator up.

Bea Somerset was answering the phone when I arrived. She had a quiet efficiency and used exactly the correct amount of sadness in her voice. She looked up and smiled sorrowfully, continuing to murmur into the phone.

I remembered seeing her at Jake's funeral, but not at the house afterward. She was a tall, thick woman with hair that was plainly styled and neatly combed into the kind of waves popular on older ladies in the early sixties. It was that gray that looked blue in some lights. She wore a man-tailored shirt and a gray skirt that exactly matched her hair. She wore no jewelry nor make-up. I could imagine her making statements about aborigines applying paint to their bodies and faces for pagan rites.

She hung up the phone with a *clunk* and smiled at me as though it was uncomfortable for her to do so.

"I'm terribly sorry," she said. "Things are upset. We've had a tragedy here. You're the client from Gilhooley's?"

"No, I'm not," I said and handed her my card. "My name is Cheyenne Bruce. I'm helping investigate the murder of Mr. Levin."

"Oh." She looked dubious while she studied the card. In her world, young women were not investigators and one didn't speak to anyone other than the police. For all she knew, I could be working for the murderer. The phone purred and she pounced on it as if it could save her life.

"Products Management Incorporated," she sang, watching me while she spoke.

"Oh, yes, Mr. Quiller," she said with relief and patted the general area of her heart. My own heart sank. She was exactly the sort of woman that Quiller liked. He could tell her to jump off the Aurora Bridge and she would do it simply because he was one of the "authorities".

"Well, in fact, there's someone here now," she was saying. "She *says* she's investigating Mr. Levin's death. I believe she said her name was Anne. Oh. Yes, she did. Oh?" She looked surprised. I had a mean fantasy of Quiller talking dirty to her over the phone. When she hung up, she rose to her feet.

"I'm sorry, I'm going to have to show you the door."

"That's not necessary," I said as pleasantly as I could manage. "I saw it when I came in." She started toward me as if she were willing to remove me bodily from the premises.

"I couldn't help overhearing that you were speaking to Mr. Quiller," I said. "He's a nice man, isn't he?" I smiled my most charmingly at her and she pulled herself up short, surprised again.

"Why, yes. He is," she said.

"I'd hate to see him make a mistake in this case and arrest the wrong man. You can't imagine how badly that reflects on a detective's record. Why, he could get a reprimand." I clicked my tongue, all concern for Harlan Quiller. That, of course, was ridiculous, but she didn't know it.

She shook her head. "That wouldn't happen, would it?"

"It certainly would if the wrong man is arrested. And they are already interrogating someone whom I believe to be the wrong man. That's why I'm doing this independent investigation." I tried to give weight to the words 'independent investigation.'

"Mr. Quiller told me I didn't have to talk to you."

Damn, that son of a bitch! He had no doubt begun calling all of the principals to tell them not to talk to me. I wondered if I could hang on and stay in business until he retired.

"And, of course, you don't have to, but Mr. Quiller is only being protective," I said, forcing myself to smile. "He doesn't believe that women should work. Isn't that quaint?" I gave her a conspiratorial wink and a smile. "He's such a lovely man. You and I both know that we women sometimes have to go behind the men's backs to help them even if they don't realize that they need it." I saw her mouth relax almost imperceptibly so I jumped at the chance while I had it. "May I ask you just a few questions? It would be of great help to Mr. Quiller."

"I suppose that would be all right," she said after a doubtful frown.

"Thank you so much!" I tried to make my smile look reassuring. "Do you know of any enemies that Mr. Levin might have had?"

"Oh, no," she said. "Everyone loved Mr. Levin." I had heard that before. She moved back to her desk, sat down and looked reflectively at her typewriter, as if it could give her some answers. I took the chair that was near her desk and turned it so I could face her. The phone rang once again, but that time she flipped a switch and her own voice stated that she was unable to answer it just now.

"Do you know who Suzanne French is?" Her frown deepened and she pressed her lips together and nodded. I saw her knees clamp together too.

"She's...was Mr. Levin's...friend."

"Did you know her?"

"No! I never saw her nor did I talk to her. Well, I spoke to her one time. No, the only reason I know about her was that he sent flowers to her and...things." She moved her mouth as if she had suddenly found it full of rabbit droppings.

"What things, Miss Somerset?"

"*Mrs.* Somerset," she said firmly.

"I'm sorry. What kind of things did he send, Mrs. Somerset?"

"Nighties and those horrid little things that look like slips but are made like shorts." She shuddered.

"Teddies?"

"I certainly don't know *what* they're called. Teddies? I don't know. I used to have to go out and pick up things for his wife, but I can tell you, he never bought things like that for her. Oh, no. He bought her furs and ear clips and perfume, yes, but he never bought her teddies." She almost spit the word out. I wondered how she knew about the teddies. Had Jake brought boxes back to the office that she had peeked into while he was out?

"When was the one time that you talked to Suzanne French? Was that recently?"

"It was that day. The day he…he was killed."

"Did she come into the office?"

"Good heavens, no!" Mrs. Somerset launched into a raucous laugh that sounded like a nanny goat in heat and there went her prim persona straight out the window. It didn't go with her appearance and I thought how fortunate it was that she was the staid, humorless person she was.

"Then she called?"

She nodded, collecting herself and looking a bit embarrassed by her outburst. "Yes, she called just before Mr. Levin returned from lunch. She asked me to tell Jake…Mr. Levin, that she would be a little bit early. She wanted him to know that she would be there at 10:45."

"How did you know it was Suzanne?"

"Why, I'm no fool!" She puffed out her chest. "I know about it every time he meets a client, calls someone or someone calls him. I set up all of his appointments for him. And I keep records of them too."

"But it could have been his wife. Or it could have been Laurel, or anyone. How can you be so sure it was Suzanne?"

"Well, I believe she said her name." She pulled a phone message pad from her desk drawer and riffled through it, then nodded. "I wrote here, 'Suzanne will be there at 10:45'. That's how I know."

"Thank you, Mrs. Somerset," I said, standing. "Can you remember the exact conversation? You answered the phone and she said…what?"

"Let me think. She said, 'Mrs. Somerset, would you tell Jake that Suzanne will be there early tonight? He knows where. Tell him Suzanne will be there at 10:45.' You know, I told all of this to the police."

"Yes, I know and you are wonderful to repeat it all for me. Thank you. Can you think of anyone who may have been even angry at Mr. Levin?"

She pursed her lips and slowly shook her head. "No," she said, "except, once his gardener came in and they had a little argument."

"Rolf Edmondson?"

"Yes, that's the name." She again flipped the pages of her message pad. "Let me see. Here it is. He called twice in one day. That was Friday, October fourteenth. Mr. Levin wasn't in either time. Then, later that same day, he came in here and demanded to speak to Mr. Levin."

"I wonder why he would do that," I said. "He lives on Mr. Levin's property. Why would he come all the way down here to speak to him?"

"I'm certain I don't know. I think he—Rolf, that is —must have wanted to borrow some money. He left looking quite fierce."

"Did you tell the police about this?"

"Why, no," she said, and a faint blush rose up on her face. "They didn't...they only asked me about what Jake had done that day. I didn't think it had anything to do with the...with what happened, since it was several weeks ago and the man *did* work for Mr. Levin."

"Thank you, Mrs. Somerset," I said. "I suggest you tell the police about that incident, and, if you think of anything that might help me or Mr. Quiller, please feel free to call me. You have my numbers on the card I gave you."

She nodded and reached again for the ringing phone. I let myself out and rode the elevator back to the street level.

I was going to have to chat with Rolf again.

Just outside the building there was a telephone booth. I called Easy.

"Hey, dude," I said when he answered.

"Hey, yourself. Where are you?"

"Downtown. I'm carrying a possible murder weapon around in my briefcase. I have to drop it off to Quiller and I want to talk to Donald Tooley. Perce said they were going to pick him up today. I thought maybe you would like to buy a hungry woman some lunch."

"Sure!" His enthusiasm always lifted me up.

"Meet me in a half hour in front of the jail."

"You are such a romantic," he said.

After I had spoken to Easy, I called Magda. She assured me that she would be fine without me. In fact, I thought she sounded relieved at the prospect of me taking a few hours for myself. The press had backed off, it seemed. In addition to the lumberyard fire, a bank robbery had taken their attention as well. I was free for the rest of the day. I told Magda I would be back later that night.

◆ ◆ ◆

I found Donald Tooley in the visitors' room with his wife. He looked like a man who had been hated all of his life and it had left a scar on his face in the shape of a frown. His eyes were permanently sun-squinted and his teeth as brown as tobacco. Even though he had no hat, he appeared to be wringing one. The sad thing was, there wasn't anything in particular about him to hate. In fact, most people wouldn't have noticed him at all and maybe that's where his pain came from. His biggest enemy, I decided, was probably himself. His shoulders were stooped from being constantly under the world's thumb. I felt sorry for him. He sat hunched into the plastic chair. His clothing was the drab color of mud—a cheap shirt and pants of indeterminate material. Not prison garb, for he wasn't formally charged.

Donald's wife was by his side. She had the air of being stuck in her situation. She probably believed that her Don couldn't survive without her and it may have been true. She probably considered him her cross to bear and her shoulders were bowed, like Donald's, under its weight. She obviously was willing to stand by his side and that was as much of a mistake as she would ever willingly make.

I introduced myself as a private investigator. "You don't have to talk to me," I told Donald. "If you want, you can call your attorney."

"You're working for her, aren't you?" Geraldine Tooley asked the question passively. There was no stinging jealousy, no rebuke, only resignation. I wondered if she was capable of killing Magda's husband. But, if she was, what would have been the point of choosing him? Why not Magda herself and rid Donald once and for all of his obsession with the woman he could never hope to have?

Geraldine was the kind of woman that you would turn away from in an effort not to stare at her when you saw her walking toward you in the Safeway store. Her hair looked tired, the way it does when a perm is in the final stages of growing out and her eyes seemed to be painted on upside down. Two heavy black smears of liner under her lower lids made her lashes look as if they had begun to run. She wore a garish dress covered with enormous flowers and leaves. The red was bright enough to make you squint and the green, stringent enough to make you pucker. She nervously straightened the fabric across her knees and licked her lips, watching me. She made me feel like weeping.

"Yes, I'm working for Magda St. Martin. She wants me to find out who killed her husband."

"She thinks I did it!" Donald said. His expression never changed. "She's the one who told the police that I sent her notes. They had that young kid, that druggie, but she told them to look at me. She thinks I did it for sure." He turned and started to stand up, as if thinking that the whole interview was a waste of time.

"Mr. Tooley, if you don't want to answer my questions, I won't ask you to, but I would like to talk to you. It might help to clear this up."

"Donny, I think you should talk to her," Geraldine

said.

"You butt out, woman," he said, but his tone held no venom. He said it the same way he might have said, "Okay, honey," if he had been another kind of man and she, another woman. Nevertheless, he settled back into the chair again and buried his face in his hands.

"You wrote letters to Magda several years ago, before her second husband was killed."

He started nodding before I had finished. "Sure. I wrote them. I ain't ashamed of that. I guess you probably saw them if you worked on that case too."

In fact, I hadn't seen the letters until Laurel had led me up to that curiously dust-free attic to take a look at them. When Angelle had disappeared, Donald's name had not come up at all. He hadn't been considered a suspect of anything nefarious by me because I hadn't known of his existence. When Peter Winthrop was killed, Donald was questioned by the police but not held. At the time, he had seemed to have no connection to either Peter's death nor Angelle's disappearance.

"Do you know Angelle St. Martin?"

"Nope," he said and shook his head. "Never met her."

"She is Magda's daughter. Were you aware that she disappeared shortly before Peter Winthrop was killed?"

"Nope," he said again and looked confused. "I don't

know her. You can't say I had anything to do with that."

"I wasn't saying you did. I just wanted to know if you knew her. What do you remember about last Monday night, Mr. Tooley?" I saw a look pass between husband and wife.

"I don't remember anything," he said. Geraldine let out a sigh. It sounded like relief. I touched her hand and found it hot and dry. From her I felt pure, crystalline fear. She glanced at me, surprised.

"Mr. and Mrs. Tooley, I'm going to have to have some straight answers if I'm going to find out who did this thing. You aren't helping your case by denying knowledge. I want to know what you remember about Monday night."

"Like I said, I don't remember anything." He looked more sullen than ever and I thought for a moment he was going to demand to be sent back to his cell.

I turned to Geraldine in exasperation. "Do you know where Donald was that night?" I asked.

"He was home in bed." The red roses in her dress shifted. She was lying.

"When he answered, you sighed," I said to her. "You sounded relieved when he said he didn't remember. His not remembering could be very bad for him. What made you sigh with relief?"

She licked her lips and pressed her fingers to her thin thighs. Her gaze slid to her husband and back to me. "I was afraid he was going to lie and say he was out at a bar or something. It's easier if he tells the truth, even if it means he don't remember where he was."

"I know I was home in bed because my wife says so, but I don't remember any of it. I'd been out all the night before and most of the day. I was drinking, ma'am. I drink a lot. I been drinking for years. Sometimes a lot, sometimes a little, and sometimes, for a couple of days, not at all." He said it "not a tall". I believed him. About that, anyway.

"The police don't believe that I was home in bed. They don't believe that Gerry rolled me in there at five that afternoon."

"But, why not, if she was there with you?"

"I wasn't there the whole time. I went over to my sister's about ten." Again, her eyes flickered and she shot a glance at Donald. I got the feeling that these two were reciting a story they had cooked up between them and then rehearsed. "Her girl come in with her two kids and one of them took sick. I used to be a nurse's aide so she called me up and asked would I come over and look at the boy. I didn't get home until around midnight or a little after."

"What was Donald doing when you got home?"

"He was laying in the same position he was in when I left. He didn't move anything and I knew that in the morning, his shoulder would be good and sore because he had his arm up over his head for so long.

He's got bad joints and when he lays in one spot all night long, he's stiff as a board the next day. Sure enough," she said, nodding, "it hurt him so bad that the Ben Gay—"

"She don't want to hear about my aches and pains, for cryin' out loud," Donald said tiredly.

"Who do you think killed Jake?" I asked Donald.

"I don't know. I can't say that I'm sorry it happened, though. I never liked the way he treated Magda. He run around at all hours of the night. Didn't pay any attention to her at all. Magda St. Martin should never be treated like that. I'm glad he's dead and she's free now."

Geraldine's face was still passive. I wondered about her loyalty. Donald was in jail for being suspected of killing Magda's husband because he was so in love with Magda, a woman he had never actually met. Donald treated his own wife badly, yet his reasoning for wanting Jake dead was that he treated Magda badly. His alibi was teetering because he'd been drunk for two days, yet he criticized Jake for ignoring Magda and leaving her alone. Geraldine herself was treated as shabbily as Donald had said Magda was, and yet was doing her best to defend the man. I wondered again if she could be capable of killing Jake herself just to please her husband.

"Donny used to work for Mr. Levin," Geraldine said suddenly. He gave her a sharp glance, but nodded.

Worked for him? "When was that, Mr. Tooley?"

"'Bout eight years ago, before Mr. Levin got married to Magda. I got myself fired for drinking on the job and sleeping my way through a vandalism attack."

"You were a watchman?"

"I was a Pinkerton," he said with a twitch of his mouth that could have been the beginning of a smile that died before it ever hit his eyes. I took it for pride. Working as a Pinkerton guard probably was the closest he had ever come to a good, steady, respectable job. "I didn't *acshully* work for Mr. Levin, but I was on the night shift in his building down in Federal Way."

"This was before you sent those letters to Magda?" I asked. I knew when he had sent them, but I wanted to find out if he lied as easily as he drank. And I wanted to see if he would tell the same story twice.

"No. I sent the letters before that. I sent them letters even before that other husband was killed. That's why the police come after me for it. They heard about the letters, just like now and thought I had something to do with it. They didn't know that I wasn't the one doing the tormenting."

"I don't understand what you mean, Mr. Tooley," I said. "Who was tormenting whom?"

"*She* was. Magda St. Martin was sending me letters bad enough to match anything I ever sent to her. She was the one doing the tormenting."

"She sent *you* letters? Did you tell the police

about it?" I was certain he hadn't. Perce would have mentioned it to me.

"No, I didn't tell them. She's got a little crazy streak in her, I know that. Besides, it woulda been just her word against mine. I didn't save them and who's going to believe a drunk over a beautiful movie star, anyway?"

"Mr. Tooley, what did those letters say?"

"Oh, this was after I sent a few, you know, saying that I..." He glanced uneasily at his wife. She laid her hand on his, never changing her expression at all. "I said I was in love with her and if anything should ever happen to her husband, why, I'd like to take her down to Honolulu or somewhere. She sent me some saying she loved her fans and needed them." Donald coughed deeply and wiped his mouth with a blue edged handkerchief. "Gerry found out about the letters and I cut out writing. A little while later she, Magda that is, wrote me and asked me why I didn't send her more letters, so I did. Gerry found out again and I promised her I wouldn't, but I kept on getting those letters from Magda beggin' like and hoping that her fans wouldn't forget her. Said she needed her fans and their love. It got worse than that. She started to demand that I keep writing to her. I wrote to her once or twice again." He looked at Geraldine, but she wasn't looking at him. "I asked her to stop writing that way, is all. After that I didn't write anymore, but she started writing dirty stuff and it got worse and worse."

That didn't sound like the Magda I knew. "Are you sure the letters were from her?" I asked. "It could have been a prankster."

"No, ma'am. I'm sure they were from her 'cause I got an autograph of hers and all the letters. It's the same writing. I know it was her. She's got a little crazy streak in her all right."

"Did you say you didn't keep those letters she sent, Mr. Tooley?"

Geraldine looked at her hands in her lap and Donald shook his head. "They got thrown out," he said and glanced at his wife.

"I threw them away," Geraldine said without looking up. I nodded to reassure her that she hadn't done anything wrong, even though it may have helped the case if they had kept them.

"Do you think Magda could have killed Mr. Levin?" I asked.

His face blanched. "Oh, no, ma'am! She didn't. She wouldn't of done it. No."

"How can you be so positive? You yourself said she has a crazy steak." He shook his head but said nothing. "Do you have any idea who did do it?"

He shook his head again. "He was always good to me. Even when I fouled up and let them young kids break the windows in his warehouse. He mighta been cheating on her, but he was a pretty good boss."

"You didn't *let* them kids do it, Donny," the ever-loyal Geraldine said. I wondered how much would have to happen before she would quit believing that he was nothing but a big, innocent child.

I stood up. "Mr. and Mrs. Tooley, before I go, is there anything you need? What about your children? Are they being cared for?"

Geraldine drew herself up and straightened her gaudy dress. "Yes, ma'am. My kids are with my sister. We don't need anything. We sure do thank you, though." Donald said nothing.

◆ ◆ ◆

E asy was waiting for me when I came out. The winter afternoon sun was the color of icy lemonade. We would be in for more rain, and soon, but for the moment, it was one of those times that made Seattle beautiful. And I had the afternoon off.

"Get anything?" Easy asked.

I shook my head. "A little, I guess. But neither Donald nor his wife are being completely honest. They aren't making it any easier, that's for sure. After I drop off this knife, let's take advantage of this wonderful weather and walk up to the Market for an early dinner. After the jail, the outdoors seems like paradise."

"The Copacabana for *paella*?"

"I was thinking of the Sound View Café for

groundnut stew and rice salad," I said. His hopeful expression dissolved into a disgusted look. I had to laugh.

"Tell you what," I said. "How about we get some shrimps and French bread and I'll make you some of my soon to be famous Shrimp Cheyenne at my place. Or, no. At yours. Yours is closer. I want to stop by Suzanne French's apartment if we have time."

He looked doubtful and made a little grunt that could have been either yes or no. "Shrimp Cheyenne? It sounds hot."

"You're thinking of *cayenne*." I pointed at myself. "Cheyenne. You'll love it. I promise."

"Garlic?"

"Of course."

"Mushrooms?"

I nodded. "Butter and cream, too. And wine."

He stopped. "You don't cook with butter and cream." His wonderful eyes narrowed with suspicion.

"Okay, not butter and cream, but it will taste like it. I promise. You'll love it. You'll see."

We stopped by the precinct and I handed off the knife to Perce. My angels must have been watching over me because Quiller wasn't there.

"I don't think this is the weapon," Perce said while I was signing the requisite paperwork, "but I'll make sure it gets logged in. It seems the weapon was thicker than an ordinary knife. Could be something bigger."

"Like what? Like a cleaver? An axe?" I frowned. "Neither one of those would make a very efficient close-range weapon."

He shook his head and shrugged. Everyone, it seemed, was baffled by the case.

We left Perce to deal with the knife and walked up Second Avenue. Between Union and Pike, it looked like a war zone. Buildings awaiting restoration or the wrecking ball were boarded up and covered with graffiti and ruin. On any other day it would have made me depressed, but the idea of an afternoon off helped.

By the time we got to the Pike Place Market, Easy had me talked into going down to the lower level for a visit to Old Friends and Grandma's Attic. Both antique stores were tucked away in the depths of the Market along with a used record store I happen to know he could easily spend hours investigating.

Easy had collected records for years and owned thousands. He had gotten himself a two-bedroom apartment so he could have a dedicated music room. From looking at him, you wouldn't think he was a Zappa fan but he owned everything the man had recorded to date along with a vast array of eclectic and popular works.

Easy also collected hats. Not to wear. He kept them in orderly rows on his living room wall. I always told him he had chosen hats because of a deep-seated confusion about his choice of vocation. He said he had started collecting them to cover up the holes in the wall. I had wisely kept silent about the holes in his head.

We wandered through the shops and stalls, breathing in the scents. No matter how old I get or how far from Seattle I go, I knew I would never forget the smell of the Pike Place Market. It was a subtle mixture of spices and textiles, fresh fish and meat, wax and string, hot dogs, pizza, new cloth and old, wood, flowers, vegetables and tea. The sound of steel drums somewhere in the Market mingled with the delicious cooking aromas that also drifted on the air from the cafés, bakeries and coffee shops.

We passed Don and Joe's Meats and Easy admired planks of beef that made his stomach rumble. To me, they only looked like slabs of something dead. We moved to the Pike Place Fish Company and bought our shrimps—prawns, actually, they were so big and plump. There were other goodies there; geoduck, looking obscenely wonderful, and Chilean Sea Bass. I couldn't afford the bass and couldn't talk Easy into the gigantic clams.

At the Market Spice Shop, I dashed in for a pound of tea. Over the years, the price had skyrocketed from around a dollar a pound to seven dollars as the tea had become famous. Expensive, yes, but worth every savory little leaf. I treasured it like precious jewels.

We bought a hot, round loaf of French bread at the Three Girls Bakery and I ducked into a grocery to pick up some items for the shrimp dish. Then we strolled up through the craft booths.

The Market kept me in tune with the world. It was the only place where you could buy anything from handmade brooms and baskets to jewelry made from paper. You could find tie dye, wooden toys, sand sculpture and umbrellas made from glass. I loved woods, yarns and fabrics, as well as anything that came from the earth. I was a sucker for the colorful and handmade.

We headed back to our cars. The sun would be going down soon and the wind was picking up. Easy lived in the University District. So did Suzanne. So did Clovis Houston, I remembered with a twinge of guilt. I hadn't done anything about trying to catch him in the act of eating for several days. I made a promise to myself to get on that.

I rang Suzanne's bell but got no response. An older gentleman, wearing a camouflage fishing hat and raking leaves told me she had left a couple of hours before. He winked and grinned at me, showing huge, perfectly white teeth. I handed him one of my cards, doubting that I would ever hear from her. I was sure I would have to hunt her down.

E asy's apartment was not what you would expect of a youngish single-man/chaplain of a city police department. His home wasn't just his base of operation, he *lived* there. He had made himself comfortable among the things that he loved. His wall of hats had grown quite impressive over the years. Here and there were small antiques that were more than just decorative. Useful tables, comfy chairs, and soft rugs showed his taste as a man who appreciated pleasure but treasured utility. His kitchen, while not a cook's dream, was functional and attractive. And it was always clean, something that impressed me no end.

We put our purchases in the kitchen and I started some water boiling for pasta and the peeling of tomatoes. Easy put something old and comfortable on the turntable then hovered until I finally told him to open the bottle of wine and sit down. Neither one of us could actually drink any of it; Easy was on call and I still had to drive back to West Seattle, but we put a healthy portion of it into the pasta sauce.

After we had eaten way too much, Easy sat back and put his hands on his stomach. "You can't tell me you didn't sneak some butter and cream into that while I wasn't looking," he said.

"It's magic," I told him. It had actually been the magic of yogurt, but he didn't need to know that. It really had been delicious. I put my hand on his arm. I swear that man gave me a pleasant little sting of electricity every time I touched him. He looked at me, his gaze never wavering from mine until I laughed uncomfortably.

"At some point," he said, "we need to have a talk."

"Talk?" I said, stalling for a little time. "About what?" I knew, though.

He looked at me for a long moment. "I understand your reluctance," he began, but I cut him off.

"Easy, we've had a really nice dinner. It was fun. Let's not talk about any of this now." I tried to look anywhere else other than his eyes but they were right there and I couldn't seem to get away from them.

"You never want to talk," he said using a gentle, patient tone. I got the feeling he had rehearsed the speech. "You have to move beyond the past, Chey. I know how you feel, but we have to talk. If not right now, then soon."

"Then I choose not right now." I tried to keep my voice light and playful but I knew I had failed.

I saw disappointment flit across his face then it was gone. "Chey," he said, his voice sounding gruff. "It's just talk. That's all. No commitments. Just talk."

"Who said anything about commitments?" I asked, alarm bells beginning to sound in my head.

"I know how you feel…"

"No. You don't," I said. "Please…"

"Chey…" I could almost see him give himself

a mental shake and switch gears. "That was a wonderful dinner," he said finally.

I gave a soft little relieved sigh. "I should be on my way."

"Wait," he said. "Let's go sit in the living room for a little while."

There were two candles burning between us. I leaned forward and blew out one. He blew out the other. It wasn't dark. The desk lamp still made a soft, warm glow on our faces. I smiled at him, wondering suddenly what I was doing. I started to rise and he grabbed my hand. I could feel more than I wanted to in his touch. I tried to pull away but he held on.

Thankfully, Easy's pager beeped. Startled, we both laughed, his sounding guilty to me. I wondered if he had been planning to betray his deeply held beliefs.

I put the dishes in the sink while Easy phoned in. "I'm needed," he said when he put down the telephone.

I nodded. "I have to get back to Magda's anyway," I said. "I'm supposed to be 'protecting' her, after all."

"Chey," he said, taking my hand again. "That was the best dinner I've had in a long time. I..." He didn't finish, but kissed me softly. I breathed in the warm scent of him. He kissed me again, longer this time and I wished that we could keep on kissing, but in a moment, he was gone.

I washed up the dishes and tidied the kitchen for him before I left. The wind had picked up and I could hear rain slashing against the outside wall. I couldn't help thinking about what the evening might have turned out to be. Easy didn't submit to his feelings easily. You could almost see the wrenching soul searching that went on inside of him. He was raised by a stay-at-home mom and a traditional suit and wing-tip wearing father. They never missed church and Easy grew up believing that no matter what he did, someone was always watching. He firmly held on to the belief that sex should wait until after marriage. I, on the other hand, had gotten my formal sex education in back of Portable Number 9 at Shoreside Elementary School. He, I knew, was aching for a marriage and a large family. I seemed to have damaged something that other women apparently had in their brains. I had been desperately in love once. He had died. I had fallen in love again and gotten married. He had left. I was a loner and I liked it that way. No partner in work, no partner in life. If you are alone, there's no one to leave you. I would have done almost anything to prevent that kind of hurt from happening again.

The gale whipped my hair around as I climbed into my car to head back to West Seattle. It was later than I had intended and I was feeling a twinge or two of guilt for leaving Magda for so long.

It was for the best that Easy had been called away. I wished that I could have been more, well, easy with Easy. While I was not averse to a casual sexual encounter once in a while, I knew for Easy it would be a much more serious matter. I knew that he would have a wrestling match with his conscience that night, even though all we had done was kiss. It was the intention that he would struggle with. Sometimes, I wished I didn't like him quite so much.

TEN

Thursday, November 17, 1983

It occurred to me that it was the same kind of stormy night it had been when Jake was killed. Maybe even a little worse. The rain pounded on top of the car and misted my headlights. The wind was making the trees lash at the air as if trying to desperately warn us humans that Mother Nature meant business.

On the West Seattle Bridge, I decided it was the perfect night for a peek at the murder scene. After all, the time was right and so was the weather. It would only take me a few minutes. If I could sit in my car in the exact spot where Jake had parked and empty my mind, maybe I could catch an echo of his ordeal. It may not give me any more information than I already had, but, on the other hand, it might.

I took the Harbor Avenue exit and wound around past Salty's and the Embers. Just before the Don Armeni Park, which really was nothing more than a boat ramp, was the parking area where Jake had been killed. I counted over to the fourth stall and pulled in to where I knew he had been found. I knew that just ahead, the lights of the city twinkled within the pillow of fog the same as they had the night of Jake's murder.

I tried to put myself into Jake's position. He had been alone, as I was and the rain had been, as now, pouring down in great splashes. The car's interior quickly steamed up, though I wasn't breathing exceptionally hard. Outside, the wind buffeted my little car, rocking it gently. His Lincoln probably hadn't rocked. But his car had held a much worse danger. I leaned my head against the head-rest and tried to reach my mind back to that night.

I let my thoughts drift, watching the dim lights of a late-night ferry as it crept across the treacherous waters. With each raindrop, the lights blurred and ran together. I may have half-dozed, God knows I was tired enough, but sometimes a trance-like state can seem like sleep. Suddenly, I felt a strong sense of the car, the world closing in on me. An odd sensation ripped across my chin. It was rough, like a cat's tongue. The claustrophobia pushed down on me and I found my hand clutching the window handle when I "awoke". Immediately, it was all gone. Sometimes it's frustrating. Just when I thought I was getting something, it left me. Like the fleeting whiff of perfume in a busy department store, it was gone before I could identify it.

I opened my eyes and looked around. Everything was as before. Everything except me. I suddenly and achingly wanted Easy and if I hadn't been so close to Magda's house, I might have been tempted to page him and ask him to meet me back at his place. I might even have been willing to do some talking. A little. Instead, I stepped out of the car, deliberately letting the rain splash onto my face. There was no better way to combat fear than to walk right into it.

The rain hammered the sidewalk and obscured everything but the closest objects. No cars *swooshed* by and the dark was overwhelming. The streetlights on that stretch of road, for some reason were not lit. The city's electrical conservation efforts may have lent the right atmosphere to Jake Levin's romantic trysts, but they weren't helping me at all.

Suddenly, I heard more than just the rain. I didn't have time to turn around before an arm snaked across my body, pinning my arms to my sides. Hot breath in my ear galvanized me to try squirming away. An ungloved hand clasped my chin, forcing my head sideways so my ear was pressed to my assailant's mouth. I pushed my backside into his body, trying to unbalance him, and felt something hard and sharp press into my lower back.

"Stand still," he commanded. I did. I didn't know what kind of a weapon he had and didn't care to find out. Not then, anyway.

"I don't have any money," I said, hoping that was all he wanted. I couldn't move. I could feel a mixture of defiance, menace and, strangely, purpose emanating from him.

"I don't want money. I want you to leave off sneaking around and trying to find out about Jake Levin's murderer."

"Who are you?" I asked, though I was pretty sure I knew.

He shook me hard. "Never mind. Just lay off. Do you hear me? Quit snooping around where you don't belong." He shook me again. "I asked you a question. Do you hear me?"

I croaked a "yes," hoping I could throw him off balance, but before I could react, he shoved me hard. My feet couldn't find traction on the slippery street and I crashed headlong into a metal trash container. By the time I struggled to my feet, he was gone. The darkness was overwhelming. The houses across the street had no porchlights lit and the windows were covered. I hadn't heard a car start, nor could I see tail lights or headlights in either direction. The rain pelted my face and my heart thudded. I climbed, dripping and bruised, back into my car and drove slowly up California Way to Magda's.

I was shivering when I locked the car and trudged up the front walk. I climbed the stairs not caring about possible water on Magda's pristine floors. As I passed Magda's door and Laurel's, I saw dim lights underneath both and thought they were probably secure enough for the night. In my own room I left wet footprints, then a soggy pile of my clothes in the middle of the bathroom floor. In the shower, I let hot water run on my back, my front and my back again, but the chill stayed with me all the way to bed. My feet ached with it and a nagging pain pulsed between my shoulder blades.

I did not consider calling the police to report the attack. At least, not then. I had been physically assaulted more than once during my career. The attack itself was a clue to this case, and I planned to dig deeper before making any official complaints.

I must have dozed, for I awoke with my head hanging over my right shoulder. My book was lying against my chest, and the glasses I wear when my contacts are out, were slipping down my nose. My alarm clock said it was 3:10. The rain had stopped and the wind, it seemed, had died.

I had dreamed of music. A waltz, I thought. It had been too far away to tell. I sat up and realized that it may not have been a dream. Had there really been music playing in the house somewhere? I listened, trying to figure out if it was music or voices that I had heard. Sometimes it had seemed like both. Then I heard the unmistakable sound of footsteps just above me in the library. I threw off the blanket and gasped at the hundreds of tiny knives poking into my joints.

My knees and hips all but creaked as I stood up. I pulled on my robe and grabbed the flashlight I had stashed in the closet. The house was deathly quiet now. I no longer heard the memory of music but I felt that someone was still moving around upstairs. I carefully opened my door and peered out into the hallway. Magda's and Laurel's doors were both shut and there was no light coming from underneath either. I had deliberately left my slippers off so there would be no chance of my being heard walking up the uncarpeted stairs. My feet were freezing. I hesitated at the bottom and listened. Yes, I definitely heard a footstep, then another, directly above my head. From my previous prowls through the house, I knew that there were area rugs and hardwood in the library. Still, it seemed that someone up in the middle of the night wouldn't have been inclined to wear shoes that could be heard downstairs.

The second stair creaked softly and I stopped for a moment, then moved toward the outer part where the pressure of my step would be less likely to make noise. I thought I could still hear faint murmurs coming from above and the quiet footfall of someone moving around. It only took me a few seconds to climb the stairs but they seemed to go on forever.

The library door was shut. I leaned against it carefully and put my ear to the wood. Nothing. I hadn't heard it open, nor had I heard it close. If anyone had been inside, they must still be there. I gently turned the knob which made a faint groan as though it felt pain from my touch. The door squeaked, but it didn't matter. There was no one in the room.

I walked in and switched on the light, carefully peering behind chairs and drapes, feeling slightly foolish. What had I heard? There had been sounds; voices, footsteps, maybe music. I was sure of it. I hadn't imagined them. Or had I? I sat down in one of the leather chairs to let my heart return to a normal beat. In the corner, I thought I heard the *swish* of fabric. I turned around but saw nothing.

"Angelle?" I whispered. "Is that you?"

No one answered.

ELEVEN

Friday, November 18, 1983

In the morning, my muscles were sore from wrestling with my dreams, library phantoms and Rolf Edmondson. I was sure that he was the man with the powerful grip of the night before. My back still hurt from whatever it was that had gouged into it. I doubted that Mr. Edmondson had had a gun with him, nor had it been one hell of a hard-on. I suspected his agate belt buckle had left its impression in my back. I was intrigued. Surely Rolf knew that his attack on me threw more than a little suspicion on himself. I was quite sure that now I could eliminate Donald Tooley and Suzanne from my suspects list. Thanks to Mr. Edmondson, Magda, Laurel and Rolf himself had moved to the top.

I put on a pair of sweats hoping to walk around the block a few times, not for exercise but to work out the kinks in my poor, aching muscles. The sun had struggled through the clouds and was throwing sunbeams on the polished floor of the foyer as I went past. I glanced at the stained glass windows as I always did. This time, though, something made me stop. I stood there before it for several seconds.

Medea and the Furies rose above me, frozen forever in their terrible moment. Around them swirled the winds and spirits. Glittering pieces of glass in glowing reds, rich golds, purples, blues and greens rippled and flowed like gleaming satin ribbons.

The sun shone on the window in such a way that I could see a crack. One of the green pieces in the center window was broken. I hadn't noticed the crack before, and Laurel hadn't mentioned it when I had been admiring the windows earlier in my visit. Magda, I was sure, would have seen to having it fixed if she had known the window was flawed. She wasn't one for keeping a damaged piece of anything in the house. I wondered how one went about repairing such a thing. Or even if it was ever done. I certainly had seen stained glass lamps and windows before with cracks in them. Maybe stained glass with cracks was similar to crazing in old porcelain. A small flaw sometimes made a piece more beautiful. It became unique. Somehow, I doubted that Magda would see it that way.

In the time that I stood there, the sun had moved and hit another section and the crack had disappeared. I stepped from side to side and back and then forward, but I could not make it visible again. For a moment, I wondered if I had imagined it after all. A trick of the light, perhaps. But, no, I knew what I had seen.

Abandoning my intent to walk, I went into the kitchen and found Laurel sitting at the table reading the morning Seattle Post Intelligencer. She looked up and smiled.

"Morning," she said. "You must have come in late." Her expression, on anyone else, might have been called a leer.

"Guilty," I said. "I hope I didn't wake you." Had it been Laurel I had heard the night before? I could see neither she nor Magda being able to get back to their rooms without my having seen them. On the other hand, I could have been hearing the residual sounds of those who had once lived in the house. That happened all the time.

"Oh, no. I was dead to the world right after the eight o'clock movie was over," Laurel said. "I didn't hear a thing until my alarm went off."

"Laurel, did you know there's a crack in one of the big stained glass windows?"

"A crack?!" Her face blanched. She rose immediately and hurried into the foyer as if I had told her that the front door was in flames.

"You can only see it if you happen to be standing right here at exactly the correct moment in the earth's rotation," I said. "I wouldn't worry about it too much." I was a bit sorry that I had mentioned it at all.

"Which piece is it?" She stood on her toes and peered at the glass.

"I'm not sure now," I said. "I think it's that lime green strip right there under Medea's left hand."

"Don't say anything to Magda about it, will you?" she said and turned to me. "She's so fussy, she would demand to have it fixed and it's such a horrible business you wouldn't believe it. Just keep it quiet, okay?"

"Sure," I said. It wasn't my window. "How do they do that, anyway? Fix those things."

"Oh, it's a huge production, believe me. They have to take the whole thing down to the shop. They have to board up the space because it takes several weeks to finish the repair. The house looks terrible with plywood across the window. Magda had hysterics about it. She noticed a tiny crack in it several years ago and she insisted it be fixed. I hope to never have to go through that again!"

"I didn't realize it was such a big job."

"It took them hours to get it out and then weeks to find the right glass. Magda had a fit. You know how she is."

"Where did she have it repaired? Is there a place around here that does that kind of thing?"

"There's a stained glass shop down there on Fauntleroy, just before you get on the bridge. That's where she had it repaired before."

We went back into the kitchen but Laurel's worried expression lingered on her face. She toasted bread and smeared hers with peanut butter. "Juice?" she asked.

I nodded. "I've got to go back to Mercer Island today," I told her. "I need to pick up a couple of things."

"Been too busy, huh?" Her worried frown had disappeared. She smiled and I saw that leer flash across her face again. Somehow, she didn't seem like Laurel. I wondered if I was blushing. My face felt hot. I hadn't done that in years. I was getting as bad as Easy. I decided to ignore her. After all, I was over thirty-five and wasn't used to being watched. I didn't like it. At all. But she wouldn't let it alone.

"I guess you like that Mr. Radford quite a lot. I saw you looking at him the other day when he was here. Have you known him long?"

I drained my glass and put it down. "Laurel, how do you happen to know who I was with last night or where I was?"

She immediately dropped the coy act. "I'm sorry," she said. "I *don't* know. I was just guessing. I..."

I didn't wait to hear the rest of what she had to say. "I'll be back later," I said.

I cut across Magda's lawn intending to have a talk with Rolf. I was curious to know where he would claim to have been at eleven the night before. I was pretty confident that he had followed me and then, possibly, had found the gall to discuss it with Laurel. Otherwise, unless she truly was guessing, how would she have known with whom I had spent the evening? I pounded on his door then gave up when I realized his station wagon wasn't parked in its usual spot. I would have to track him down later. I had a few things to ask him. And a few things to say.

◆ ◆ ◆

The sight of my little apartment abruptly reminded me that in a few weeks I would have to be living somewhere else and my mood soured a little bit more. I listened to the few phone messages my recorder had collected and wrote down the particulars. I gathered the mail from the floor and stuck it into my briefcase. I dug into the file cabinet and found Clovis Houston's file. His case had been weighing on me. I needed to get out to the U District again, talk to Suzanne and try to find Clovis in a compromising position. It was going to be a busy day.

In the car, I leafed through my mail, knowing I would be able to throw most of it into the trash bin on my way out. One letter intrigued me. I ripped it open. The name and address on the envelope had been typed but the letter appeared to have been printed by a child. It took me all of two minutes to read it, get back through the door, put the letter into a plastic evidence bag and call Easy. Thankfully, he was still at home.

"How many people know how Jake Levin was killed?" I asked him without bothering with the niceties first.

"Just the police. The press hasn't been given that information. Why?"

"I just got a letter. It says that if I don't lay off the case, my throat will be cut too. Easy, this has to be from the killer. No one else knew. Unless...Does Magda know?"

"I don't think so. They told her that there were knife wounds but the MO wasn't given to anyone else. When she identified him, the wounds weren't visible. I was there." I heard rustling on the line and realized he was putting on his clothes. "Listen," he said. "I want you to stay where you are. I'm coming over to Magda's right now to get you."

"No, you aren't. I'm not at Magda's anyway. I've already gotten my prints on this letter, but I'm going to run it down to Harlan Quiller right now."

"Where are you? I'm coming over. I don't want you to be alone. Listen..."

"Easy, for God's sake! I can take care of myself." I was regretting that I had called him. "Look, I promise I'll be watchful."

He started to mutter something but I hung up.

I was on the freeway before I realized it might

have been one of the rare times for me to carry my weapon.

TWELVE

Friday, November 18, 1983

Quiller wasn't in so I handed the letter to Perce, glad that no one else was in the office.

"Fan mail, huh?" He eyed the childish writing. "Your good buddy and mine is going to be real interested in this," he said, nodding at Quiller's desk.

Just as I had finished signing the required paperwork, Easy crashed through the door. It swung back and hit the wall, almost breaking the glass window.

"How the hell did you get here so fast?" I asked, exasperated.

"I was just on my way out the door when you called. I'm going to Magda's with you."

"Easy—" I started to say, trying to keep my voice calm.

"I want you off of this case."

I laughed. Perce glanced from me to Easy and back to me, then did the seven-foot-tall version of making himself invisible. He shut the door quietly behind him.

"Chey, this isn't something to laugh about. I want you to tell Magda that you're off the case. As of today. You're finished." He moved over to Perce's desk and leaned over to look at the letter.

"The hell I am." It was getting hard to control my voice.

He turned back to me with a look of infinite patience and something else I didn't recognize at first. "You've been threatened," he said. "Doesn't that mean anything to you at all? Your life is in danger." His knuckles were white as he clutched the edge of Perce's desk. I was doubly glad Quiller wasn't there. He would have thoroughly enjoyed the scene and he wouldn't have made the graceful exit that Perce had.

"I'm not quitting this case, Easy." I heard my own voice beginning to shake with fury. "And I don't want you going with me. This is none of your business. You didn't hire me, Magda did."

"I never should have called you in on it in the first place. You don't have any business working on a murder case." He shoved at the desk and paced over to the blinded window.

"Oh, for Christ's sake! You did call me in because you knew I could handle this. I don't intend to quit until I find out what the fuck is going on around there."

"Don't use that kind of language!"

I almost laughed again but I was too full of rage. Instead, I grabbed at his arm. "You look here," I said. "You do *not* have the right to tell me what to do or what to say."

He jerked his arm away and slammed his fist onto Perce's desk, making the half full coffee mug jump.

In the few seconds my hand had been on his arm, I knew what it was that I had seen on his face and I didn't like it. It was love. That did it.

"God damn it to hell!" I said as controlled as I could be, which wasn't very. "I won't tolerate a man patronizing me. If you think you have some rights to me, you are wrong!" I strode to the door. "I'll see you around!"

I slammed the door behind me. The glass in the window shuddered. I was sure that someday it would break and I would get immense satisfaction from it. I saw Perce waiting for the elevator, but I marched past and took the stairs.

◆ ◆ ◆

The minute I pulled up to the front of Magda's house, I knew things weren't going to get better. I had the kind of feeling you get when you turn down your street and see ambulances parked in front of your house.

No ambulances were at Magda's. Neither were there any other emergency vehicles. There was an unfamiliar car parked in front but that could have been anyone's. I knew it wasn't, though. Something unpleasant was going on inside. Sometimes, being a psychic is great. Sometimes it sucks.

I hurried up the walk and even before I reached the front door, I could hear their voices. It sounded like Saturday night in Highpoint. That was an old West Seattle low-income housing project that was notorious for street fights and gangs.

"Get out of this house immediately!" Laurel was saying. I yanked open the front door and came face to face with a startlingly beautiful woman who was on her way out. Laurel stood with her fists clenched like she was ready to give someone an uppercut. Behind her, Magda had her hands covering her mouth.

"What is it?" I asked. I put a detaining hand on the woman's arm. I didn't want her leaving before I had a chance to talk to her, whoever she was. As soon as I touched her, though, I knew.

"Just get her out of here." Laurel's face was pale.

Magda came forward and skewered the woman with a look. "Cheyenne, this is Suzanne French," she said in a low, controlled voice. "Will you please see to it that she leaves?" She turned her look onto me. I felt a quiver of guilt that I hadn't been there for the protection Magda was paying me for, but, hell, I couldn't protect and investigate at the same time.

Suzanne jerked her arm away from me and glared. "Who are you?" she said. I could tell it was pure bravado. She was scared. Badly.

"My name is Cheyenne Bruce," I said, steering her outside. "I'm investigating Jake Levin's murder."

Suzanne visibly relaxed. "Thank God someone is," she said.

"Let me take you somewhere so we can talk," I said. "I was going to come and see you today anyway. I have some questions I would like to ask. Do you mind?"

She shook her head. "I shouldn't have come here," she said, "but...I had to find out what was going on." She looked deflated all of a sudden. I gathered that she wasn't used to holding her poise for very long.

"We'll go get some lunch," I said. She nodded gratefully.

She followed me in her car to a posh little restaurant in the heart of "downtown" West Seattle. The menu there was famous for its salads. I happened to be extremely fond of the Northwest Crab Salad and, after the morning I'd had, I thought I deserved a little indulgence.

Suzanne halfheartedly ordered the spinach salad.

"I didn't see you at the funeral," I said, thinking that she would have made a perfect "woman in black" who is supposed to attend all murder victims'

LELLA RAE

funerals. A huge picture hat and a revealing black dress would have suited her to a T.

She hung her head then tipped it back and faced the ceiling as if to keep the tears in her eyes by sheer force. "I didn't go," she said.

"Suzanne, I want to tell you how terribly sorry I am for your loss," I told her.

The tears spilled over instantly. "Thank you," she whispered. "No one has said that to me. One of the reasons I didn't go to the funeral was because everyone would be telling Magda how sorry they were and I'm the one who will miss him most."

"I have been wanting to talk to you. Didn't you get the card I left at your apartment? I left it with your landlord."

She gave me a shaky smile. "No. He probably kept it. He likes to collect the phone numbers of attractive women."

"You said you wanted to find out what was going on. You didn't have to go to Magda's house to find out. The newspapers and TV news could have told you anything you wanted to know."

She shrugged.

"Then, whatever possessed you to go over to Magda's? Surely you knew you wouldn't be welcome there."

"I went because I wanted to tell her that Jake and I...that we weren't having an affair."

I must have looked startled because she wriggled uncomfortably.

"But you were, weren't you?"

"Yes," she said. "We were. I just wanted to assure her that we weren't." She looked at me with blue-green eyes that were incredibly beautiful. They were the color of pure turquoise. I had a necklace of Mexican silver and turquoise that matched them perfectly. I was tempted to give it to her.

Out of the corner of my eye, I saw a man seated at a nearby table who couldn't seem to stop looking at Suzanne. After a moment, I turned and stared him full in the face, not answering his surprised smile. After that, he turned away.

Suzanne didn't seem to notice him. She acted not at all like a woman used to having men stare at her, though I couldn't imagine why not. It was almost as if she hadn't been beautiful until recently and didn't quite know how to react to admiration yet.

"I'm certain that Magda already knows you were having an affair with her husband." Could this woman be so dim that she didn't realize how it looked to be meeting a married man on Alki Beach for the purpose of having sex?

She sighed and the last remaining bit of starch left her. It was as if she had been keeping up a stiff false front and when there was no longer a need for it, it simply drained away, like soapsuds going down a drain. "I know," she said. The woman looked miserable. Not only that, she wasn't making much sense. She played with her wine glass but didn't pick it up to drink. She seemed more interested in watching the display of her manicure than eating or drinking. I sipped my wine. It was delightful.

"How long have you known Jake?" I asked.

"I met him before I got out of high school," she said, looking somewhere into the past. I raised my eyebrows and she caught the look. "Oh, I haven't been sleeping with him that long," she said. "We have only been together for a few months. Since spring. We have...*had* a wonderful relationship." She regarded me a moment, as if she had made a decision. "It wasn't all sex, you know. We played. We did fun things. In the summer, we went to the Seattle Center at night and played games in the Fun Forest. We won stuffed penguins from playing Skeeball." A tear rolled slowly down her cheek and she fumbled in her bag for a tissue.

"How did you meet him?"

"I was a friend of Sondra's. That's his daughter. She was in my class at school. Angelle and I both knew him. We all knew him. He used to pick Sondra up from school or parties and sometimes he'd give us rides home too. That was before he even met Magda." She looked at her lap for a moment. "I've known him longer than she has," she said, sounding petulant, as though that somehow gave her more right to Jake than Magda had. "Did you know Angelle?" she asked.

"I was the psychic investigator they called in to locate her," I said. She passed right over the word "psychic". Usually that got people off the track. They suddenly didn't care anymore about what we had been discussing. They only wanted to know who they were going to marry or if their career was on the right course. "I wasn't aware that you knew Angelle. How well did you know her?"

Her turquoise eyes gazed into mine. "She was my best friend," she said.

"Have you seen her since she left home?"

Suzanne shook her head. The waiter had returned with our food and we waited while he busily set down plates and rearranged utensils on the table. I have always been amazed at the power that wait-staff seem to have. They somehow know when you are discussing something important and seemingly take every opportunity to help you lose track of what you had been talking about.

Suzanne moved her fork around on the plate and then put it down. "I always believed Angelle was dead," she said.

"Why is that?" *Interesting. So did I.*

"She would have contacted me if she was alive. We *were* best friends. I didn't make a move without her and she didn't without me. We told each other all about our men, our lives, everything."

"How is it that I investigated Angelle's disappearance and I never ran into you? If you were her best friend, you would have been one of the first people I would have spoken to. I don't think your name was on the list that Laurel gave me."

"Magda probably told her not to put it on the list. She didn't like me. Said I had a bad influence on Angelle. I was in England when Angelle disappeared. I was studying." She made a face that indicated studying was secondary only to scooping up dog shit as an occupation. "My mother didn't notify me because I would have used it as an excuse to come home."

"That you could have had vital information didn't cross her mind?"

She shrugged.

"If I had known about you then, I might have gotten a lead or two on Angelle," I said.

"Oh, I didn't know anything about it! Angelle wrote to me that she was thinking about running away with some man but I don't think she ever did. I know that if she was alive, she would have found some way to contact me."

"She was thinking about running away?" I asked. "I guess that isn't something you would tell your mother. Magda certainly didn't mention it." I watched Suzanne closely. She didn't notice. She seemed to be telling the truth. I put my hand on hers and felt that she was. When I touched her, she looked up, startled.

"She always said she couldn't talk to her mother."

Suzanne looked sad, as if she were sorry she had agreed to have lunch with me.

"She was having an affair with someone, then? Do you know who he was?"

She shook her head.

"If she wouldn't tell you who the man was, why would she tell you she was planning to run away?"

"I don't know," she said, thinking. "I always wondered why she wouldn't say who he was. She wanted to tell. She used to write hints and clues and things, but I never did know who he was. I always thought he was married. I'll tell you what I really thought. I always thought it was Peter."

"Peter? Magda's second husband? Angelle's stepfather?"

"She used to make remarks about how love was greater than age and things like that. I think if she had run away, she would have written. At least to me. Besides, he didn't go with her. What's the use of running away if you don't take your love with you?"

"And, if she was in love with Peter, why didn't she come back when he was killed?" I added. "Her aunt, Morgan Chatfield, seems to think that Angelle is in California trying to break into films."

Suzanne made a very unladylike snort. "Not Angelle. She always thought that models and actresses were trashy. She and Magda had a terrible fight about it once. Magda wanted her to go to modeling school with Laurel and Angelle called actresses and models whores."

"I bet that went over big with Magda," I said.

"Laurel too." She smiled sadly at me.

"You were engaged to Rolf Edmondson once," I said, watching her expression. A bit of annoyance passed over her face and was gone.

"That was a long time ago. We were just kids."

"Why did you break up with him?" It was hard to imagine Suzanne and Rolf together. They didn't seem to be suited to each other at all. And their ages were wrong. Rolf had a good fifteen years on her. But perhaps they had both been different people then.

"He was jealous." She watched her plate while she spoke as if she was wondering why her food just didn't go away. I don't think she had eaten three bites.

"How so?"

She looked up at me. "You know about Rolf's record?" I nodded. "He was always threatening people. I mean, a guy would just look at me and Rolf would go, 'Leave her alone!' Like the guy had asked me out or something. I broke up with him and he went crazy."

I knew that was no pipe dream. She was not a girl who imagined that her discarded lover was mad with grief. The torment in her eyes was real. Besides, I had witnessed his intimidation tactics first hand.

"He almost kicked my boyfriend to death," she

said. "That's why he went to jail. I was really scared when he came over the other night. That's why I was late meeting Jake."

"You saw Rolf on Monday night?" I almost inhaled a piece of lettuce.

She nodded. She was going to make me pull every answer out of her like teeth.

"What did he want?" I asked, controlling my impatience.

"He wanted some pictures."

"Suzanne, I think you'd better tell me the whole thing. From the beginning." *This could take forever*, I thought.

"He came over to get some pictures." She shrugged. "They were snapshots that Jake and I took last summer, with one of those cameras that develops the picture right away." She looked at me questioningly and I nodded.

"What time was this?" I asked.

"He left at ten. A little before, I guess. I had just enough time to get ready to meet Jake at eleven." She blinked her big eyes. "It takes me awhile to get ready."

"Okay. And what about the pictures?" If he had left her at ten, that would have been more than enough time for him to get to Jake's parking garage and hide himself in the Lincoln. That left open the question of how he had gotten home after the murder. Unless he had walked.

"Jake and I spent the afternoon in a hotel on Aurora one day last summer. We were just being silly. It was fun. We laughed..." Tears filled her eyes and I handed her another tissue.

"They were pornographic photos?" I asked as gently as I could.

"Oh, no! Not like that. We were naked, but they were just silly. Funny."

"How did Rolf know about them?"

"I think he must have seen them somehow. Maybe he snooped around Jake's house. Or maybe he was spying on us. I don't know." She sounded remarkably unconcerned.

"Do you think Rolf could have had anything to do with Jake's murder? After all, Jake was seeing you and Rolf's a jealous man."

She slowly shook her head as if she had never before considered the possibility. I watched fright dawn on her face. "I don't know. I didn't think anyone knew about us."

I wasn't so sure about that. "What about your friends? Did you ever tell any of them?"

"Oh. Well, yes. They knew. But I didn't think..."

"Did you tell the police that Rolf had been to see you right before you left to meet Jake?"

She looked startled, then abashed. "No. I guess I should have."

I nodded.

"But they'll think Rolf killed Jake then!" Her eyes went round as the idea dawned on her. "Do you think I should tell them? I don't like talking to them. That Mr. Quiller isn't a nice man. He acted like *I* killed Jake."

"I definitely do think you should tell them," I said. I took a card from my briefcase and wrote Perce's name on it. "You ask for this man when you call. You can tell him and he will tell Mr. Quiller."

She nodded and looked relieved. I then decided to get back to Angelle and let her digest the idea of Rolf committing murder.

"Magda says she's gotten a letter from Angelle," I told her.

Suzanne looked up. There was hope splashed all over her face, but it drained away as before.

"You doubt it?" I asked.

"I don't know. I'd like to see the letter. I could tell you if it was Angelle's writing or not." She thoughtfully chewed on a bit of mushroom.

"I'll try to get you a copy of it. I'd like to know what you think of it."

"Don't tell anyone that you're going to show it to me, or it will disappear. Especially Magda. She's a terrible woman."

"Why do you say that?" The wonderful Magda St. Martin was sounding less and less wonderful these days.

"You saw how she threw me out of the house." She put a pout on her lips that could have been in a lipstick ad.

"Suzanne, surely you can understand the grief she's going through. She's lost four husbands and her daughter. That has to be devastating. And you were, after all, having an affair with her husband. Besides, it was Laurel who threw you out of the house."

"Before you got there, Magda screamed at me to get out," she said, in a petulant, little girl voice.

It was hard to imagine Magda screaming about anything. "You can't expect her to welcome you like an old friend, even if you were," I said.

"I wasn't. Not *her* friend anyway. And, don't forget," Suzanne said in a hard, frigid voice. "Magda St. Martin is an actress."

"Did you expect Jake to leave her?" I asked.

"Yes, I did. He said he was going to." She stirred her salad and I let her mull over whatever was going on in her mind. In a moment she spoke again.

"You know," she began and looked off in the direction of California Avenue. "Jake always called me 'Sudie'." She glanced at me with tears in her eyes. "Isn't that cute? Sudie? One of the reasons I loved Jake so much was because he was so loyal. I love that in a man, don't you?"

"You think he was loyal, when he was playing around with another woman?"

"What other woman?" Her voice scaled up in indignation and her face paled. "Jake never looked at another woman. He loved me. I know he was going to leave her. He loved *me*."

"He was cheating on Magda. With you. *You* were the other woman."

"Oh, well, but that's...He loved me. He was going to leave her and we were going to get married. But he was killed." A fat, slow tear dribbled down her chin and fell into her spinach salad. I *did* feel sorry for her. She was so young, and so dumb and now she was alone.

"I know that I was the only 'other woman' Jake ever had," she continued, making quotation marks with her fingers. "He loved me. He *was* loyal." She glanced at me. "To me," she added. "I know the old stories about 'the other woman'. I'm not stupid. I heard what my friends said about us. But none of those people knew Jake. They didn't know what he told me in bed. They didn't know the things we did with each other. He never had that with any other woman. He was a gentleman."

"A gentleman doesn't go to bed with a woman other than his wife," I said, trying to be gentle. Surely, she didn't believe that the man she loved was really that virginal. She looked at me, then looked away.

"You were the one who found Jake's body," I said. It had to be done. I was sorry to be the one to initiate this part of the conversation, but I had to start getting some answers.

"She nodded. Her lip began to tremble. "I already told the police."

"I know," I said and let my hand brush hers. "But, please go over it again. Sometimes it helps." She nodded and took a sip of wine.

"I was late," she said. "If I had been on time I might have been there and it wouldn't have happened." She bowed her head over her discarded salad. "Jake used to laugh at me because I could never get anywhere on time. And, really, I was only a few minutes late." She wiped her eyes on her napkin and sniffed. "He thought it was cute."

"Suzanne, if you had been on time, you might have been hurt. The police think the person hid in Jake's car. There was no mud or water in the back of the driver's seat, so they concluded that whoever did it, hid in the car while it was in the parking garage. The plan might have been for both of you to be killed. There's no way of knowing now." It occurred to me suddenly that Suzanne was one of the few people who knew the way Jake had been killed. Could she have written that note to me? I didn't think so. Besides, if Suzanne knew, then others most likely knew as well. Even if the police had impressed upon her to not say anything, I doubted that she would have been able to abide by that.

Her eyes grew wide and her mouth stopped trembling. "I could have been killed if I was on time," she said and shuddered.

I nodded. "Suzanne, did you tell anyone, any of your friends, how Jake had been killed?"

She shrugged and, from that alone, I gathered that she had. "I don't know. Maybe."

"Did you tell Rolf?"

"No!" She shook her head. "No, I didn't tell Rolf."

"But you did tell your friends," I said.

She looked at me with alarm. "I wasn't supposed to say, but I think I did."

"I wouldn't worry about it," I told her. "Just don't tell anyone else." A little of the weight of that letter was lifted off of my shoulders. Anyone could have sent it. It could easily have been a prank.

"Why did you call Jake's secretary and instruct her to tell him that you would be early if you weren't going to be?"

"Call? I didn't call her. I never called Jake's office! He didn't want me to ever do that. And I never did."

"Suzanne, do you know Jake's secretary's name?"

"Sure, it's Bea. Jake always called her Bea."

"Do you know her last name?"

She shook her head again. "No. Jake only called her Bea. Why?"

This time I shook my head. "Nothing." But it was

something. The wheels were spinning a little faster now.

"Did the police tell you that I got in the car and sat in all the...blood?"

"Yes, they did," I said. "You were fortunate you weren't there. If you had been, you would have been killed too. I'm certain of that." I reached over and laid my hand gently on her arm. She accepted it almost as if she wanted to absorb something from me. Strength maybe. I hope she did. By touching her I could see clearly into her mind. She was telling the truth.

"So, you think the killer knew that I would be meeting Jake. Do you think he was planning to kill me too?"

"I don't know. I suppose, if Jake had gone straight home, he would have been killed in his own garage. I just don't know."

I saw the waiter hovering nearby and signaled for the check. There was no need to let him in on all of the gory details.

When he had gone, I pressed Suzanne's hand again. "Suzanne, why *did* you go over to Magda's today?"

"I told you. I was going to tell her that we weren't having an affair."

"What difference does it make now? You obviously don't care about Magda's feelings. It wasn't human kindness that made you go over there. You weren't trying to spare her. What was it?"

She looked at me for a long time until she spoke. "I'm afraid of her. I thought if I talked to her, she would see that I really did love Jake. Maybe she would feel sorry for me or, I don't know, that she wouldn't hate me. Or maybe I wanted her to think that Jake and I hadn't been sleeping together. I don't know what I thought." She stopped and closed her eyes for a moment. "I was afraid that," she said slowly, "if she thought we were having an affair, she would kill me too."

THIRTEEN

Friday, November 18, 1983

After I left Suzanne at the restaurant, I headed down Fauntleroy Way. I wanted to take the longer route to Magda's so I could think. Also, Laurel had said there was a stained glass shop on Fauntleroy. I wanted a little more information and, besides, I was fascinated by the stuff.

My friend, Molly, had once been into stained glass. She had tried to get me into it too, and I would have succumbed and undoubtedly enjoyed it except the supplies had been way too expensive. That was in the days when every penny went toward my mother's medical bills. Those days had been getting close to being over until I had found myself in need of finding another apartment. Nothing I would be able to find would be as inexpensive as where I was living. Nevertheless, seeing Magda's lavish windows had reminded me of how much I had enjoyed watching Molly's stash of gorgeous Christmas ornaments and boxes grow. I wanted to find out if repairing that tiny crack was the big deal Laurel had said it was.

Sure enough, Avenue Art Glass sat nestled between a dry cleaner and a used car joint like a jewel set in a wad of chewing gum. I spent at least ten minutes on the outside looking at the display windows and trying not to drool. There was a lamp in the corner that I would have given my good reputation for. It was a luscious pink and green masterpiece made like a tree full of cherry blossoms. Seemingly hundreds, maybe even thousands of tiny pieces of glass had been used to create a work of spectacular art. Bits of red, like rubies, glittered among the textured green glass pieces that were the leaves and creamy pink glass that represented blossoms. I calculated it to be worth at least a thousand dollars. Maybe two.

I was wrong. The shade, Ab Eberstein, the proprietor, told me, was a reproduction of a Tiffany Cherry Tree lamp and it cost five grand. Oh, well.

"There are smaller, less costly lamps that are very lovely, babe," he said. He reminded me of one of those old-time shopkeepers. He was a handsome man of about fifty-five with a scraggly gray beard and a stained green apron. He had a rubber mallet sticking out of his hip pocket. Usually, I hated it when strangers called me honey or babe, but for some reason, I didn't mind Ab doing it.

"I would love to know how to do this," I said, knowing Easy would snort if he could hear me. I was almost as bad as Molly at taking up some new hobby or another; crewel embroidery, weaving, pottery. I had even been into macrame and tie-dyeing at one time.

"We give lessons," he said.

"Actually, I'm here to get a little information. I have a window that needs to be repaired. I understand that this is something you do not come out to the house to do. It has to be brought in here."

He nodded and cocked his head to one side, waiting for more details.

"It's an immense window. I wouldn't be able to handle it myself."

"No problem. I can go get it, fix it and reinstall it. I would do that no matter what size it is. You have to be careful handling glass. If you don't hold it a certain way, you could not only destroy the window, you could cut yourself very seriously in the process."

"You repaired this window once before. It belongs to Magda St. Martin."

His eyes lit up immediately. "Of course. The Medea. Beautiful windows. I wish I owned them." Concern suddenly creased his forehead and he frowned. "It isn't badly damaged, I hope."

"No. As a matter of fact, the crack can only be seen when the light hits it just right."

He brushed the whole matter aside with a wave of his hand. "I wouldn't bother, then," he said. Then his forehead creased again. "Does Miss St. Martin know about this?"

I laughed. "No, she doesn't. I saw it just this morning. I was hoping to get it repaired before she found out."

"Not possible. For one thing, I'd have to take the window out and bring it down here. Another thing, she's very picky about the glass. When that window was in here before, it took me weeks to find the right glass to repair it."

"The right glass? But which piece was it?"

"Oh, there were a couple of pieces cracked. Mostly minor ones that I wouldn't have bothered with if the window had been mine. Let's see, the one in the child's robe I had a devil of a time with. I would have just added a line and let it go. Would have cost her about a fifth of what it cost to do it the way she wanted it done."

"I'm sorry. I don't understand. 'Added a line'?"

He smiled and motioned me out of the showroom and up two or three steps to the workshop. "Come on up here," he said. "I'm repairing a window over here."

A massive table stood in the middle of the room surrounded by bins of lethal looking sheets of colored glass. On the table was a window in what looked to me like a state of irreparable wreckage. It had once been lovely; a clear glass background in the shape of a trellis, with grapes and leaves climbing up the lines. It looked as if someone had taken a sledgehammer to the trellis.

"Little kid threw a Tonka Truck through it," Ab said, seeing my look. "It's not as bad as it seems. I'll have it fixed in a couple of hours. This one here," he digressed and picked up a smaller piece lying nearby on the same table. "This one, I just finished repairing. Can you find where it was fixed?"

I searched, then pointed to an area in the corner.

"Amazing!" he said. "You really have an eye, babe. Tell me what gave it away."

"I have to confess. The pieces in that area just seemed a little cleaner than the others. I don't know which piece was broken."

"Ah. I should have cleaned it all up before showing it to you. Here, try this one."

He held up an exquisite oval frame filled with yellow morning glories. Simply wonderful! I shook my head.

"I can't find it."

He pointed to one of the leaves. It was still invisible to me. There was no way I could tell it had been repaired.

"Could you show me how you do that?" I asked.

He went back to the grape window, lying in obvious pain on the table.

"There are two ways you can do this. This area here," he indicated a cluster of grapes, one of which had a crack across it, "will not need to be replaced." He took a strip of metal—lead, he told me—and cut off a short piece. He handed me a chunk of it and I saw it was shaped like an H on the cross cut. The pieces of glass, he said, fit into the two channels, meeting at the cross piece of the H. He took a small wire cutter and carefully cut away one of the sides of the H, leaving him with a piece that was flat on one side and slightly rounded on the other. He laid the flat side over the broken grape, curving it slightly. He brushed the junction with a dangerous looking toothbrush—the bristles were wire—then painted it with a liquid. When he touched the hot soldering iron and the end of the solder coil to it, the liquid sizzled and the solder flowed into the spot where the pieces of lead met.

"Voila!" he said. The crack had disappeared. Instead of a whole grape, it simply looked like two grapes, one overlapping the other. "Now, I'll do the same on the other side and it will look like new. This doesn't weaken the structure of the window, since the pieces are so small. On this area here," he indicated a large piece of the background that had been shattered when the Tonka Truck had sledgehammered it, "I'll have to build in reinforcement."

"What about this part here. If you just add a line to this leaf, it will take away from the grace of this curve."

"You *do* have a good eye! You an artist?"

I shook my head, but said nothing.

"All right," he said. "This is the second method. This is the way I repaired Miss St Martin's window. She wouldn't have it any other way."

"What we have to do here," he said, picking up a wicked looking curved knife, "is cut away the surrounding lead." He made a cut straight down, through the lead, to the glass. "Now, this part is tricky. I have to cut the top of the lead off without damaging another part of the lead or breaking any other pieces of glass."

It might have been tricky, but he made it look like a piece of cake. He quickly sliced through the crossbar of the H and lifted off a piece of lead shaped like the piece of glass. He set it aside.

"Now, I can either use the same piece of lead or cut another. Either way." Deftly he pried out the offending leaf, then took it to one of the bins along the wall. He selected a piece of glass and held them both up to the light. To me, the colors of the leaf and the new glass were identical.

"Close enough," he said. He laid the glass on the table and roughly drew around the broken pieces, holding them together while he did so. Then he set them aside and reached for what looked like a pistol grip with a glass cutter attached to it. After making a few "*whissing*" sounds on the glass with the cutter, he picked up the piece and broke off section after section with a pair of pliers until he had a new, perfectly shaped leaf. He dropped the new piece into the spot left by the broken one, then put the old section of lead back on top and quickly soldered the joints.

"Wow!" I said, "I'm really getting interested in this."

"You'd be a natural, babe," he said. "Now, of course, this large section here will have to be rebuilt but that isn't really a problem either. I have the glass in stock and, in fact I still have the pattern here, so I'll just recut the pieces and lead them together."

Nearby was a lamp in the process of being assembled. I ran my hand over the pansies in the lampshade. "This doesn't look the same," I said, looking closely at the glass flowers. "Is this a different method?"

"That is copper foil, or Tiffany method," he said, coming over. "This part here is actually solder, not lead." He pointed to the "lead lines" between the pieces of glass. "You wrap the edge of each piece with copper foil and then solder over it. It's usually used for lampshades because it's a little stronger and much easier to use for small pieces of glass."

"Can you use this method for a window too?" I asked.

"Oh, sure."

"Magda St Martin's windows are made with lead,

though, right?"

"Hers are lead. A magnificent group of windows. Worth tens of thousands."

"Are they old?" I asked, surprised. I hadn't thought they were that valuable.

"Not antique, but quite old. I would guess they were built in the twenties. I ran into some trouble finding matching glass for her when she had the windows in the shop here."

"Is it usually hard to find?"

"She's quite a perfectionist, you know?" he said and laughed. "One piece that was broken was a yellow cream streaky that isn't made anymore. I had a hell of a time finding some. It took two shipments before I could locate the color that would satisfy her."

"Where did you finally find it?" I asked, not so much because I wanted an answer, but because I wanted to stay and look at the glass, the equipment and the fascinating bits of half-finished work that lay on the table. I even liked the way the place smelled. A mixture of metals and cork, wood and paper. It was the scent of creativity.

"I had to send to Germany. Then, when it came, she wasn't satisfied. She'd come in here, get a look at the glass and shake her head. Then I'd have to send for more. Another lot. Not cheap stuff, either. She could have settled for domestic glass, or even had the crack leaded over and it would have cost maybe thirty or forty bucks rather than the hundreds of dollars it cost her." He shook his head. "She was so damn choosey about it, she actually ended up with inferior glass in a couple of places. She wouldn't listen to me that the glass I wanted to put in there was a far better quality. Oh, no. 'The color is off,' she said. Had to have the color match exactly. I ended up using some cheap Canadian glass. Actually, the cheaper glass takes away from the value of the windows. Not that anyone will ever know. Anyhow, it isn't by much." He peered at me over the top of his half-glasses. "You don't work for an insurance company, do you?"

I did, actually, but I merely said, "I'm investigating the death of Miss St Martin's husband, Mr. Levin."

"Oh, yeah. I read about that. Awful. Yeah, I saw that in the paper."

"When did you do the repair work on Magda's window?" I asked.

"Well, let's see. I guess it was about four, five, six years ago. 'Bout six. It wasn't too long after I moved the shop to this spot. I remember, she said she saw the place while she was driving by. Never had seen it before."

I picked up the window he had previously repaired. "Fascinating," I said.

"Hey," he said. "If you're really interested in this, you should join one of our classes."

"I might," I said. "Seriously. There are some really

beautiful pieces here. I love the way the glass looks."
I knew I probably would never be able to join a class.
It was simply too expensive for me.

"Here," he said, going over to the bin again. He
pulled out a sheet of blue, green and gold swirled
glass. "Great, huh?" It was more than merely great.
When he held it up to the light, it looked like the way
the sky in heaven is going to look. "How about this?"
he asked, pulling out another piece. "This is called
cranberry glass."

I could see why. It was a deep rich red that
gradually faded into warm pink where the glass
thinned out.

"This is a very valuable piece," he said. Just as he
spoke, he stepped back and his heel hit the end of
a long box of lead that lay under the table. Before I
could react, the sheet of cranberry glass had crashed
to the floor and shattered.

"Oh, Jesus!" he said. We stood there, mute before
the destruction of the wonderful piece of glass. It lay
on the concrete floor in thousands of pieces. Even
shattered, it was gorgeous. The shards glittered like
rubies scattered by a mad fairy.

"It happened so fast, I didn't have time to make a
grab for it," I told him.

"Good thing. You never want to do that. You can
cut yourself very seriously grabbing for a piece of
glass."

I helped him sweep it up. He saved even the

smallest pieces. What we threw away had once been valuable, but ended up being nothing but dust.

"I'm sorry that happened," I said. "If you hadn't been showing it to me, it wouldn't have."

"Oh, don't worry about it. That isn't irreplaceable. I just hate to see a fantastic hunk of glass like that get broken. I've seen worse, though." He laughed, but, to me, he didn't sound very convincing. Or maybe I was the one who wasn't convinced. He squeezed at a small cut on his thumb.

"How come you don't wear gloves handling glass all day?" I asked him. He wiped the bleeding thumb on his jeans.

"Not usually necessary. Oh, sure, when I handle the great big sheets, yeah. But this stuff," he waved his hands at the rows of bins lining the walls. "If you know what you're doing, you don't usually get cut. Most people, now, are afraid of glass. They pussyfoot around with it and end up breaking it. I'd much rather get cut by a nice sharp piece of glass than a piece of metal any day. Or paper!" He shuddered. "Hey, you want to try?"

I started to protest, then felt somehow responsible for his having broken the glass he had been showing me, so I nodded. He found me a piece of what looked like regular window glass with a pattern on it like frost. "Glue chip" he called it.

"Always cut on the smooth side," he said handing me the pistol grip cutter. I hefted it, then set it on the glass where he had drawn a straight line. "Don't press too hard now. All you're trying to do is score it, not cut all the way through." I pressed gently and the wheel rolled effortlessly over the glass. "Perfect!" he said. "Now look." He showed me where to place my hands and which way to bend. The glass snapped cleanly into two pieces.

"See? Easy! You're a natural."

Before I left, I took one of the brochures explaining the classes. He walked me to the door.

"Before I go, I have one more question. Did Magda watch when you repaired that window?"

"She sure did. Stood right there and watched every move I made. I was scared to death I was going to put too much pressure on one of the other pieces and have to replace it too. I would have had that window here for another three weeks. Hell, not only that, it makes you nervous having a famous person like that standing there watching you. She's a fine looking woman."

I thought about how the fire had changed her and didn't comment. I gave him my card with Magda's number scribbled on the back, and he handed me one of his. He assured me he would put me on the mailing list.

"Listen, babe, anytime you want to take classes, give me a jingle. I live upstairs here. You can call me anytime."

I thanked him and, still thinking about the

classes and how much I liked stained glass and Ab Eberstein, I drove back up to Magda's. That afternoon I would look at those windows with new respect.

I thought about calling Easy and making up with him, but the more I thought, the angrier I got. I figured he probably had come over to the house and found me gone. He might even be hovering somewhere nearby. The idea made me smile. Then I thought of the other person who might also be hovering nearby. The letter probably resided with the other case evidence at the police station by now, but I still felt it burning into my mind. Even though Suzanne had given me reason to believe the chances of it being from the killer were less than I had originally thought, I was extra careful on the way back.

FOURTEEN

Friday, November 18, 1983

I t was about four when I stepped onto the porch. The sky was darkening fast and rain clouds were pushing the night closer. I didn't bother ringing the bell, but let myself in. The house was silent and cold. I found the thermostat and somewhere deep in the bowels of the house, I heard the furnace switch on.

This whole thing was damned discouraging. I didn't feel I was making much progress. All I seemed to be doing was "protecting" Magda and not doing it very well, apparently, since I had no idea in the world where she was or what she was doing. And now, it seemed, I was in some need of protection myself. I turned on the lights and found the note lying on the foyer table. Laurel and Magda, it said, had gone out and I was to get my own dinner. *Good*, I thought, *this will give me a chance to explore the house and go over those letters from Donald Tooley without anyone looking over my shoulder.*

My first stop was Magda's bedroom. It was dark and quiet and, even after I switched the light on, there was nothing much to see. It was a lavish room with beautiful furnishings but a bit devoid of personality. Her closet was another matter. It was much more than a closet. It was more of a sitting room where she kept her clothes, mirrors, dressers, lamps and everything else she needed and treasured. There was even an easy chair. It felt as though that room, almost as big as my entire apartment, was where Magda actually resided. I felt her there more than anywhere else. Overall, it was a sense of sadness, of passion and of loss that dominated there, as though that was the part of the house where Magda allowed herself to really feel. I imagined her secreting herself there in order to hide her tears from everyone else.

Orderly racks held rows of garments made of lush fabrics in rich colors. Many were the caftans she wore so often to cover her burn scars, though I saw a few evening gowns in jewel hues as well. There were suits and lovely, filmy dresses, tailored pants and gorgeous jackets. The woman knew how to dress. There were shelves of hats and rows of shoes. A wig-stand with a luxurious dark auburn wig gave me a start when I caught a glimpse of it in the floor to ceiling mirror. A perfume seemed to emanate from her clothing, something light but exotic. I opened the drawers one at a time, not touching anything, just looking. I don't know what I thought I was going to find. A bloody knife? A note saying "I confess?" I smiled to myself when I shut the door.

Jake's clothing had apparently been removed from the premises. I felt nothing of him, though I thought his closet may have been the one off the other side of the bedroom. I peeked into it but it was empty. Laurel must have seen to the removal of his belongings already. There was only a faint breath of the man left for me to sense. The bedroom itself held nothing of Jake either. I wondered if he had slept separately from Magda. Perhaps in the guest room next to hers.

If Magda's room was empty of Magda, Laurel's was definitely full of Laurel, though the feelings I got were mostly in conflict with one another. There was certainly passion there, but there was pain and disappointment and loss as well. I wanted to leave.

I never snooped in people's rooms lightly. It took me a long time to get over the guilty, sneaky feeling when I entered someone's inner sanctum. I was an investigator. I investigated. When Magda had hired me, she had given me tacit permission to do exactly that. I needed to delve deeply into people's backgrounds, question their neighbors and friends. When I opened dresser drawers and peered into closets, I was searching for who the owner was and what drove them. I sometimes had to handle an article of clothing or a hairbrush, a toy, or a pillowcase in order to discover the inner workings of the owner. So often clients and family members were not strictly honest and sometimes they didn't even know they weren't. There were always questions and part of what I did was find out the answers. Not only was I an investigator, I was a psychic as well. I needed to be able to enter the intimate spaces my clients inhabited.

I quickly looked through Laurel's closet and drawers but found nothing but the stew of emotions that pervaded the whole room. In the hall, I took a deep breath, as if I had been physically stifled in the bedroom.

I shook off the feeling and looked into the guest room next to Magda's. It was nicely furnished in a dark red theme that gave it a rich, masculine feel. I was certain that I had found Jake's bedroom, though none of his belongings remained there. I did get a hint of vitality, well-being and self-possession and knew that Jake had probably been a man who had enjoyed his life and his home. I wished for a moment that I could have known him.

I gently shut the door and headed for the third floor stairs. I tried the door to the apartment which seemed to take up the space of several rooms, but it was locked.

I bypassed the library, since I had visited it recently and the ballroom. I was eager to get to the attic and find those letters.

The light in the attic not only worked, the

lightbulb was actually clean. I had to wonder at people who clean light bulbs. Some days, I was lucky if I got my hide-a-bed folded back together. Most of the time, my apartment looked presentable enough, but I knew there were dust kitties, spider webs and— gasp! dusty lightbulbs!

Frankly, the attic looked like a movie set, although, even a movie set would have had a few realistic looking cobwebs. Everything was neatly stored, as I had seen before. I moved to the trunk labeled "Angelle," hoping to find some of her personal items that may have lent me more of a clue to where she was, but it was locked. I made a mental note to ask Laurel for the key and turned away. I found the chest labeled "Fan Mail" and opened it.

I thought I heard voices, very faint, very far away. The house was an old one with lots of echoes of many people who had lived and died there. Every old house had its spirits and I was used to feeling them around me.

I wanted to find some of the later letters Donald had told me about. The ones which begged Magda to leave him alone. The packet of letters Laurel had shown me was gone. There were hundreds of notes from hundreds of people. Some were written in childish scrawls asking for autographed photos, some in praise of one movie or another. There were a few expressing disappointment that Magda had said certain words or had fallen for a particular man. While interesting to read, they were not the letters I needed. I wondered if Laurel had taken them downstairs. Could either Laurel or Magda have destroyed them? I was sure not. After all, they had kept all of the boxes and trunks and cartons full of treasures that remained in the attic. I would ask both Laurel and Magda about the letters. It was possible that they could be valuable in clearing Donald Tooley's name. At any rate, they were evidence.

I heard a noise that was not a voice, and paused, thinking Magda and Laurel must have returned. I packed the letters back into the chest and reminded myself to ask Laurel about the key to the Angelle trunk. I heard the front door shut as I was coming down the stairs. At the top of the staircase to the first floor was a window that overlooked the front porch. I moved the curtain aside and saw Rolf going down the front walk toward the street. I knocked on the window. He stopped and looked around.

I ran the rest of the way to the door. When I opened it, he had resumed walking.

"Rolf," I called. He stopped but didn't move nearer so I went to him. "What were you doing in the house?" I asked. He looked at me as if I were a rock that had suddenly spoken. "Where did you get the key?"

"I got a key to the house," he said. "How do you think I take care of it when the Mr. and Mrs. are gone?"

"Do you also have a key to Mr. Levin's car?" He glanced at me but didn't answer.

"What were you doing in the house just now?"

"I saw some lights, so I came over to check. What the hell do you think I was doing?" In the afternoon light the agate in his belt buckle glittered.

"I think maybe you were looking for some pictures," I said. He started to turn away, but I grabbed his upper arm. The muscles in it were rock hard and I felt threat emanating from him. He yanked away from me and started down the walk again. "I think you'd better talk to me," I said. "You lied to me."

"Lady, I don't have to say anything," he said. He frowned and I almost expected a snarl and a baring of his teeth. "If you know what's good for you, you better leave me alone."

"Why? Have you been refining your strong-arm tactics? I would think you'd be man enough to talk to me face to face rather than threaten me in the dark." He seemed to deflate, and I was astounded. I was in the wrong, after all. He was the caretaker and had a right to be in the house if he saw unexpected lights. But he had also threatened me. That, he had no right to do. "Let's go back into the house," I said.

"Now," I said when he had followed me into the living room, "I know it was you who threatened and then pushed me last night." I watched his face carefully. "I hope you realize how guilty that makes you look. Do you have anything to say about that?"

To my astonishment, he looked ashamed, but only for an instant. He covered it up with a glower.

"I didn't kill Mr. Levin!" he said.

"Then why attack me? If I reported it to the police, you would be back in prison before you had a chance to blink."

"I don't want them thinking that Suzanne or Mrs. St. Martin or Laurel had anything to do with it," he said, looking at the floor. Then he raised his eyes and looked directly into mine.

"You willing to go to prison for them?"

"No, I…I didn't think about that. I wanted you to stop. I don't want you getting them into trouble."

"Rolf, if they are 'in trouble', it's because they got themselves into trouble. If you think those women are innocent, then you should welcome my investigation. You've only succeeded in getting yourself in deeper. Physical attacks and lies don't exactly make you look innocent."

"I didn't lie about anything!"

I felt hostility and extreme dislike, maybe even hatred pouring off of him. But strangely, he seemed to be telling the truth.

"You lied about being at the video arcade the night Jake was killed."

"I didn't lie," he said. He looked like a sullen little boy. "I was there."

"Suzanne said you were at her place until ten."

He looked down into his lap and cracked his knuckles. "I was at the Silver Dollar from about 10:15 until probably 11:30."

"You didn't tell the police you'd been to see Suzanne," I reminded him. "Why not?"

"I knew they'd think I killed Mr. Levin."

"How did you find out about the photos?" I asked.

He winced at the word. "I saw them. They were in Mr. Levin's car."

"Come on, Rolf. He didn't have naked pictures of himself and his girlfriend just sitting around in his car for everyone to see."

"No. They were in the glove box," he said. The muscles in his jaw were working hard. "I was cleaning his car and I unlocked the box to get at the tire gauge. They were right there."

"Why didn't you take them, then?"

"Mr. Levin came and hollered at me for unlocking the glove box. I didn't have a chance."

"And so, you went to his office to ask for them? What made you think that he would give them to you?"

His face twisted in what I took to be misery. "I didn't think he would give them to me. I didn't want them anyway. I just wanted him to throw them away. Burn them. Shred them. I don't know. I wanted him to destroy them. I couldn't stand him having pictures of Suzanne like that. Besides, what if Mrs. St Martin saw them?"

"Rolf, are you still in love with Suzanne?"

He looked startled and immediately shook his head. "No, I'm not. Not that it's any of your business."

"If you aren't in love with her, why do you care if there are pictures of her?"

"She doesn't deserve that," he said. "She's a good kid."

I continued to look at him to see if I could see anything further in his face.

"I'm not in love with her. That was kid stuff. A long time ago. She's not the one." I moved my hand to his arm and, before he could fling it off once again, I learned the truth. He wasn't in love with Suzanne. He was in love with Laurel!

"What did Jake say when you asked him to destroy the pictures?"

"He said it was none of my business," he muttered. "Just like it's none of yours." He stood, and, a moment later gave the door an admirable slam on the way out.

I spent the rest of the evening going over my notes, typing them and putting them into order. Lots of the detectives I knew put pictures of their suspects up on a board and kept it in view to study while they were assembling evidence. I didn't do that. In movies and on television I had seen walls plastered with photographs of victims and their killers gloating and slavering over them. To me, a suspect board was way too similar to those walls of crazy. I preferred to keep them in my head.

I started with what I knew about Magda. There was a woman who had some mental problems. And who wouldn't, with her history? She'd lost most of her loved ones and her career. I thought about my brother, Larry, in Wyoming. I loved him, but I wondered how devastated I would be if something happened to him. It wouldn't change my life much, I had to admit. He was a few years older than I. We had lived together in Portland for a while but then he had gone back to Wyoming and I hadn't seen him since our mother's funeral. Quickly, I sent him a little mental hello and paused to see if he would respond. In a moment I felt a warmth, like a kind of mental hug. Smiling, I went back to my notes.

Magda was compulsive. Everything in her world had to be perfect and she couldn't tolerate imperfection of any kind. She was an actress and good at hiding her emotions, although I had seen a glimmer or two from her. Briefly, I thought about the chipped knife that she had been using to chop apples. A person who is compulsive about perfection would most likely be unwilling to use a damaged knife. On the other hand, the knife itself may have had some sentimental value for her that she was reluctant to give up. There were lots of forms of compulsion, I knew, and I was not trained in that area.

Magda said she was in love with Jake but I believed she was seeing another man. I had watched her at the post-funeral gathering with de Las Alas, though, and her feeling for him had seemed superficial at best. Jake, too, had been having an affair. The brief sense I had gotten from his bedroom had told me he had been content and happy with his life, so I wondered if the depth of his feelings for Suzanne may have been something less than she thought.

According to Suzanne, this was the first time Jake had ever strayed from Magda. Of course, Suzanne wasn't the smartest person I had ever met, nor was she impartial. She was convinced that Jake was going to leave Magda for her. What if Jake had refused to leave Magda? Could Suzanne have killed him and faked the discovery of the body? Not likely. The police had said she had blood on her, but it was mostly on her back and seat from when she had entered the car without realizing what was inside. She would not have gotten in if she had just killed Jake herself. Suzanne was not terribly bright and I didn't think she could have devised a devious plan for getting away with murder.

What did the killer do to disguise the fact that he or she had blood on at least his or her hands and arms? If the killer was behind the front seat, he or she would have been protected from most of the blood. Some, granted, would have spattered back after hitting the windshield, but not in the amount that would have been present had the killer been in front of Jake. He or she had to have gotten out of the car and presumably traveled at least a little way to get to his or her own car. What if the murderer had traveled on foot? Then, either he or she lived very nearby or else was in real danger of being spotted by someone. Or there may have been a collaborator who had picked up the killer. The most likely scenario was that the killer had had a car positioned somewhere close at hand. In that case, there undoubtedly would have been blood in the car. Maybe not a lot since the killer was no doubt intelligent enough to remove his or her outer clothing before getting in. Laurel had no car of her own, but she could have used Magda's or, possibly Rolf's. Magda, of course, could have used her own car and Rolf, his. The police had checked over Magda's car and cleared it. Rolf's as well. So, whose car had been used in the escape?

Rolf had sounded sincere when he had been telling me about the night Jake was murdered. But then, I know there is nothing more sincere sounding than a man with something to hide. Rolf had access to Jake's car. He had motive and a flimsy alibi. I was certain Rolf had not been lying when he had said he was no longer in love with Suzanne. He had said he couldn't stand having compromising pictures of her out in the world. I could understand that and it didn't seem reason enough for him to kill Jake. To me, Rolf was an enigma. He was almost pathologically protective about the women in his life. He was willing to risk a return to prison to steer suspicion away from Suzanne, Magda and Laurel. I wondered how much he knew about Jake's murder that he wasn't saying. I would most definitely be keeping a very close eye on Mr. Edmondson.

About 10:40 I heard the sounds of someone downstairs and knew Magda and Laurel had returned. A few minutes later, I peeked into the hall and saw a light under Laurel's door. Magda had not yet come upstairs. I wanted to be sure to catch Magda before she settled in for the night so I could ask her about the letters. I would ask Laurel as well, but I wanted to hear what Magda had to say about them. With one ear cocked to hear Magda's door, I went back to my notes.

The police had determined that the killer had waited in Jake's car while it was in the parking garage downtown and I agreed. If so, why not kill him there? Because Alki would be far more private than a parking garage, even at 10:30 or 11:00 at night. If the killer wasn't Rolf, Laurel, or Magda, who could he be? Unless it was Donald Tooley.

The killer would have had to be someone who had known Jake's habits intimately and, again, all three of them did. Laurel had known that I had been with Easy and Rolf had known where to find me the night before so he could threaten me. I had gone to Alki on a whim so he must have been following me. He certainly could have followed Jake and so could any of them. Did Donald Tooley know Jake's habits? He had once been a serious student of Jake's wife, but I didn't see him knowing Jake that well. Plus, he didn't have access to Jake's car, although a former Pinkerton man may have been able to get around that. And the killer had to be small enough to hunker down in the back of the car without being noticed. The four of them still fit. Whoever did it, knew Jake was going to Alki and knew he was going to meet Suzanne. He or she had wanted Jake to be early, in fact, so the murder could be a *fait accompli* when Suzanne arrived. Would someone be able to hunker down behind the driver's seat and remain undiscovered for the time it took to travel from downtown to West Seattle? I thought yes. It had rained particularly hard that night. I believed the sound of the rain would have successfully covered any inadvertent noise from the back seat.

A woman had called Bea to make sure Jake would be early. That could have been Magda, Laurel or Geraldine. Rolf could have persuaded a female friend to make a quick, innocent sounding call for him.

I shook my head. I hated to think that Magda had

something to do with it. She was hardly the type for murder. None of them were, really. With the possible exception of Rolf. Besides, if Magda were the killer, why on earth would she hire me? As a cover? She said she wanted protection, but often left the house on her own. She seemed unconcerned when I wasn't around as well.

She could have hired someone to do the actual killing, of course. Again, my thoughts turned to Rolf. He was so cowed by the world and so devoted to Magda, he apparently would risk his whole life for her. He wasn't a big man, but he was strong enough to hold me immobile and he had once nearly kicked a man to death. I could imagine him sneaking into Jake's Lincoln and waiting until the opportune time to slice into his neck with a knife. He could have had his car parked nearby. He could have gone home, showered and no one would have seen him. He would have had to detail his car, though, to rid it of any residual blood. The day I had gone with him to the video arcade, I hadn't seen any trace of blood and, frankly, his car had looked like it hadn't been cleaned for a while. In any case, the police had checked both his and Magda's cars and had found no traces of blood. Any one of them could have walked home, of course, but that greatly increased the chances of a passerby seeing them with blood on their clothing. It had, however, been a stormy, rainy night and blood on the hands or coat may not have been noticeable to any casual observer.

I tried to imagine how I would have gone about accomplishing the grisly business. A rain slicker would do the job of keeping most of the blood off the killer. A slicker, gloves and a garbage bag could easily have been all the tools the killer would have needed to accomplish the deed and get away clean. Those items and, of course, a knife.

The most puzzling question of all was the murder weapon. What was it and where was it? The police had found nothing. Even the autopsy had not been able to pinpoint what it was. Magda owned a large knife. The police had it in the evidence room. But Perce had said it probably wasn't what killed Jake.

About 11:00, I heard Magda come upstairs. After a few minutes, I stepped out of my room and tapped gently on her door.

"Come," she said. "I found her in the walk-in closet, sitting at her dressing table brushing her hair. It was the first time I had seen her look less than perfect. She was wearing a long sleeved, high collared robe of emerald green. She had removed her make up and her face was bare. She looked older and very vulnerable. It was the first time I had seen her without any of her masks.

"Cheyenne," she said and reached to dim the dressing table lights. "Oh, dear, I did it again, didn't I? Left without letting you know where I was. I'm sorry. I'm not used to this protection business at all."

"As long as you are safe, Magda," I said. "That's

what I care about." I smiled at her, hoping I looked reassuring. "I didn't come in here to scold you, anyway. I wanted to ask you about those letters."

"Letters?" she said, watching me in her mirror. Her scarred fingers played with the pearly brush handle.

"The ones Donald Tooley wrote you," I said.

She turned to me then. "Why, I gave them to the police. That's what we were supposed to do, isn't it? Mr. Quiller said he wanted them."

My heart sank. If Quiller had them, he would do everything in his power to keep me from seeing them again. And they did not look good for Donald. Although, if the later letters, the ones where he had appealed to Magda, were included, they could actually help his case. I apologized for disturbing her and said goodnight.

My mind was still whirling when I climbed into bed with one of Richard Bach's books. I let myself sink into it and relax.

◆ ◆ ◆

The red numerals on my clock announced that it was 2:13. The dark pressed down on me and I turned over, not even thinking about what had awakened me. Then I heard a muffled sound from deep in the house. I pulled the blankets up around my face and snuggled down into the bed, leaving not much more than my nose exposed.

Smoke! I sat up immediately, suddenly wide awake and strained my senses toward the source. Someone was smoking cigarettes. Knowing that neither Magda nor Laurel smoked, I silently stepped out of bed and fumbled with my slippers in the dark. The only one who smoked in the household was Rolf. Was he finishing, in the middle of the night, his search for the pictures that tormented him so? If he was, he had no business, caretaker or not, being in the house at this hour.

I padded to the door and peered out into the dark hall but saw no one. The smell of smoke was no stronger out there than it had been in my room. There had been just a breath of it after all, as if it had been left over from a long-ago party. I had almost decided to go back to bed and allow Magda or Laurel a clandestine smoke in peace if they wanted one when I heard the faint sound of music. *Probably Laurel or Magda watching television*, I told myself. But a second later, I heard the very real sound of laughter.

I sighed and started down the hall. *I am here to protect*, I thought, *so protect I will*. I wasn't necessarily trying to be quiet but my slippers made no sound when I passed Laurel's door. I could see her light was off. Magda's door was ajar. I pushed it open with one finger and whispered, "Magda?"

The door swung open easily and I could see by the window's dim light that she was not in bed.

FIFTEEN

Saturday, November 19, 1983

With a growing feeling of unease, I glanced toward the stairs to the third-floor ballroom and library. What would Magda be going upstairs for in the middle of the night? I weighed the idea of returning to my room again when a stronger puff of cigarette smoke drifted to me. Still very faint, but there, nevertheless. I moved toward the stairs and started up.

The foyer was carpeted in lush, though old, deep, rich red plush. The ballroom doors, heavy oak, were intricately carved and beautiful. One of them hung open. The floor was shining, silky wood. Inside the room, was a woman with long, dark hair. Not Magda? Nearby, a recording of Johnny Mathis singing "Wonderful, Wonderful," played softly. The room was filled with the sounds of laughter, as if a crowd of invisible people, ghosts perhaps, were enjoying a party.

The woman had her back to me. She gestured and laughed as if speaking to a group of admirers. In her hands, balanced in her slender fingers, was a long cigarette holder with a burning cigarette. She suddenly laughed softly and moved to a chair. She wore a pale blue dress. The slender skirt, flared at the bottom, *swished* when she walked and, when she sat, the fabric pooled around her on the floor like a mysterious fluid. The gown, low cut in the back, left her arms bare. I saw then what I had failed to notice at first.

"Oh, thank you," I heard her say and she laughed again. Still watching her imaginary guests, Magda turned around. The front of her dress was as low cut as the back. The light blue fabric was in startling contrast to the white and purple scars that covered her chest and arms like a garment. Her breasts had been burned away.

The moment she spotted me her face contorted with fury. "What the hell are you doing?" she shrieked. Her pitiful arms moved to cover the damage on her chest. She flew at me, her rage as tangible as a third person in the room.

"Magda, I—"

"You get the hell out of here right now!" She grabbed my arms and tried to physically steer me from the room. I could feel heat and hurt and humiliation raging through her. Her breath in my face was heavy with alcohol and I was sure I saw green fire blazing in her eyes.

"Magda," I said, keeping my voice low and as calm as I could. "Listen to me—"

"Get out of my house!" she said in a savage whisper. I felt her words on my face. "You be out of this house first thing tomorrow morning. I will not have you in my house any longer. I will not tolerate a spy!"

I watched her for another moment then turned and retreated to my room. I had followed men and women and had seen much that was disgusting and much that was shameful. I had never, in my life, seen anything as heartbreaking as the scene I had just witnessed.

It was impossible to get any real rest that night, of course. After a short while, I heard Magda come back to her room, but I imagined she was sleeping no better than I was. When I did doze, my dreams were peopled with ghosts of my past; my mother, David, Angelle, Cam and, of course Magda.

In the morning, Laurel was in the kitchen cooking sausages. She watched me as though she knew what had happened in the depths of the night. I refused her offer of meat and made myself a cup of tea, then put some bread in the toaster.

The morning paper was full of Donald Tooley. He had been arraigned the day before and his face filled much of the front page of the PI. I looked into his eyes. He had been caught gazing straight at the camera. The misery on his face was almost palpable. I put down the article unread.

Laurel continued to watch me. I wondered, not for the first time, if she knew everything that went on in that house or if she simply had some psychic ability herself.

"Magda's late this morning," she said, just as Magda herself stepped into the kitchen.

She greeted us and looked at me. There were dark circles under her eyes and her voice was raspy and hoarse when she spoke a brief "good morning" to us. She wore a bright red turtleneck and a loose black jumper, black tights and flat shoes. Her gray hair was groomed and she wore red lipstick. A far cry from the pathetic vamp I had witnessed the night before.

She sat down at the table and waited for Laurel to serve her a cup of coffee. Leaning on her elbows, she surveyed me silently as if waiting for me to make some first move, take some opening shot. If she was expecting me to produce my suitcase and slink out into the day, she had another think coming.

I saw Laurel slide a look at both of us and I swear I saw her smirk. In a moment she wandered away to have a conference with Rolf, muttering something about moving one of the rhododendrons.

Magda swept a sulfurous glance over me then it settled on her cup. "I'm not used to having guests in my home spy on me," she said, her voice even huskier than usual. "Especially in the middle of the night."

"I'm not a guest, Magda," I said. "You hired me to do a job. I'm terribly sorry that you were embarrassed, but I'm here to investigate Jake's murder and protect you. When I hear noises in the night, and smell smoke, I'm going to investigate." I felt sorry for her. The poor woman had had much pain in her life, though this "poor woman" could very well be a murderer.

"I'm sorry you saw what you saw," she began in an icy tone. Her eyes hardened and I could see a trace of anger creep back into them. Her hands clutched at her upper arms.

"I am not going to quit, Magda. I believe you ordered me from your house out of anger and embarrassment. If I quit now, I will be abandoning you for a second time."

She looked at me for a long moment, then nodded.

I smiled at her, pushed my toast aside and rose, but as I did, she clutched my arm. "Cheyenne," she began and stopped. I sat down again and waited. When she spoke at last, her eyes were focused on mine. "I appreciate what you are doing. I'm sorry for what I said last night. You are quite right. I hired you to protect me and to investigate what happened. I'm sorry that you saw me last night. I…"

I patted the hand that still rested on my arm. "I understand the losses you have suffered, Magda," I said. "I sense them. I only wish that by feeling them myself, I could remove some of the pain for you. Unfortunately, it doesn't work that way. Please, let's put this behind us." This time, when I stood, she didn't stop me. "I'll be out most of the day. Will you be all right here?"

Again, she nodded.

◆ ◆ ◆

My plans for the day included another visit with Alphonso de Las Alas, another with Suzanne and I wanted to see if I could track down Clovis Houston. I sped along I-5, past downtown and the new convention center. Its green glass and modern architecture made it look like an immense crystal growing out of Freeway Park. It hovered over the freeway like a giant terrarium for humans growing ideas.

My friend, Molly, lived just outside downtown, not far from Suzanne's apartment. I had known Molly for as long as I could remember. She had become something of a mother figure for me since my own had been gone even though she was nearer my age than my mother's. Over the years we had become close. For one thing, she found everything I did utterly fascinating and who could resist that?

Molly's house was filled with small tables covered with home-made bric-a-brac. She had hung so many curtains and drapes over the windows and covered the floor with such thick pile carpets and rugs that her home seemed more a cocoon than a house.

Molly herself spent her life making pottery, crocheted tea cozies, afghans, embroidered lamp shades or whatever her current craft craze happened to be.

"Hey, Moll," I said when she had answered the door. She smothered me in a warm hug and pulled me into the house.

"Cheyenne, do I have a man for you!" she said. Good will steamed off of her like a cloud.

"Oh, Molly—."

"No protests," she said, and I didn't bother with any. When Molly has decided to enhance my happiness, there's no point in doing anything but just allow her to have her way.

I let her wind down then mentioned the St. Martin case. I often told Molly about my cases. She sometimes had insights that had helped me on more than one occasion. She was well aware that she was receiving confidential information and I knew that all of the secrets I imparted to her were safe. She landed on Magda's case with both feet.

"I think it was the wife," she said, bustling about in

the kitchen.

"Magda? Why?"

"She had the most reason. Motive. He was sleeping around on her, wasn't he? I'd bump off my husband too if he cheated on me."

"You don't have one, Molly."

"You damn betcha," she said as if that settled the whole question. She set a mug of hot tea and an apparently homemade mini cinnamon bun in front of me. I took a bite and couldn't help a little groan of pleasure. I had had no breakfast, after all.

"Donald Tooley has motive too, according to the police," I said after I had dispatched the luscious bite. "And so does Rolf, the handyman. His is a compelling one, especially when you know that he's an ex-con."

"Ooh, do tell. What did he do?"

"Assault."

"Oh, well," she said, waving it off. "That isn't murder. What's his motive?"

"It could have been murder if the guy had died. It's a fine line."

She ruminated on that for a minute while I took the final bite. "What would his motive be for killing Mr. Magda?" she asked.

"The oldest and the best. Jealousy. Jake was screwing the woman he loved." I frowned. "Only he says he's not in love with her anymore and I believe him. That shoots a few holes into that theory." I purposely didn't mention Rolf's attack to Molly. She was almost as bad as Easy when it came to overprotection.

"Oy. Sex." She nodded. "Always a good motive in any case. What about the secretary? Laura? Laurel? Does she have a motive?"

"You know, it's interesting you should ask that," I said. I shook my head at her offer of a second cinnamon bun. "She has lived with and worked for Magda and her various husbands for years. She's put aside any career plans she may have had and has virtually been in service to Magda. Both Magda and Laurel insist they're like mother and daughter, or like sisters at least, but Laurel is treated like a servant. I can't figure out why she would put up with that."

"Maybe she hopes to inherit."

"Maybe. In which case, I should be back there protecting Magda like crazy right now," I said, but didn't make a move to go. That little cinnamon bun was sitting so very comfortably in my stomach and the tea was perfect and hot.

"There are some women who are like that, you know," she said. "They're willing slaves. Some do it for a man. Most, I'd say. But there are women who like women, you know."

"You think Laurel is in love with Magda?"

"It isn't impossible."

"Of course not. It hadn't occurred to me, though. But you could be right I suppose. Although, neither Laurel nor Magda act like it. In fact, I'd say Laurel is more afraid of Magda than in love with her." I heaved myself and the cinnamon bun out of the chair. "I have to go interview a guy I met at the funeral. I believe the man is having an affair with Magda."

"An actor?" Her eyes lit up.

"Sorry, he's a real estate broker. Guy named de Las Alas. Then I'm going to interview Suzanne, the woman who was having an affair with Jake, and who discovered the body besides. After that, I get to go try to catch a guy in the act of hoodwinking an insurance company." It made me tired to think of all I had to do that afternoon, especially after having gotten only a half night of sleep.

"You get on out there and interview, woman," she said. "I want your name on the front page of the paper with a big shitty grin on your face from having solved the whole thing." She gave me another smothering hug on the way out and I headed up north.

◆ ◆ ◆

Alphonso de Las Alas' office was in the heart of Greenwood. I hadn't called ahead and realized too late that he might not be in. His office was practically deserted, except for a secretary who looked up at me but didn't say a word.

"Is Mr. de Las Alas in?" I pronounced it 'day-los-AH-las' the way I had heard him pronounce it, although he had been drunk at the time.

She punched a button on the intercom and said, "Mr. Duh-LOSS-uh-loss, you got a customer." Then she pointed with her nose and I went through a cheap hollow door into a room only a little larger than a closet.

"Afternoon, young lady," he said, standing. "What can I do for you? Hey, didn't I meet you at Magda's? Yes, you were at Jake's funeral."

"Good memory," I said. "My name is Cheyenne Bruce."

"Oh, yeah. I was thinking it was Laramie."

"That's my brother's name," I said. "I'm hoping you can give me a little insight into Magda St Martin."

"I don't know what I can tell you." The grin never left his mouth but it disappeared from his eyes.

"Are you having an affair with her?"

He shot me a look and the grin finally vanished. "You get right to the point, don't you?"

"I try."

"Sure, I had an affair with her." He sat down at his desk and indicated a chair for me. "I guess it can't hurt to tell you. It's all over with, though. Has been for a while."

"How long is a while?" I had the feeling he wasn't telling me the truth. So far, practically no one had. But I couldn't be sure unless I touched him and I wasn't in a hurry to do that.

"Couple of months," he said. He looked at a painting on the wall over my right shoulder.

"Mr. de Las Alas, I think you were with Magda just recently."

He blushed. I thought people outgrew that.

"Okay, I still see her once in a while. She's not easy to, uh, get away from."

"Is she that intriguing?" I asked.

"Hell, no. She's demanding. I tried to break it off with her a couple of times. She's like that woman in that movie. What was the name of it? She wouldn't let the guy go back to his wife or something like that. She killed the wife or killed the husband, I forget. Fortunately, I don't have a wife."

"Oh, yeah. That movie with that actor," I said, nodding sagely, but he didn't seem to get the irony. "She won't let you go?"

"Oh, well, I guess I could if I really tried. But, like I said, I don't have a wife so there really isn't any reason..." He wound down.

I kept silent and, in a moment, he spoke again. "We got together several months back. Jake was cheating on her and she was lonesome. She thinks men don't like her because of her, you know, her scars." He shook his head and lifted his feet to the edge of the desk, tilting his chair perilously far back. "She's got 'em bad. You know, she used to do commercials of hand lotion and dishwashing detergent and stuff like that? She had gorgeous hands, she says. And, when she was first starting out, they used her body in movies when the actress was too modest to do nude scenes. Guess there aren't many of that kind of actress around anymore."

"You didn't know her then?" He had a hole in the bottom of his right shoe. A serious one. I wondered what Magda found in him to interest her. He was good looking, but didn't seem to have much else going for him.

"Naw. I didn't meet her until after the plane crash. And I never have seen her body. Never. She keeps herself pretty well covered up. I guess the only one who ever saw her body after the fire was Jake."

And me, I thought.

"Did she want to leave Jake and marry you?"

He boomed a laugh that bounced off the wall behind me. "Hell, no!" he said, still laughing. "You don't think she had anything to do with his death, do you?"

"Mr. de Las Alas, you yourself said that she was like 'that woman in that movie' and that the woman was a killer."

"Oh, yeah. Well," he said, looking a little frightened and a little ashamed at the same time. "I guess she was."

Mr. de Las Alas didn't give me a heck of a lot more information than I already had. He was willing, but he just didn't know anything. It sounded to me like he and Magda had a halfhearted relationship at best. I wondered if it was his ego talking when he said she was "hard to get away from" and that she was "like that woman in that movie" or if she had, as Laurel, Morgan and Donald had all said, a "crazy" side.

I left his office and thought about what to do next. I was already hungry. The little cinnamon bun would count as breakfast but now I was ready for lunch. I headed over to the Greenwood Mandarin Restaurant. I'm a sucker for garlic and there was nowhere in Seattle to get good Chinese food that loaded with garlic than the Greenwood. They treated it like a vegetable in its own right.

After a half order of Chinese Vegetable Deluxe, I felt better. It's wonderful what food can do.

To my surprise, Magda had let me take Angelle's letter after I had promised to return it safely. I had it in my briefcase, so I decided to hop over to Suzanne's and show it to her. Besides, I wanted to see if she was getting along all right. I always worried about women who couldn't seem to make it without a man in their lives. Of course, I didn't think Sudie would be without one for very long.

On the way, I drove past Clovis Houston's house but saw his car wasn't in its normal place in the driveway. I decided to stop by on the way back.

I parked on Fifty-third and was just passing a Super-Sub Sandwich Shop when I actually saw Mr. Houston himself standing at the counter. *Oh please, oh please, oh please*, I thought. *Make this easy on me. Get something and sit in a seat by the window.* I casually opened my briefcase and took out my little camera. I lurked at the corner, looking in the window of the dry cleaner next door as though the racks of plastic covered clothing were the most fascinating things I had ever seen.

When he came out, Clovis had obviously bought his lunch to go. He held a white paper bag. *Damn*, I thought. *The man just will not cooperate.* I walked behind him for a half block and watched in futile frustration while he unlocked his car and got in. Just before I turned away, he reached into the bag, extracted a large paper wrapped sandwich, unwrapped it and took a huge bite, right there in front of me. I almost dropped my camera in my rush to get it to my eye. Fortunately, his greed got the better of him and he took another gigantic bite before wrapping the sandwich back up and starting the car. "Thank you, Clovis," I whispered. "Enjoy your day."

Suzanne's apartment was in a well-maintained building just off of Fifty-third on a quiet little street in the University District. She had a ground floor unit with a window onto the front patio. I wondered if living so close to the University would slowly, over the years, allow her to soak up a few smart rays. I hoped so, for her sake.

I pounded on her door and when I got no answer, I peered into the front window. Her living room looked ordinary enough, but I sensed something ominous. I berated myself all the way to the manager's office, thinking that I was just going to get myself into trouble.

I remembered what Suzanne had said about the manager liking attractive women, so I gave him a wide smile. He didn't protest too much. Maybe he was used to people demanding to be let into his tenants' apartments.

Once the door was open, I knew I hadn't made a mistake. I turned to the manager and told him to call the police. When he was gone, I turned back to the poor pathetic thing that lay on the bathroom floor, carefully leaned over to feel her neck for a pulse. Then I wept.

SIXTEEN

Saturday, November 19, 1983

S uzanne's pitiful body lying on the bathroom floor had made me cry like nothing had since my mother's death. Even so, I knew I had to take a quick, cursory look around before anyone else got there.

I went back to the door and removed my shoes. I snapped photos of the area just inside the door making note that any foot prints already there had been obscured by the manager's and mine. I photographed Suzanne and the surrounding area from all angles. I knew the crime scene investigators would be doing the same and, in fact, more thoroughly, but that was what I had been trained to do. I placed a dollar bill next to some blood spatter and photographed that as well.

The apartment didn't look as though it had been searched. Of course, that could mean that whatever it had been the killer had wanted had simply been lying around ready to be taken. Or, I realized, he could have known where to look. Another option, was, of course, that he or she had not wanted anything beyond Suzanne's death.

I put on a pair of latex gloves and quickly slid my hands down into all of the dresser drawers. I carefully lifted out stacks of clothing, replacing them exactly where they had been. I found nothing. I checked closet shelves and pulled out the few books she had in her bookcase, then stood in the middle of the apartment, feeling helpless. Ranks of stuffed toy penguins watched me from a shelf at one end of the living room. I was about to head for the desk when I heard the approaching sirens and knew that Quiller was on his way, and by then I had recovered my equanimity.

"This wasn't done by the same person as the Jake Levin case," Quiller told me. He watched dispassionately while the ME looked over Suzanne's body.

"I don't know how you can tell that at this stage," I said. I was still sore with pity for Suzanne, but the physical effects of finding her lying in what looked like a million spilled bottles of scarlet nail polish hadn't affected my brain. "It looks like the same MO to me. Besides, why did you come if you didn't think it was connected?"

"Ah, Miss Bruce. Do we have to suffer through your amateur detecting just now? We all admit that she was stabbed in the throat." He put up his hand to stop me and sighed deeply and dramatically. "*Somewhat* like Mr. Levin was killed. But there are differences. Significant differences." I hated it when he tried to sound like Sherlock Holmes.

"Name one," I said.

"Well, now. This little lady was at home, wasn't she? We have the murder weapon right here. He used one of her own kitchen knives. Obviously, she put up a struggle. I wouldn't be at all surprised if some of this blood isn't from the killer."

"What are you going to do, Quiller, crawl around on your hands and knees with an eyedropper and sample every little speck? She was afraid someone was going to come after her. If you had listened to her instead of dragging her over the rack the other day, you would have known that. It's obvious to me this is connected to the Levin case. And it's highly likely that the same person did it."

"The old *psychic ability* telling you that?" He said the words as if they were in capital letters, italicized and underlined. "Or is this just women's intuition?"

"Yeah, Quiller," I said with a long, tired sigh. "It's what I do best, conform to gender stereotypes."

He looked at me for a moment and I wondered which of the words I would have to explain to him. Then he turned away and lit a cigarette, pretending that my "amateur detecting" wasn't worth listening to. He knew it was the same person. He just couldn't stand it that I knew it too.

The ME estimated the death had occurred sometime the night before. The building manager had seen her arrive home at about 9:00 or 9:30. Whoever had killed her was either waiting for her in the apartment or it was someone she knew and had let in.

"Just what are you doing here, anyway?" Quiller asked. His eyebrows arched in a quasi-interested expression that made him look surprised rather than smart.

"I came over here to show something to Suzanne. I wanted to get her opinion on it."

"Let's see it. What is it?"

"Uh-uh," I said, shaking my head and smiling. "Forget it. This isn't any of your business."

"It might have some bearing on the case," he said. His tone was warning, but I didn't care. "If you're withholding evidence, we could take legal action against you."

"Fine. Do it." Did he think I was so stupid I didn't know what I was doing? Of course, he did. The letter was Angelle's case. And Angelle's case wasn't Quiller's.

He pulled his unconcerned act again and I couldn't resist jabbing him one more time. "I guess this takes care of your theory that Donald Tooley murdered Jake Levin, huh?"

"Not at all. Like I said, it obviously wasn't done by the same person."

I gave up. I was too drained for any more combat, from him or anyone else. I made my formal statement and left him there.

Poor, little Suzanne. My heart ached for her. She had suffered so much in the past five days. I thought of her having lunch with me the day before. She had been scared. Magda, she had said, might try to kill her. At the time, I had thought her hysterical. I had been wrong. Even if I had come over here to Suzanne's instead of running to Molly's first, it wouldn't have made any difference. She had been dead by the time I got up to watch Magda do her lonely dance in the night.

◆ ◆ ◆

I was exhausted when I got back to Magda's. There were three telephone messages for me. All were from Donald Tooley. Easy had paged me three times as well. I was debating whom to call first when the telephone rang. There didn't seem to be anyone home so I answered it.

"Miss Bruce!" Donald hollered. I pulled the receiver away from my ear. "...something more," he was saying. "Would you come?"

"Mr. Tooley, I don't think—"

"Oh, you've got to, Miss Bruce!" There *was* desperation in his voice. It rang like a cracked bell. "I have something to say. I think it'll change things.

Please."

"Whatever it is, I'm sure you can tell me over the phone."

"No, I've got to tell you to your face. I don't trust these phones."

"It's okay, Mr. Tooley. No one is listening." Why do people always think phones are tapped? I remembered then what I had told Easy not long ago. I hadn't wanted to use the house phones either.

"The jail phone is bugged! I can't tell you unless you come here!"

"All right," I said and sighed. "I'll be there right away."

I hung up and glanced at my watch. It was 3:30. I debated with myself about calling Easy. If I did, there would be long explanations and I was simply too tired for that. I didn't want to go down to the jail and talk to Donald either. The jail would be too depressing. But then I thought of the poor man staying there for days and, though I felt like a flat tire, I decided to get it over with.

I went up to my room and got out my notebook, turning to the Donald Tooley section. His alibi didn't look good but, as far as I was concerned, Suzanne's murder had exonerated him. He couldn't remember where he'd been and his wife was the only one who knew that he'd been in a drunken stupor the night of the murder. Not only that, I got the impression that he had been lying about either that or something else. I wondered what he had to tell me that would "change things." I doubted that anything he could tell me was going to save him. Quiller was convinced he had his man. He would invent another killer for Suzanne if he had to.

The jail was busy on Saturday. Pitiful wives visited pathetic husbands. I shifted uncomfortably waiting for Tooley. It was foolish, being there, I knew, and I was angry at myself for having caved in to it. Why not just leave Tooley alone to face the music? He had a lawyer. If he was innocent, he would get off. Of course, I knew the judicial system didn't work that way. I had once had a friend who was completely innocent of the hit and run charge he had been slapped with. He had simply been in the wrong place at the wrong time. Due to the import of the charge, the lady who had accused him had been awarded damages. My friend had not even been allowed to speak in his own defense. No one believes an alleged negligent driver. No one believes a drunk.

I saw Donald before he saw me. If possible, he looked worse than he had the day I had seen him with Geraldine. His facial lines had deepened, and he looked like he had lost weight, something he could ill afford to do.

"Miss Bruce," he said when he saw me. His eyes lit up and his face seemed to relax into a softer frown.

"Mr. Tooley," I said, knowing I was frowning myself. "How are you doing?"

"Okay," he said. "Okay. Thank you for coming."

"You said you had something new for me."

"I do," he said. He took quick, darting looks around him, as if unwilling for anyone to hear what he had to say. "Remember what Gerry said the other day, about my alibi?" I nodded. "Well, I don't have an alibi."

"Well, I agree, it isn't much of an alibi, but it's better than nothing."

"No. I mean, that isn't the truth. I wasn't asleep, drunk, like Gerry said."

I stared at him. "Where were you?"

"I don't want to say."

"Mr. Tooley, you got me all the way down here to tell me something new. I think you should do so." I knew I was speaking sharply, seemingly unable to stop myself. I was still disgruntled about the way the whole day was going and this man before me was not helping.

"I'll get to it," he said, holding up a hand as defense against my anger. "I don't want you to tell Gerry this, or anyone. Do I have your promise?"

"I won't promise anything," I said. "Maybe you should be telling this to your attorney."

He waved the suggestion away. "Him! He's just a young snot they appointed for me. He don't care if I go to the clink for the rest of my life. He gets paid anyway. I got to tell you this, but it's got to be a secret."

I sighed. "Okay. Tell me." I wondered what Easy was doing right this minute. I wished I could be sharing some Shrimp Cheyenne with him, but then I remembered how miffed I was with him and tried to focus on Donald.

"On the night that feller was killed, I was out... making a delivery."

"What do you mean, 'a delivery'?"

He looked right and left again. There were other couples in the room but no one seemed to be paying any attention to us. "Drugs," he said.

I simply stared at him. He didn't seem the drug runner at all. More the father of the boy who smoked a little weed but not the pusher, not the bagman.

He nodded in answer to my look. "You need to tell your lawyer this," I said.

"No. That ain't going to happen. I want you to prove that I didn't do that there murder so they'll let me out of here."

"That's your lawyer's job, not mine."

"If I told that kid about the drugs, he'd see to it that I never got out."

"Maybe you shouldn't," I said. I hadn't felt so mean in a long, long time. I was instantly ashamed.

He put his head down. "Maybe I shouldn't. But you'd understand if you'd been out of a job as long as I have. I got kids home that I got to feed no matter what. Whether I work or not, them kids still got to eat. Rent's got to be paid and we got to have heat. I got to do something to get money. You don't know how it feels." He stared into my face until I dropped my gaze.

I did know how it felt. I had been in his shoes at one time. Not in jail, but without work. Homeless. And I was once again looking at being out on the street unless I could find another apartment and soon. "Geraldine doesn't know?"

"Nope. Nobody does. I want you to find the guy that did this murder so's I can get out of here."

"So you can run more drugs?"

He shook his head. "No, I ain't going in for that anymore. I had enough of it. It's good money, but you can't trust them bastards." He looked at me quickly. "Pardon me, ma'am."

"Mr. Tooley, did anyone see you at all that night? Did you stop anywhere along the way? Meet anyone?"

"Nope. I went to down to Kent, did what I was supposed to do, then came back." He ruminated a moment. "I did stop in at a 7-Eleven to buy cigarettes, but that was only for a second."

"What time was that?"

He shrugged. "Maybe midnight."

"Did you charge your purchase?" I asked him.

He shook his head. "Cash."

"Look," I said, thinking. "If the store clerk could recognize you, that might help." There was more than a good chance that Donald Tooley would be released anyway in view of Suzanne French's murder. I didn't want to give him false hope but I did want to give him something. "I'll see what I can do." I said, patting his shoulder.

When I left him, he was still sitting in the chair, staring after me.

From there, I stopped by Evidence before heading up to Quiller's office. The letters weren't there. Somehow, I had known they wouldn't be and it had nothing to do with ESP. Quiller had hung on to them. I went straight to his office. Might as well ruin the rest of the day, I thought.

Quiller sat at his desk like the king toad of Swamp Lake.

"Quiller," I said, wanting to get out of there as quickly as I could. "Where are the Tooley letters?"

"The what?" He looked genuinely surprised. This wasn't your routine Quiller bullshit.

"The letters from Donald Tooley that Magda St. Martin gave you. I'd like to take a look at them." I spoke slowly and deliberately.

"I'm sorry, my dear. I don't have the letters. I asked her for them, but I don't have them."

"Quiller, cut the shit. I really don't feel like it today. Magda said she gave you the fan letters Tooley wrote to her five or six years ago. I think there is something in there that will shed some light on the Levin case. You aren't helping anyone, including yourself, by withholding them."

"I don't know what you're babbling about," he said. "I don't have the letters."

The terrible thing was that I believed him. I didn't want to, but the astonishment and puzzlement on his face was more genuine than I had ever seen on him before. The thing about Quiller was, when he was faking, it was usually obvious.

I walked from Quiller's office all the way up Pike and stopped at the Market. Especially on a Saturday, it was teeming with people. The walk and the presence of humanity did me good. When I had left Donald, a headache was inching its way to the top of my head. When I had left Quiller's office, it had completely surrounded me and was dunking me under.

I stopped at a phone booth and dialed Easy's number. I was doomed to disappointment. He wasn't home. I tried his office but he wasn't there either. Damn! You don't need them for much, but when you do, they just aren't there. I knew that was unfair as well as untrue but I was in no mood to be rational or fair. Instead of trying his pager, I got some dinner at a vegetarian place at the Market and felt better.

All the way home I nagged myself about the murder weapon. Not only had it not been found, so far, no one could definitively say what it was. Apparently, it was a knife of some sort. A dull one at that. The picture of Magda chopping apples with just such a knife jumped into my mind. But, then, Perce had told me the lab techs had said the weapon was something heavier than a knife. Something thicker. Suzanne's killer had grabbed one of her own knives out of the block in the kitchen.

I wondered why the killing had been done in the bathroom. Was that where Suzanne had run in panic? Or had the killer chosen that room to hide in, then grabbed her when she had innocently entered? Why would the killer choose that room? Because it was more cleanable than the bedroom or the living room? Someone like Magda would have done that very thing. Magda and Laurel had not been at home all evening. I remembered that Laurel had come upstairs about 10:40 and Magda about twenty minutes later. Could Magda have killed poor Suzanne, then celebrated with a cigarette and Johnny Mathis? And what had Laurel been doing? Maybe she had done it. Maybe Suzanne had been a collaborative job for the two of them. I hadn't seen Rolf at all. So much for my keeping a close eye on him.

By the time I reached Admiral Way, my knuckles were aching from clutching the wheel so hard. Without the weapon that had killed Jake, we had less than nothing. With it, I felt, the answers, at least some of them, would fall into place. I was determined to find it.

When I pulled up in front of the house, I stayed in the car a moment to think. The wind had picked up again on the way home and the gusts rocked my little car. I suddenly didn't want to go in anyway. Rolf's car was there but there were no lights on in the Caretaker's Cottage. Was he in the house again? I could see lights in the big house, though. If anyone was home, he probably wouldn't be snooping there.

After a moment, I got out. The wind almost yanked the door out of my hand. I didn't head for the front door right away. Instead, I walked up the wide drive, circled to the side and tried the lock on the door to the small shed attached to the three-car garage. I wondered why I hadn't thought to check this out before.

No one was in the kitchen. The rack of keys hung just inside the back door. I knew which ones belonged to the garage, the house, Magda's and Jake's cars. Jake's car was still in impound, but the spare key still rested on its hook. This, of course, was where Rolf would have known to come for the key to Jake's car. Rolf and anyone else who had wanted it. There were several that looked like luggage keys and one by Shoemaker, the brand of lock I had seen on the shed. I studied the rest of them. I slipped the garage key from the hook and spied a key for a Ford. *Hmmm*...I thought. I rummaged in the tool drawer for a flashlight.

I leaned into the wind and went back to the shed.

I had no idea what I was looking for. Something long and dull but sharp enough to be deadly. Beyond that, my imagination would not go. I flashed the beam around the room, stumped. The shed was as tidy as the rest of the house. I couldn't imagine Magda out there anymore than I could see her venturing into the attic. She had mentioned at one point that she had a fear of spiders. Lots of people do, of course, but hers, she had said, was more of a panic than a fear. Myself, I don't mind them. They eat other beasties that I don't like. Flies and mosquitoes for instance. I knew this shed would be a spider haven. At least, it normally would have been if it hadn't been so neat.

A thought startled me so much I almost dropped the light. Its beam faltered and fell on a pair of gardening gloves tucked behind a can of concentrated weed killer. I picked one up, then both. I had seen these gloves before. Obviously, they were used for gardening, but they were as clean as new. Yes, I had seen Laurel washing them the day I had arrived. The day after Jake had died.

The gloves were the kind that are made for gripping. I knew Paul Harvey had advertised them on the news radio every morning. I ran my fingers over the tiny plastic bumps on the palms, then slowly lifted the glove to my chin. Thoughts like fragmented pictures flickered through my mind. Jake, blood, panic, darkness. The glove felt like a cat's tongue.

I crammed the gloves into my jacket pocket. I could call Quiller tomorrow. I thought of bypassing him altogether and taking them down to the lab myself. Jane owed me a favor. She would run the tests if I begged. Even though they had been washed, there was a very good chance some blood still lurked in the seams. Quiller would be pissed off but, at that point, I didn't care what he thought.

I relocked the shed and unlocked the side door to the garage. In the blackness, I saw Magda's car. Next to it was the empty space where Jake's car would normally sit. Next to that was a wall dividing the garage. I moved carefully through the dark, around the work bench that stood against the wall, a large trash container and a stack of assorted flattened cardboard boxes. The divider reached from the back wall almost all the way to the garage door. I shone my light through the narrow space and played it around on a tarp covered car. It stood to reason. If Magda had kept Angelle's room intact for five and a half years, it came as no surprise that she had kept Angelle's car for her as well. My mind raced as I relocked the garage and headed for the house.

I shoved the flashlight into my pocket and the keys with it. The kitchen light had gone on. I didn't want to answer any questions. I didn't want to talk and I didn't want to think. I could return the keys to the rack in the morning. I trudged past frantically waving bushes to the front door. The foyer light was on and Medea shone eerily down on me. She colored a patch of sidewalk with blood red and hard, cold green. I glanced at Mr. and Mrs. Graft's house. I saw a figure in the window and wondered if Iola was watching for ghosts. I waved but she didn't respond.

SEVENTEEN

Saturday, November 19, 1983

Inside, the house was quiet, though the wind moaned around the porch. I wanted only to get upstairs for a little quiet and a little rest. I could hear Laurel in the kitchen. I climbed the stairs hoping I wouldn't meet Magda in the hall. I wanted to confront her with the fact that she had lied to me about giving the Tooley letters to Quiller, but I didn't want to do it right then.

So many lies, I thought. Laurel had lied about Magda being in bed that night. Donald had lied more than once. Magda had lied about her affair with de Las Alas and she'd lied about the letters, too. How many other lies had I been told? I was supposed to be helping those people.

It wasn't Magda, but Laurel who caught me. She must have been listening for me.

"Cheyenne," she called, just as I was reaching the top of the stairs. Wearily, I turned to look down at her. She gestured for me to come back down and I plodded, hoping something would call her away so I could escape. The doorbell, the phone, anything.

When I reached the bottom of the steps, she steered me into the living room, glancing back at the stairs as if she expected to see Magda lurking there. Her eyes were bright and manic. "Oh my God!" she whispered.

"What is it, Laurel?" I asked, becoming alarmed.

"They've arrested Rolf and I've gotten a phone call from…from Angelle!" Her eyes glittered.

"Rolf? And Angelle?" I said stupidly. Out of habit, I tried to feel the essence of Angelle and couldn't. That meant nothing. That night I wouldn't have been able to feel a bolt of lightning.

"Angelle called this afternoon. She says she's all right! Then, they came to get Rolf about an hour ago. They're saying he killed that Suzanne French woman!" She was talking fast, as if she were frantic to get the words out as quickly as she could. "Of course, Rolf didn't do it. It was Angelle who did it. I know it was. She sounded crazy, Cheyenne."

Crazy? This whole business was crazier than a truck load of demented rats. What could anyone possibly do that would make it any crazier?

"You know about her grandmother," she was saying, still talking at speed. She said it defensively as if that placed blame on the entire schizophrenic population for any off the wall activity.

"What did she say? Did she talk to Magda?" I asked.

"No, she didn't want to talk to Magda." Laurel threw another look at the stairs. "It's just as well. I think it would make Magda too upset. She's already upset about Rolf being arrested."

"Laurel, try to calm down and tell me what Angelle said." I heard myself and what I was saying and realized how bizarre it sounded. Was Angelle's "call" like her "letter" had been—contrived and misleading? Who was doing this?

"She said she couldn't help it, but she might do it again!" Laurel's voice scaled up until it was something like a whispered scream. "I'm scared, Cheyenne!"

"Do what? Do what again, Laurel?"

"Kill." Tears began to leak down Laurel's face and she gathered a handful of tissues from her sweater pocket.

"Are you sure it was Angelle? Did you recognize her voice?"

"Oh, yes! I knew it was Angelle. This is terrible! I'm afraid she's going to hurt Magda. Or you." She looked at me with something more than tears glittering in her eyes. Was it fear? Interest?

"Would she hurt you, do you think?"

She shook her head. "No, she would never hurt me. She…"

"Would she hurt her mother?"

"Yes, definitely. She's crazy. She could do anything." Laurel took a deep, ragged breath.

"I think you should tell Magda," I said.

"No. I don't think so. I think we'll lock the house up good tonight and keep the bolts on the door. You aren't going anywhere tonight, are you?" While she spoke, she moved to the front door and shot the dead bolt. She peered behind each of the heavy drapes and checked the windows. The fabric whispered on the floor like a reunion of ghosts.

"Your friend, Mr. Radford, called us to say Suzanne French was dead. I didn't tell Magda. They're going to come and question us about it tomorrow. I told them Magda was too ill tonight. Besides, they already arrested Rolf. I don't know why they would want to question us." She looked around, her gaze darting everywhere as if she expected Angelle to step out of the shadows.

Laurel's movements were quick and frenetic. Was this a reaction to Rolf being accused of murder? *Curious*, I thought. *More than curious.*

"You told Magda that Rolf was arrested but not that Suzanne had been killed?" I asked. "What does she think he was arrested for?"

"No, I didn't tell her Rolf was arrested."

"Laurel, you said you did. That she was upset about it."

"Oh, I don't know what I said!" Her eyes continued to flit back and forth.

"I'm going up to talk to Magda," I said.

"No, she's too ill! You can't talk to her now. She's too upset." She stopped her frantic aimless searching and gazed at me steadily.

I had moved toward the stairs but she put a hand on my arm. I felt heat—a kind of jittery, fire-like intensity coming from her.

"Magda's having one of her headaches. She took a sleeping pill, I think. We don't want to disturb her." She seemed to be watching me carefully now. "You're going to be here with us, aren't you? In case Angelle decides to do something?"

"I'm not going out," I told her. "I think I'll go upstairs and read for a while then go to bed early. I suggest you do the same."

She breathed a sigh of relief while I went back up the stairs.

Something is very wrong here, I thought. *Very, very wrong.* I thought of stopping off at Magda's room and speaking to her about this new development, but if she truly did have a bad headache, I didn't want to disturb her. Nevertheless, I had to make sure she was safe, so, when I reached her room, I gently opened her door. She was in bed and apparently sleeping. I whispered her name. She sighed once and shifted. I backed out and continued to my own room.

I kicked off my shoes and sat down in the armchair by the window, determined to stay awake until I heard Laurel come up to bed. I intended to check her light periodically, too, to make sure that she had settled for the night before I would allow myself to rest. I was afraid to lie down for fear I would fall asleep. I wanted to drag the spare blanket over myself, but knew that if I were cold, I would be less likely to drowse.

Moments later, I roused from what I knew had been a light doze. I turned on the overhead light and tried to force my eyes to remain open.

In spite of my best intentions, I slept and my dreams tormented me. They rose before me in blinking colors. Even in the dream, I winced away from the light. Hideously bright colors shifted and moved—alive.

I felt as though I had slept for only a few minutes. The overhead light was off and the red glow of my clock had disappeared sometime when I had been dreaming. I shivered, stumbled to the wall and flipped the light switch. Nothing. The wind was slamming against the side of the house. I had worn my jacket upstairs earlier and it was still draped across the back of the desk chair. I found the flashlight in the pocket and switched it on.

The case notes were still scattered on the desk the way I had left them before visiting Donald. My head throbbed as I gathered them up. Something about them disturbed me. I stood staring at the notes and the letter from Angelle, letting amorphous thoughts solidify in my mind. After a few minutes, I fumbled for the card Ab Eberstein had given me. I dialed, hoping he wouldn't be angry at being awakened. But, by then, I didn't care.

Neither did he. I asked him three or four questions.

A glance at my watch told me it was 1:38. The house was cold, but the chill had nothing to do with the air temperature. I moved down the dark, silent stairs, went to the front window and looked up. The glass dagger was gone from Medea's hand. I wondered if Iola Graft had been watching when the ghost woman had climbed down for the last time.

I listened for any sound in the house at all, but there was nothing but the mournful cry of the wind outside. Then I did hear a distant thump as a small branch landed on the roof. Or had it been a branch? I strained my ears when a lull came in the wind and I thought I heard the faraway voices of the past. Soft, like the faint sigh of whispers. I went toward the stairs and started to climb, stopped to listen, then climbed again.

Once I thought I heard the far away hint of a laugh. At the top of the stairs, I listened at Magda's door but heard nothing but the wind battering the eaves outside. Behind Laurel's door too was nothing but silence. When I reached the third floor, I stopped at the ballroom door. It stood ajar. The room was as dark as a crypt. I reached out with one finger and pushed it open. Nothing. No light, no sound came from the blackness. As I headed toward the attic stairs, I heard a quiet murmur and a soft laugh.

The attic was dark but for a single candle that had been placed on a box. It sputtered as I silently pushed the door open a little wider. A slender woman in a pink gown, her long dark hair covering most of her face, knelt on the floor cradling something that looked like a large doll. Magda? I caught a glimpse of wispy hair and another of stained red plaid.

I realized with an icy start that what she was embracing was not a doll at all. It was the frail, desiccated body of a woman dressed in the dusty tatters of what had once been a white sweater and bell-bottom pants.

Laurel looked up then, Magda's dark wig hanging in lank waves around her drawn face. I watched rage infuse her features when she saw me.

She was on her feet in less than a second, lunging at me with the glass dagger, a living Medea. The glass dug deep into my arm as I raised it to shield my face. The flashlight spun out of my fingers, landed with a *clunk* and went out. I hissed in a breath and scrambled backward, tripping over an open trunk. She raised the dagger again even as I felt the warm blood gushing from the line of fire on my arm. Ab had been right. You can kill with a piece of glass. My stockinged feet slid on the wooden floor but I was able to scoot backward to an area beyond the range of the candle. A second later, she had blown it out.

"I can't let you leave here," she said in a voice that sounded sad. The dark shape of her moved nearby and I heard the whisper of her long silk dress along the floor.

"What are you doing, Laurel?" I asked her quietly. I could just make out her silhouette moving again as she turned toward me.

"I'm playing with my friend," she said, sounding like a parody of a child.

"Who is your friend?" I asked as though she truly was a child.

"Angelle. I love Angelle." She laughed, a chilling sound that made my skin crawl. "She lives here with all of us. She's perfect now."

"Did you kill Angelle, Laurel?"

She giggled—a horrible sound. "She was sleeping with Peter. She was wrong to do that. Now she is perfect. They're almost all gone now. Only one left. Then everything will be all right."

"Who, Laurel? Who is left? Magda?"

"Why, you, of course. I would never hurt Magda. Magda will love me when all the rest of you are gone." I saw the darkness that was her head nodding in the blackness.

"Why do you want to kill me?"

"You slept with Mr. Radford," she said. "He's a man of God. You shouldn't have done that. After you die, the devil will get you."

"Don't you think Magda will be angry at you for killing Angelle? And Jake and Peter and me, too?"

She frowned. "I don't *want* to hurt Magda, but maybe I'll have to. I *had* to kill them. I *had* to do it. You all kept doing things that were wrong."

"What about Rolf?" As I talked to her, I began to very slowly move toward the doorway. "Did he do anything that was wrong?"

"Rolf isn't dead. Suzanne is dead. She wasn't a good person. Rolf *is* a good person." I knew that if I could see her eyes, they would be even more frightening than her words.

"Rolf is in jail for killing Suzanne, Laurel. You don't want him to pay for what you did, do you?" I carefully got to my feet. My arm was throbbing and my hands were slick with blood. As I stood, I realized that standing had been a mistake. If I passed out, I would never awaken. She began to move toward me and I backed in the direction of the door.

Suddenly, she rushed at me and I felt the memory of her breath on my neck and her madness reaching out to me. She didn't plunge the dagger into me as I had expected, but stopped at the door, blocking it. She was breathing in short, hiccupping gasps, and I saw with horror that she still clung to the upper part of Angelle's body.

Mummified human remains weigh at least twenty-five pounds. Even in the shock and terror of my horrified mind, I was aghast at the strength of the woman.

"I love Rolf," she was saying in a surprisingly

conversational tone.

"You don't act like it," I said, wishing my head would stop spinning. I took a hitching breath. "I don't think you do at all."

"Yes! I do!" she suddenly shrieked and rushed toward me again, this time with the dagger held high. I dodged her but felt a searing swipe on my shoulder. With the slice of the blade, her left hand touched me and, for a moment, I saw into the boiling chaos that was her mind. I felt her white-hot fury, a maelstrom of agony and more. I knew what I had to do.

"I do!" she said again. In those two words was her need to be loved. That need overshadowed everything. She had killed Angelle because Angelle *had* been loved, regardless of what she did. Pity for Laurel filled me then in a sudden rush and I knew that she wanted to actually *be* Angelle. She had tried so hard to make everything perfect in order to earn Magda's love, not realizing that she already had it. She had even tried to make those around her perfect and when she couldn't, it had unhinged her.

"Angelle?" I said softly. "Angelle, I'm afraid you're getting cut by that glass you're carrying. Won't you let me help you?"

Laurel looked at her hands. This time she wasn't wearing gloves and the glass had cut her palms. Thin lines of blood crept down her forearms toward her elbows as she looked at them.

"Oh, dear," I said as gently as I could. My heart was beating way too fast. "You've hurt yourself quite badly. Here," I held out my hand to her. It seemed very far away. "Come here and let me help you."

I had hoped she would step closer but instead she reached behind her and pushed the door.

Instantly, all that was left was the dim light that came from the night beyond the window, and she melted back into the depths of the dark. I wanted to try for the door again but would I come too close to her?

I turned and searched through the blackness for an even darker part of the huge attic. There were obstacles everywhere and I floundered among them, bruising toes and shins and knees. I was grateful for the pain. It banished, however briefly, the hot buzzing inside my head. I frantically tried to peer through the gloom for somewhere to hide for a moment so I could sit. I felt if I could sit, then the attic would stop spinning around me.

I stood still to try to hear movement from her; breathing, something to help me locate her again in the darkness. All I heard was the soft, slow *pat, pat, pat* of my own blood dripping onto the floor. Then I heard an almost noiseless sigh very near and at last saw a faint silhouette of Laurel.

"Angelle," I breathed, unable to summon the strength for my voice. I cleared my throat and tried again. "Let me help you."

She sighed again and I thought I heard a little of the madness leave her. "I'm afraid," she said in an eerily childlike voice.

"I know you are, but I will help you." I took a step toward her and she started forward, but she hadn't let go of the dagger. "Come here, Angelle. That's a good girl," I crooned. She screamed then and rushed at me a third time. I moved aside just in time but felt the nearness of the blade as it *swissed* past my ear. "Angelle! You mustn't do that," I said, trying to sound stern, but I heard my own voice come out shaky. "You'll only hurt yourself more. Come here to me so that I can help you. Don't be afraid."

She sobbed a word that sounded like "Mommy." She stood now in the sliver of lighter darkness that came from the edge of the door. I could see her eyes and their manic glitter.

"Let me help you, honey. Everything will be all right." My voice was getting weaker and I was beginning to shiver.

She looked at her hands again and seemed confused by the blood. She slowly opened her hand and the dagger fell, and shattered on the wooden floor. She looked down at it as though she hadn't known she was carrying it.

"Oh, no!" she cried. "Now I've broken it. Mommy is going to be so mad!"

"No, she won't be mad, honey. I'll tell her it was an accident. Come here."

She came to me then. We sank down to the floor together. I could no longer stand and my knees simply gave out. I gently eased what was left of poor Angelle from her arms and cradled Laurel's trembling body. She began to cry then, in pitiful, weak little sobs.

EIGHTEEN

Sunday, November 20, 1983

Laurel cried quietly in my arms, then. Alternately murmuring and weeping, she slowly wove a complicated tapestry of jealousy, deception, betrayal and delusion. Gradually a story emerged dyed with false colors and elusive patterns but with the pure thread of truth running through it. She told me a tale of lies and of love and, in the intricate chaos that was her mind, I'm not sure even she knew what was real and what was not.

At last, I managed to help myself and Laurel rise slowly to our feet and we had taken a few small, tentative steps toward the door. If Magda had not appeared in the doorway then, I may not have been able to hang onto consciousness. I will never know. She quickly pressed a cloth to my cuts and gathered the increasingly hysterical Laurel into her arms. She had heard us upstairs and had listened at the door long enough to grasp what had happened, then rushed back to her room to call the emergency services who, thanks to Ab Eberstein, had already been on the way.

Laurel cried and pleaded with Magda to go with her to the hospital. She wouldn't allow herself to be separated from the only love she had ever known. When she was sedated, she looked so young and vulnerable, my heart broke. The wig had been removed and her hair, always so shiny, was dull and matted, yet still gold against the pillow of the gurney. Her child-like face belied the storms I had seen raging in her mind.

◆ ◆ ◆

Though I was on the second floor being bandaged by the paramedics, I heard a car scream around the corner. In a moment, I heard Easy hit the porch at a flying run and his voice echoed through the downstairs.

"Chey!" He clambered up the stairs and finally found us in my room, now crowded with people. By then, the lights had flashed back on and the world had seemed to return to something resembling normal.

The cuts were beginning to hurt, though the darkness that had been growing around the edges of my vision seemed to be receding. Easy's comforting arm felt good, warm and strong.

"I remember now why I hate working murder cases," I said. "I don't like being up in the middle of the night."

"It's all my fault," he said.

The paramedics were instructing me to go to the hospital for some stitches.

"Oh, Easy," I said, sighing, but I didn't feel like going into how ridiculous his guilt routine was. Especially right then.

"If I hadn't called you in on this, none of it would have happened."

"No, and Donald Tooley would have gone to prison for a murder he didn't commit. Magda would probably be dead, too, for that matter."

"You going to drive her to the hospital or are we going to take her in the wagon?" the medic asked Easy.

"She can't go yet." Quiller's voice grated on my already frayed nerves. "She's got to give her report." He had finally arrived to spread unpleasantness around.

I told the medic that I would get to the hospital on my own. I wasn't about to risk nerve damage.

I didn't protest when Quiller sat down on the bed next to me and set a tape recorder on the bedside table. He spoke his name, mine and the date and time into the recorder then asked me to describe what had happened.

"I awoke in the night and heard noises upstairs, so I went up to the attic. Laurel Gold attacked me with a glass dagger taken from the stained glass window in the foyer." My mouth was dry and felt like it was full of cotton balls. "She killed Magda's third and fourth husbands, Peter and Jake, and Suzanne French, as well as Magda's daughter, Angelle." I swallowed. My throat made a little click. "It's Angelle's body in the attic."

"Laurel Gold confessed to all this?" he asked, looking and sounding doubtful.

I nodded. "Yes. She killed Jake with the glass dagger," I told him. "She probably killed Angelle with it too."

He shook his head. "That's highly unlikely, my dear. How could she possibly do that?"

"She stood by and watched Ab Eberstein at Avenue Art Glass when he repaired that window," I said. "She told him she was Magda." I looked up and thanked Easy for bringing me a glass of water. "I called him tonight, uh... last night, I guess that was, and asked him what Magda had looked like. When he told me she had blonde hair, I realized that Laurel had pretended to be Magda. She watched him fix the window and knew how to get the glass out and put it back. She must have used glue or double stick tape to keep the lead in temporarily so she could use it anytime she wanted to." I looked at Quiller. His little eyes had narrowed. "I'm sure you and your boys can check that out."

"I honestly thought it was Tooley," Easy said.

I shook my head. "It wasn't Tooley. There's no doubt about it, but I can't prove it and neither can he. Forget it, Quiller," I said when he opened his mouth. "You'll have to ask him about it yourself. And, you don't really need his alibi now, anyway, do you, since Laurel has confessed to everything?"

I turned to Easy. "What's going to happen to her?"

Quiller cut in before Easy could answer. "Let's stick to the facts here," he said. "Keep going."

"Laurel told me, more or less, that she had killed Angelle. She believed that Angelle had been having an affair with Peter. Laurel must have lured her up to the attic, killed her and placed her body into the trunk. With Angelle out of the way, Laurel then got rid of Peter. She killed Jake because he was having an affair with Suzanne and Suzanne because of Jake."

My head was beginning to get a bit fuzzy again. "Laurel was willing to do anything to keep Magda from being hurt, including murder. To Laurel, death was preferable to scandal."

I stopped for a moment, to let my head clear.

"Keep going," Quiller said. "Did you suspect Laurel Gold all along? If you did, you should have told me. You may have jeopardized—"

ALWAYS A BAD SIGN

"Just let me tell you, Quiller!" I said. I knew my tone was sharp, but I didn't care. "No, I didn't suspect Laurel. Not until last night. She started acting...well, deranged."

"How? In what way?"

I stared at him a moment until he backed off.

"Laurel had been acting paranoid," I told him. "If you will quit interrupting and let me tell you, we can get this over with." I was fully aware that all of what I said was being recorded.

"I was disturbed by the letter Magda got that was supposedly from Angelle. It was obviously cut from a larger sheet. Laurel had cut off the date and trimmed the margins then sent it or gave it to Magda saying it had just arrived. Apparently, she had found it more than five years ago, learned what she thought were Angelle's plans, then killed her. The way it originally read, I suspect, is that she was planning to run away with Peter. I'm not sure Angelle really was planning to run away or if it had been just a fantasy. Nevertheless, when Laurel found the letter, most likely in Angelle's trash basket, she couldn't allow that 'imperfection' to come into Magda's life. You see, all along, Laurel had been telling me that Magda was a perfectionist. It wasn't Magda at all. It was Laurel."

"My dear, you aren't making any sense at all," Quiller said.

"The day that I went to the attic to see the Tooley

letters, I should have realized it right away. Magda told me that she had been abused as a child and had never gotten over it. She could barely go near the attic. It took immense courage on her part to come through that attic door to help us after she had called the paramedics."

I paused to let what I was saying sink in and to catch my breath. Quiller was frowning so hard I expected his cherubic face to crack. Easy had his head in his hands.

"Where is this letter you were talking about?" Quiller asked, sounding disgruntled.

"On the desk." I nodded toward it.

"I want to see it," he said. "It's evidence."

Easy picked up the letter in its plastic evidence bag and handed it to Quiller.

"You see," I said. "It makes quite good sense this way. That is, if you allow for grammar and punctuation errors, and, according to Magda, Angelle was never very good at those things anyway. Easy, grab a blank sheet of paper for me, would you?"

I placed the letter on top of the paper. "Now if you just add a word or two to each of the lines... This is just conjecture, of course. I don't know for sure that Angelle wrote it exactly this way, but it's likely that whatever she wrote was very similar."

Dear Mothermine

I know you have been terribly worried about me *lately*
but things will be all right! The trouble between *Peter*
you & me has hurt us all. I can't take it anymore & *we*
must do something about it. You are the strong one. *Peter &*
I love you. I don't want to take away one you love but *we*
can't help it. At first it will hurt but if you know *Peter &*
I'll be happy that should make you happy too. Forgive *us.*

Love Angelle

Quiller read the note with Easy looking over his shoulder. He turned the paper over as if he hoped to find some further cryptic messages on the other side.

"I'm not certain that Peter and Angelle *were* having an affair. The important thing is that Laurel believed they were. In her mind, they had sinned and had to be punished. He was another imperfection that Laurel had to deal with. She believed he was cheating on Magda. With her own daughter, no less. Laurel followed him to his parking garage, waited until he came to his car, took him by surprise, killed him and slipped away. She had taken his wallet to make it appear to be a robbery and it had worked. To the police it had looked like a random crime."

"If this is what the letter said, then they *were* having an affair," Quiller said, stabbing his finger at the words I had written.

"Not necessarily," I told him. "It could have been a girlish fantasy. She threw the letter away, after all. Look how crumpled it is."

I sighed. I felt as though I had been babbling. If I was, it wouldn't have been surprising. I had been up for two nights, not to mention spending several minutes dodging someone who had wanted to kill me.

"When she killed Jake, she hid in the back of his car. She had called Jake's office, pretending to be Suzanne, and left a message for him that she would be early to their meeting. She had followed Jake several times and knew his habits as well as Suzanne's. She knew Suzanne would be late. She always was and even if she showed up on time for once, the deed would already have been done. Laurel told Jake's secretary that she would meet him at 10:45. Suzanne, of course, wasn't coming until 11:00 at the earliest. As it was, she was trying very hard not to be late and possibly only missed Laurel by minutes. Bea said the woman called her by her last name, but Suzanne didn't know her last name. Also, neither Bea nor Laurel knew that Jake always called Suzanne 'Sudie.'"

"She mention anything about how she got down

there to Alki and then back home?"

I couldn't believe Quiller was asking me a straight question without any sarcasm.

"She told Rolf that she had to take Angelle's car into the shop. Apparently, she kept it maintained and kept the license up to date. She parked it in a slot down there on Alki near to where she knew Jake would be parking and walked home. Then she had Rolf take her downtown, supposedly to pick up the car. He dropped her off and she hid in Jake's car until he parked to wait for Suzanne. She killed him, then got into Angelle's car and drove home. She probably used Angelle's car to get out to Suzanne's apartment too. The car had been in the garage for more than five years behind a dividing wall. No one had thought to look for it. The police hadn't even known of its existence when they processed Magda's and Rolf's cars."

Quiller was nodding.

"I don't know if Rolf knew what he was doing," I said. "If he knew that he was helping Laurel commit a crime." I looked at Quiller. "I suspect he did." *It wouldn't be his only crime*, I thought, thinking of his threats and attack on Thursday night. This was not the time nor the place to make my report about that.

When I stopped, Easy must have seen something in my face that he didn't like. He told Quiller that he would personally bring me down to the station the next day to finish my statement. Quiller must have seen whatever Easy had and uncharacteristically acquiesced. Muttering about my statement not making a lot of sense, he put away his recorder. Then he trailed downstairs again, hollering at the crime scene techs to be thorough.

Easy wanted to drive me to the emergency room at Harborview, where I could get my arm stitched and he could pick up Magda. I let him. Normally, it would be a matter of pride to me to be able to get into my own car and drive wherever I needed to be without assistance, but Easy had gotten a lot of grief from me lately and I wanted to make up for it.

I stopped in the emergency room where an alarmingly young doctor stitched up my arm and rebandaged the wound on my shoulder. I hate needles and probably wore a quarter inch off of my teeth from clenching them. When he finished, he directed us to the psych floor and even alerted the nurses that we were on the way.

We found Magda sitting on a drab sofa in the psychiatric wing. She looked up when we entered and even smiled.

"Cheyenne," she said, taking my hand. "You're always there when I need you." She gave Easy a sad smile. He gave her one of his wonderful big brotherly hugs.

"You were the one who was there, Magda," I said. "I don't know how long I could have lasted."

"You were holding your own when I got to the

attic," she said. "I suspect you would have made it all the way downstairs just fine. You'll have to thank Mr. Eberstein. He called 9-1-1 first. He got to worrying about you after you talked to him and had the police already on the way by the time I called them.

I shivered a little at the memory of that nightmarish scene in the attic. "How are they doing with Laurel? How is she?"

"She's sedated now. She has a very hard road ahead of her, I'm afraid." She closed her eyes for a moment as if collecting herself. She quietly gathered her bag and coat and started walking with us. "She'll have to be in a hospital for some time, I imagine."

"Magda, I'm so very sorry about Angelle."

Magda nodded and gave herself a moment before she could speak. "I have suspected that she was dead for a long, long time," she said. She passed one of her scarred hands over her face. "I sometimes think I have dealt with it, and sometimes not."

"I don't imagine it's something you will ever get over," I told her. She gave my hand a squeeze.

"I'm sorry about Laurel, too," I said. She continued to hold my hand as we walked. I felt her warm affection and it soothed my heart a bit and I hoped it soothed hers as well. We walked toward the entrance. Easy followed at a discreet distance as though to give us a little privacy.

"Did you suspect Laurel at all?" I asked her.

She shook her head. "No. But, sometimes, I think,

I was a little bit afraid of her. Why would I have lived with her so long if I honestly had thought she was a killer?" She laughed softly. "It's amazing what the human heart can convince the human brain to believe."

We got into Easy's car and Magda looked out the window for a long moment.

"Laurel has always been like a beloved sister to me, she said. "She was pretty much ignored as a child. Our mothers were friends." She shook her head at the memory. "Laurel's mother wasn't quite as bad as mine. Well, she was, but in a different way. Her mother was a social climber and she didn't have any time at all for her daughter. Laurel was raised by teenaged babysitters who, for the most part, didn't care. She was constantly striving for attention. In a way, I've always felt responsible for her. I imagine she thought if she made everything perfect, she would be praised for it."

"She told me once that she had had a perfect childhood," I said. "That her mother taught her to cook and so forth."

"Not true," Magda said, shaking her head. "That's the way she wished her life had been, I imagine. But it wasn't so."

"She should have stayed with acting or modeling," Easy said. "She would have been admired and praised as much as she would have liked."

"Oh, no! Not always the case," Magda said. "She

would have been devastated the moment anyone made any innocent remark about her weight or her aptness for a part or, oh, anything! She did do it for a while, but the pressures got to her very quickly. She was good at it, but she wasn't perfect. She had to be perfect. She thrived on the attention, but it was much too chaotic for her. She's never been very stable. Never satisfied with herself. When she quit, she stayed on with me and gradually took over caring for the house. She refused to let me hire a cleaning staff because they never did a good enough job. For her, anyway."

"You can only find perfection in a very few things," Easy commented quietly. "In everything else you find disappointment."

"That's so true," Magda said. "She always looked for perfection and never found it in anything or anyone."

I remembered Magda picking up a nearly invisible piece of walnut the first night I had stayed at her house. She hadn't been doing it for her compulsion, but for Laurel's.

"Laurel was terribly jealous of Angelle," Magda said. "Angelle was so free. She could stand to be imperfect. Sometimes I think she gloried in it. She scorned modeling and acting too. Laurel couldn't hack it."

"I suppose the letters Donald Tooley says you sent him were from Laurel," I said, thinking.

"The letters *I* sent?" She looked genuinely puzzled.

"Donald said you sent him letters after he stopped writing to you."

She nodded. "Of course," she said. "She must have written them." She glanced at me. "I didn't get much fan mail after a while. None really. She was rather incensed about it. Yes, she must have written him."

"But what about the handwriting? It seems he would have noticed the difference."

"Laurel could imitate my handwriting perfectly. She was my secretary, you know. I used to have her autograph pictures for me when my hands were bandaged. Not quite fair to the fans, I guess."

"With a little different temperament, she may have made a great actress," I said.

"Oh, yes. God knows, she had the drive. She somehow got it channeled the wrong way. She never stopped trying to make the world a perfect place and the sicker she became, the stranger her attempts. She couldn't allow her world to be peopled by sinners." Magda smiled sadly. In the passing street lights, I thought I saw a tear glimmer in her eye. "Imagine," she said, "my Angelle, a sinner."

"I never knew Angelle," I said.

"You would have liked her. She was a free spirit. Like you. It's hard for me to grasp that someone I love could kill. And kill others that I love."

I wondered if she knew about Laurel's belief that

Angelle and Peter had had an affair. I didn't think this would be the proper time to tell her.

When we reached Magda's house, she invited us both in for coffee and tea and a bit of breakfast. The sky was beginning to lighten on a cold, forbidding November day. The investigators were just finishing up and the ME had mercifully already seen to the removal of Angelle's poor, desiccated remains.

"What are your plans now?" I asked Magda over scrambled eggs and buttered toast that tasted like the best food I had ever eaten in my life.

"You know, I think I may try to get back into the acting world," she said slowly. "Show business, anyway. I stayed home and tried to be a good wife to Jake, tried to stay out of the limelight. I thought I wanted an ordinary life, like everyone else's. I guess I didn't do such a good job of it. Now I have a chance to do what I want to do. At first, I thought my scars and I could stay hidden away from the public, but times have changed a bit. Women are directing more now and there are other opportunities."

"Morgan will be glad," I said. She laughed, the same bell-like sound that I had heard from her long ago.

"Yes, Morgan will be happy about that." She sighed sharply then and said, "I plan to move Laurel to a private hospital, of course, if I can. The law may have some say about that, though, I'm afraid." She made a little *tsk* sound. "Rolf will be devastated about Laurel. He'll be heartbroken. I wish there was something I could do for him." She glanced in the direction of the Caretaker's Cottage.

"I hate to say this," Easy said, putting down his fork, "but Rolf will be considered an accessory. He did abet her crimes. One of them, at least. That violates his parole."

"I wish I had known what was happening, Mr. Radford," she said. "If I had suspected Laurel, I could have gotten her some help and none of this would have happened. I don't know if Rolf knew what she was doing or not. I suppose he must have known. I guess that does make him complicit. In hindsight, she may have shown signs that I should have seen. Oh, dear," she said and sighed. "Maybe I didn't want to know. We don't want to believe ill of anyone we love, do we? There certainly was no concrete evidence."

"You should be prepared for Rolf's eventual return to prison," Easy said.

I kept silent about Rolf's attack on me. I was still undecided about reporting it at all. I knew, though, that if he was exonerated for abetting Laurel's crimes, I would have to speak up.

Just then, Easy's pager went off and, in a moment, he was gone, but not without a tussle with his guilt about me driving myself home. I assured him that I could stay one more day with Magda, though I had no intention of doing so.

"Something still confuses me," I said when Easy had reluctantly departed. "Mr. de Las Alas told me that you were demanding and relentless when he tried to break off your relationship."

She actually laughed and it was as genuine and healthy a laugh as I had ever heard from her. "Al," she said. "Honestly! He is very much into fantasies and, I guess what you would call role playing?"

I nodded again and knew that we were both thinking about the party in the ballroom the night before last.

"He so wanted to be in the fantasy world of acting and movies," she went on. "He loved the idea that I was like the women in films. He wanted me to be like those characters; flamboyant, devious, mysterious, well, whatever the female character in the latest film he had seen was like. He never, for more than a day or two, remembered the names of characters, actresses or titles but he would try to get me to role play. It was fun, in a way. A little like being back into acting. So, yes, for a little while, I was a stalker. He loved it." She chuckled and shook her head, her face going a bit pink as she remembered. Finally, she said, "What about you, Cheyenne? Got an interesting case to work on?"

I thought about people like Clovis Houston and shook my head. "Just the usual. Finding missing people." For a moment, I was actually reluctant to go back to locating absent wives and husbands and proving insurance fraud. "As far as you are concerned, my track record with finding missing persons isn't so good. It took me five and a half years to find Angelle."

"You did, though. I knew you could do it."

"I almost didn't. It took poor Jake dying for me to find her. I should have seen through Laurel much sooner. I saw her, at the post-funeral gathering, jump back when that glass bowl fell off the table. Anyone who has any experience with it knows that you never try to catch a falling piece of glass. She had watched Ab Eberstein enough to know that. Of course, *I* didn't know it at the time. I didn't know that the window had been repaired then, either. And, when I did find out, Ab told me it was you who had watched the whole repair process."

She smiled. "You thought I had killed Jake myself, didn't you?"

"For a while. You lied to me," I reminded her.

"I did. I'm sorry, too. I didn't think my affair with Al would matter. It didn't, really."

"Except that Laurel would have been willing to kill you because of it if she had known. I knew she was lying that first day when she told Detective Quiller she had checked on you," I said. "I thought she had checked on you but you weren't there. The truth was she hadn't checked at all. She wasn't even home. She was downtown, waiting for Jake. And then, the day of Jake's funeral, I saw you chopping apples with that big knife. It struck me later that, being the perfectionist I thought you were, that you wouldn't use a chipped knife. I should have realized. And then, you seemed to believe that 'letter' from Angelle was real." I made finger quotes for the word letter. "I suppose that was for Laurel's benefit."

Magda squeezed her eyes shut and when she opened them, I saw the glint of tears. "That letter broke my heart," she said. "I think it was at that moment that I truly realized Angelle was dead. I had suspected it, of course, for years, but that letter…" She sighed. "Poor Angelle," she said.

We sat in silence for a moment, Magda thinking about a well-loved daughter and I thinking about a girl I had never known, but felt I knew all the same.

"And the letters you said you gave Detective Quiller," I asked at last. "What about those?"

She frowned. "I asked Laurel to take them in," she said. "Oh, my, another one. She asked me if she could use my car to run them down to the police station. She didn't take them, of course."

"I thought Laurel didn't drive. When I got the note about you and Laurel being out on Friday night, I thought you had gone out together. But you hadn't. Laurel had used Angelle's car once again to go to Suzanne's and kill her."

Magda nodded. "I had no idea she used Angelle's car. Frankly, I never thought of Angelle's car at all. I knew it was there, of course. But Laurel always said she didn't like to drive and usually she took cabs or a bus. Once in a while she borrowed my car, but not often. On Friday, she must have left just after I did and wrote the note. I didn't know anything about it."

"She came home only a few minutes before you did," I said. "I heard her come upstairs and then, only fifteen or twenty minutes later, you came up. I thought you had gone out and come back together."

We sat on in the kitchen, sipping tea and buttering more toast. Suddenly, Magda turned toward me. "Cheyenne, when I do go back into films, perhaps you would consider moving into my house. I wouldn't be home much. You'd have the run of it. You could set your office up here and live here. Rolf has the Caretaker's Cottage, of course, but... Oh, but Rolf may have to go back to prison!"

"Most likely, Magda. Parole violation is a serious offense." A thought occurred to me. "You know that Rolf was arrested for killing Suzanne, don't you?"

"No!" Her wonderful green eyes went wide.

"Laurel never told you, did she?" I said. "He was arrested yesterday afternoon. That may have been all that Laurel needed to go off the way she did. She told me she's in love with Rolf."

"And he's in love with her," Magda said. "Poor Rolf."

I kept silent.

"I guess that means you could move into the Caretaker's Cottage then, she said. "It's big enough so you could keep your office there too. I wouldn't charge much rent." She looked at me. "If any. Will you think about it?"

I thought of my little apartment, soon to be someone else's home. A great weight lifted from me, just knowing there was another option. I promised her I would think.

"I imagine that Rolf, if he isn't returned to prison, would probably move anyway and follow Laurel to wherever she was being treated," she said.

I nodded. "How did you know he was in love with her?"

"I could see it every time he looked at her." She glanced at me. "I'm an expert on love, you know. That Mr. Radford has it bad for you, my girl." Her eyes twinkled in the morning light. "Trust me."

I held up my hands in surrender. "You may be an expert on love," I said, "but I'm not."

"Still hanging on to memories of the lost one?"

I shrugged.

"Is it the husband or the soldier?"

I shrugged again. "There's no point in hanging on to memories of either of them, is there?" I asked, getting to my feet. "I think I'm going to get my things together and get myself home. You don't mind being here by yourself?"

"I can stand it. I'm going to have to hire someone to take care of the house now, I guess. Cleaning and what not. And a gardener-handyman to replace Rolf.

Would you check them out for me, Cheyenne?"

I nodded. "I have to admire your perseverance, Magda," I told her. "Like you said, you've lost the people you've cared about the most, yet you are still able to give and accept love. I myself, have lost two but I can't seem to allow love into my life again."

"That's fear, my dear, nothing more. You work on that and you'll find it. That Mr. Radford..." She didn't finish. I knew what she meant.

She held out her arms to me. I stepped into them and we embraced for a long moment.

"Thank you for finding Angelle for me," she whispered. When she stepped away there were real tears in her eyes. The first genuine tears I had seen her cry. My own eyes were wet. Even so, the week seemed to be starting out quite well.

Afterword

The St Martin case has never stopped haunting me. Decades later, on cold, windy November nights, I can still see Angelle's poor body and hear Laurel's pitiful cries. I know I helped, but I felt helpless all the same and don't feel I helped enough. But then, we can only do what we can. Should I have been able to see our future? I have never been able to see what lies before me or those I love. Maybe that's the best way, after all. If I had seen what was ahead for us all, would I have begun the investigation? I think yes. I couldn't have abandoned them; Laurel, Magda and Rolf, to Laurel's nightmare. We are not meant see what events, both wonderful and terrible, lie ahead for us. It would break, if not our spirits, then our hearts.

Cheyenne Bruce

November, 2019

BOOKS IN THIS SERIES

Cheyenne Bruce

From the case files and personal journals of Cheyenne Bruce, Private Investigator

Sign Your Life Away - Coming September 2022

See following excerpt

The Book Of Signs - Coming March 2023

SIGN YOUR LIFE AWAY

From the Case Files and Personal Journals of
Cheyenne Bruce, Private Invesigator, Book 2

Prologue

February, 1972

I was in my car when the news came over the
radio that Royal Blue was dead. Shocked, the
world stopped moving for a while. The traffic
slowed, then lined the shoulder as if the drivers
and passengers were waiting for a prolonged funeral
procession to pass.

It had been the middle of winter. A fine rain had
misted the windshields and polished the pavement.
Time had hung suspended while we absorbed the
terrible facts, listened in open-mouthed wonder at
the rumors and arranged our private grief. I had
sat with my hands gripping the wheel, looking at
the buildings of Seattle's skyline dismally rising
like empty boxes through the watery air. The city
had seemed suddenly, subtly altered, though I knew
the change was only in my perspective. A blue

convertible, its rag top glistening with wet, full of sobbing teenaged girls, had sped by with the radio blaring. It had swerved sharply to avoid a slowing bus, skidded a little, then continued its frantic race with mortality.

Royal Blue, dead! It hadn't seemed possible. I had owned none of his records or tapes. My tastes ran to Neil Diamond, The Beatles, Simon and Garfunkel. Royal Blue's music was more popular with the younger crowd but I had recognized his genius. His were the records that stayed at the tops of the charts week after week and then were studied and analyzed long after that.

After the news bulletin, the radio station had played one of his quieter, more lyrical ballads and I had let his voice fill my head. His words took on a new, profound meaning for me. Had he known, when he had written that song, that he would take his own life? I wondered.

Once or twice in a lifetime, there arises a star the brilliance of Royal Blue. His style and good looks had shot him to the top where he had stayed for more than a decade. Everyone knew of his humble beginnings, his devotion to his family and now, we listened, in stunned silence, to the news of his death. We had all heard the dirty whisperings of drugs and liquor and too much pressure on a man too sensitive to endure, but they no longer mattered.

Whatever the truth, he was dead. Gradually, other stars would appear and glow while still others would wink out. But none would match Royal Blue's radiance. The world would become used to his loss, but, like the ripples on a pond, his essence would never really die. The surface of the music world would never again settle into stillness.

I drove on that day, little knowing that with the passing of years, my life would become entangled with the lives of those Royal Blue had loved. Though I didn't yet know the players, they were waiting in my future to affect me to the end of my life. Although the case was finished long ago, I dream about it still. In my sleep, I'm standing on the edge of hell with a madman.

ACKNOWLEDGEMENTS

Thank you to my darling husband, Guy, for his enduring patience, copyediting skills and sense of humor.

Thank you to Gale Peck of Iceberg Strategic Creative for my logo and cover design of the paperback format.

I hope the Seattle Police Department will forgive me for the many liberties I have taken with its personel, locations and procedures. Like Cheyenne, I have the utmost respect for them.

I would also like to thank my readers. I hope you enjoyed reading *Always a Bad Sign* as much as I enjoyed writing it. Please visit MasterPiecesUnlimited.com to get updates and emails about future books by me as well as future offers.

ABOUT THE AUTHOR

Lella Rae

 Lella Rae is the pseudonym for Delores Peck.

Delores was born in Tacoma, Washington and has lived in the Pacific Northwest most of her life. She graduated from the University of Washington with a Bachelor of Arts degree in Humanities. She lives in Seattle with her husband, Guy.